D1525703

FATAL

BEAUTY

R.C. HARTSON

BLACK ROSE writing™

© 2015 by R.C. Hartson

All rights reserved. No part of this book may be reproduced, stored in a retrieval system or transmitted in any form or by any means without the prior written permission of the publishers, except by a reviewer who may quote brief passages in a review to be printed in a newspaper, magazine or journal.

The final approval for this literary material is granted by the author.

First printing

This is a work of fiction. Names, characters, businesses, places, events and incidents are either the products of the author's imagination or used in a fictitious manner. Any resemblance to actual persons, living or dead, or actual events is purely coincidental.

ISBN: 978-1-61296-486-7

PUBLISHED BY BLACK ROSE WRITING

www.blackrosewriting.com

Printed in the United States of America

Suggested retail price $16.95

Fatal Beauty is printed in Gentium Book Basic

Cover Concept by Dean Kuch

For my beloved wife, Lynie.
Without her encouragement, patience and love,
this book would not be possible.

4/25/15
To Rachel
a friend & neighbor
Keep reading
and smiling
(Bob)

FATAL

BEAUTY

CHAPTER ONE

It was a perfect night to bury a body.

Bart Hodgkins walked stooped over, his breathing was labored and his body soaked in sweat. The weight he carried, though not substantial, was awkwardly draped over one mammoth shoulder. The rain had shriveled to a heavy mist and the sky was beginning to lighten. It had rained all afternoon. At times soft, then drizzly—and at one time, vicious, as it bombarded the trees and leaf-covered ground.

It was never easy carrying a lifeless body through the woods in the middle of the night, especially when the terrain was so uneven, but Bart was in superb shape. At a muscular six-foot four and weighing a hefty two hundred and fifty pounds, he also had a cocky confidence that guided each of his steps. The Austrian nine-millimeter Glock he carried was certain security.

Twisting his ankle en-route was unexpected, of course, but it didn't trouble him; he kept moving. Years ago, as an inmate at Menard Correctional Facility, he had trained his mind to ignore physical discomforts. And when the mind didn't pay attention, neither did the body. The mind controlled pain and the mind could make it go away. He had survived agony with that simple philosophy, and although. the cold and mist was a pain in the ass it made the going that much more challenging. Bart grunted as he trudged into the darkness like the devil into hell.

He stopped and twisted his bull-like neck to look back. Standing in place for several moments, he listened, and stared into the darkness from beneath heavy lids. Of course nobody was following him. That was ridiculous. He had a sixth sense for danger before he could see it, smell it, or hear it. He was pumped; blood slugged through his veins as he scanned the area. Using this burial site was brilliant, he thought. The densely wooded area, sixty-six miles south of Chicago, was a quiet downstate location where everything was green. Sparsely located buildings were gray, gross little shacks accompanied with pickups on blocks situated miles away from the little town with no 7-Eleven. An area full of hills they called mountains, but weren't.

Nobody in their right mind would have reason to venture this far into the woods, not even the local hicks. And if they did—even years from now—they'd find bones, but nothing to implicate him. Animals would find the bodies long before the cops, did.

A hundred yards ahead lay the gully, Bart's private cemetery, overgrown with brambles, brush and ferns. A well-hidden shovel would be there, stashed from his last visit two months before.

Side-stepping down the hill, Bart reached the bottom and flat ground, where he dumped his load like a burlap bag full of potatoes. The odor of voided bowels was strong as he squinted to study the sky. Despite the persistent cloud cover, daylight would squeeze in shortly. It was essential to finish his work before dawn and be gone. He began to use the shovel.

As he dug the shallow grave, Bart dwelled on how easy this one had been. The bundle at his feet contained the body of a whore from Ernie's Bar on Halstead Street- just one of the many flesh markets he prowled. During the daylight hours, it looked like most crappy bars look in the daytime . . . crappy. Ernie was a lush who talked too much and observed very little. His place smelled of flat beer, grilled onions, illegal cigarette smoking and body odor. A bald-headed bartender was busy, bullshitting with a man in a cheap-looking suit, and two uniformed CTA bus drivers were arguing about something or other at the other end of the bar. Some chairs were turned over on table tops. Two-thirty in the afternoon and the place was damned near empty when the young woman came in. Her flip-flops announced her approach. She eased up to Bart who was perched on a stool, nursing a mug of *Old Style* draught. He had been watching the Cubs' game on the TV above the bar.

His appearance, though gruff, sometimes attracted women. He wasn't handsome by any means- in fact, he was rather odd looking and ugly. He had no lips, and ears that stuck out perpendicular to his head like a chimpanzee's. His chin was littered with serious zit-craters, and he wore a wife-beater and dirty jeans. A ratty-looking fedora covered his spiky red hair that hung ragged over his ears, looking as though it had been trimmed with pinking shears.

The young woman was just what Bart liked: pretty, in the girl-next-door sort of way, yet too sexy for her own good. She had shoulder-length, baby blond hair, tortured into waves, worn parted in the middle and tucked behind her ears. She wore designer jeans and a T-shirt that said: *"Love Sucks--True Love Swallows."*

She didn't need a bra to keep her boobs in perfect position and looking perky. The condition of her skin and the smoothness of her hands told him that she had not worked outside at all. She probably spent most of her days in bed, and the rest in the bars. He suspected she wouldn't be missed.

The muscles of Bart's gaunt forearms twitched, like worms under his skin, as he relived the earlier events with her body squirming under his.

"Hi, can I buy you a drink?" he half-whispered. He smiled, showing incisors and lowers crooked enough to give an orthodontist wet dreams.

"Sure, why not," the young woman chirped. "Whatcha' doin, watching the Cubbies lose again?" She smiled as she edged a bit closer.

Bart glanced away like he was suddenly shy and uncomfortable. "Yeah, same old, same old," he said, as he pulled back a neighboring stool. "Here, have a seat. Let me buy you a drink. He remembered thinking she might be a pro, but it didn't matter.

Without hesitation, she slid onto the stool and began to check out the bottles behind the bar- as if her experience with drinking was limited. "Thanks," she said. "Hey, how about Absolut and tonic? I hear those are the bomb."

"Sure thing, I'm Tom, by the way." Smiling, he extended a big, calloused hand then waved to the bartender and ordered her drink.

"I'm Chelsea. Good to meet you, Tom." She smiled again and leaned in closer "I don't suppose you've got a joint, do ya'?" Bart felt her hot breath on his neck. When she gave him her hand it sent vibrations to his crotch.

"Sure do." He pretended to sweep the bar with his eyes before he said, "Not here though."

"No, no-of course not; later, that'll be cool." She winked.

Five hours later, as the bar began to hum with the after work crowd, she walked on wobbly legs as she clung to his arm and they left together.

The eaves of the motel were lit with pink neon tubing. It was two stories of frayed carpets, stained sheets, and a pink flamingo out front that looked tacky, if not out of place, on the south side of the city.

The place was shaped in an L around a narrow parking lot. Typical customers were whores renting by the hour, wannabe pornographers shooting amateur videos and rent jumpers needing a place to stay while they found a new landlord to rip off.. You rented a room, you didn't find it clean, and you weren't expected to leave it that way. Smears of blood on the bedding were commonplace at the Sleep E-Z motel.

After she used the bathroom, the girl plopped down on the edge of the bed and said, "now, where's that joint, you promised?"

That had pissed him off. Bart didn't have any pot and he didn't want the sex to cost him a damned thing, nor be consensual. He lived for the thrill of having complete control over these situations. Everything would be *his* way. He turned up the volume on the TV, and stood at the end of the bed, towering above her.

Gritting his teeth, he growled, "Shut the fuck up!" He smacked her with an open hand that caught her off guard and knocked her off the bed. She was in shock when she hit the floor, too stunned to cry, too frightened to protest. He continued to clobber her with his iron-hard fists, over and over again, until, her face was smeared with blood.

She was still conscious and moaning when he dragged her up and tossed her on the bed like a ragdoll. It didn't take long to duct-tape her hands and ankles, then cram a washcloth into her mouth. He didn't bother to remove his clothes. Loosening his belt, he dropped his jeans and jockey shorts, then, fumbled with a condom and slipped it on his fully-charged erection. Shoving her legs apart, he forced himself inside of her and clutching a handful of her hair, took his time raping her.

Tears streamed down her cheeks; her muffled screams counted for nothing but Bart's intense pleasure. As usual, he had difficulty reaching orgasm, until he flipped her over and sodomized her. When he was satisfied, Bart took a pre-loaded syringe from his jacket pocket and jabbed it into her neck.

Nearly two hours later, Bart once again raised the volume on the TV when the girl stirred and groaned. He had been slouching in the dilapidated lounge chair, but stood and slowly edged up to the bed. His toothy smile widened as he stared into his victim's terrified eyes-his face only inches from hers. "You still want that joint, babe?"

Now, as he dug the grave, he remembered those eyes—open wide and pleading, her head tossing from side to side. He had snapped his head this way and that, mimicking her protests. He loved it—gave her a moment or two—savoring his power--the raw excitement in witnessing her fear.

"Mmffff Mmfff" She grunted and groaned much louder when Bart cocked the gun with the silencer, and crammed a pillow over her head. He squeezed the trigger, firing one hollow point round into her head. *Whump!*

After he scraped the last few shovels of dirt over the girl's body, Bart lit a Marlboro and gazed up at the edge of dawn. *I won't tell Lew about this one. No way. . . Fuck him.*

CHAPTER TWO

She came in while I was sitting at the bar of one of my favorite watering holes, *The Redhead* on West Ontario. A great piano bar, but it was late afternoon and the piano man wasn't set up to play yet, so I settled for the Muzak.

Nursing my second Johnnie Walker and soda, I was in deep thought, studying my reflection in the mirror behind the bar. I checked my outfit that looked like it belonged to the street-person edition of GQ. A T-shirt that boasted Corona beer, a gray, sweatshirt, unzipped over the T-shirt- jeans with a rip in the knee and scuffed up shit-kicker boots. I also had a two-day-stubble and my sparse buzz-cut hair was covered with a Cub's baseball cap. My mood was gloomy, even foul. I felt like beating up a nun.

When the young woman came up behind me, she leaned over my shoulder, like an umpire hovering over a baseball catcher.

"Cleve?" Her voice was an attention-grabber—throaty and sexy-sounding.

"Yeah." I slowly turned to face her. "Sorry—do we know each other?"

"Sure." She smiled just a bit, as if it pained her to do it. "I'm Betty Rohrman, and you're a private detective, right?" She nodded once and looked down at her cigarette, then at the bartender. "Guess I'd better put this out, eh?"

"Good idea," I said. I was still at a loss.

"I used to work for Joe Gallup's office. You handled some fraud cases for him. In fact, you guys bought me lunch one day last summer. Remember? We went to Lou Malnati's for pizza."

"Oh, yeah!" I lied. She extended her hand and I took it, even though I was still scratching around in my mental library trying to place her. She was jittery—not

looking into my eyes, kind of nervous I thought. There was silence for an awkward moment before I asked, "So, how did you know I would be here, Miss . . . "

"Rohrman . . . Betty Rohrman, and I need to talk to you, Cleve. I don't know where else to turn." She paused and gazed at the empty stool next to me. "May I?" She slid onto the stool and crossed her legs, showing me a lot of thigh. Nice legs.

Betty Rohrman—yes, I suddenly remembered. The receptionist, a sort of Miss Moneypenny type—the model of efficiency and repressed sexuality, and all that. Her eyes were big and brown and pleading. She was around five-four, one hundred and five pounds and looked very young. Early twenties. Classic good looks. Not much makeup—I didn't think she needed it. She had freckles across her cheeks, giving her a kid-like quality up close. I realized that buying her lunch must have had something to do with those legs.

"Sorry, Betty. It's been a while, what's Joe up to these days?"

"I'm not sure. I'm not there anymore." She lowered her head as she began to fumble around in her purse. "I think I've got his card here someplace if you want it."

"That's alright, I've got one at the office, I'm sure."

We sat in silence for a moment before I asked, "So, how did you manage to track me down?"

Her eyes narrowed. "I couldn't find your card, and didn't know where your office was," she explained. "But I remember you telling me *The Redhead* was one of your favorite hangouts, so I just took a chance. I did check a couple of other places first, like Butch McGuire's." She smiled. "It wasn't that hard, really."

"I see. Well, can I buy you a drink?"

"No...not right now, thank you."

"Okay, since you went to so much trouble in finding me, Betty, what can I do for you?"

"It's my sister. She's disappeared and we're really worried about her. I want you to find her."

"We?"

"Yes, my mother and I."

"How long's she been gone?"

"Seven days, counting today, and we usually talk every other day. Sometimes *every* day, and I haven't heard from her. We're really afraid something may have happened to her. I hate to think about it, but the papers are saying they still haven't caught that serial killer, and what if—"

"Whoa, take it slow, Betty. You shouldn't jump to conclusions. I'm sure there's a perfectly good reason your sister hasn't gotten ahold of you. Have you called the cops yet?" She was watching my mouth, taking in every word, and I sensed she was legit, but scared to death.

"Yes, I called them four days ago, but I haven't heard anything back. I know the police are too busy to spend a lot of time looking for one woman, and my mom's frantic."

"I don't know. When I was there, we took missing persons cases pretty seriously. I doubt that attitude has changed."

I studied her a moment. Tears welled up in her eyes; there was no convincing her.

She was a worrisome mess, for sure. "Come on," I said, as I stood. "Let's take a table in the back—a little more privacy."

She followed me to a two-topper in the corner, by a satin-covered piano.

I pulled out her chair and she gave a heavy sigh as we sat down.

"Where does your sister live?"

"In an apartment, over on Belmont."

"By herself?"

"Yes."

I had to consider that. It wasn't the best neighborhood in the city, but there were a lot worse. I said, "What makes you believe I can help any better than the police?"

"I just know, that's all. Joe Gallup told me you were a good man who's dependable. 'Solid', he said. You used to be a cop, yourself—right?"

"Right on the cop part, but I resigned." More silence. "What else did Joe say?"

She studied me furtively and then lowered her eyes. "He said you were tough, abrasive, and fearless . . . and could be well--downright mean."

"Good. Glad I come with such a great recommendation."

Neither of us spoke for a moment until she said, "You look too young to be retired."

"Yeah. I get that a lot."

She paused as if she was waiting for something more. "Why'd you quit then?"

I swallowed some Scotch and shook my head. "Long story, Miss Roman."

"No, it's Rohrman."

"Of course it is...sorry, Miss *Rohrman*. Anyway, so maybe I had no choice.

Life can take some bullshit turns, you know?" I held up a hand. "Pardon the language."

I watched her face as I spoke, and seeing no reaction, I continued:

"See— to be honest, I've damned near given up detective work. I did it for a little while after I resigned, but I haven't done much of anything except fishing for the past few months or so. Know what I mean? Private-detecting life is a lonely deal. I mean, after cleaning the guns and shining the badge, what's a man to do?"

"Yes, but..."

"And...then...I 've had some problems with this stuff." I held up my glass, which was nearly empty. I hesitated. "A drunk front breezed through the north side of Chicago, just last night, as a matter of fact."

Her eyes met mine. "Maybe you shouldn't drink."

"Yeah, that's like telling a priest he shouldn't work on Sundays."

"You seem to be in good shape—physically, I mean."

"I do the gym thing four days a week is all."

"Well, I need to find my sister and I just know you can help." She leaned in.

"I won't take no for an answer."

I shook my head. "You should get somebody else, Betty."

She paused as I gave her the "don't push me" look.

"See, truth is--I don't respond well to demands."

She quickly reached across the table and covered my free hand with hers. Shaking her head, she said, "I'm sorry. Really, I shouldn't have said that. Please? Please? But I really need somebody like you, Mr. Hawkins."

She sounded choked up, and her eyes began to leak. *Now* I was Mr. Hawkins instead of Cleve. That was the icing, I guess, and I began to mull it over while she talked.

"You don't understand, my sister's a free spirit and we have always worried.

I've told her she takes too many chances, but she doesn't listen. I'm really afraid for her."

"Chances?"

"With men, you know. She believes everything they tell her. She's been like that all her life...even in school, she just ...well, you know, was really popular with the guys."

She pulled a Kleenex from her purse and dabbed the corners of her eyes.

I found myself feeling sorry for her—buying into her story, in spite of my usual armor that guarded against boo-hoo bullshit.

"Anyway, like I was saying, I've had problems. There was some trouble at the department." I paused.

"What do you mean? What happened?"

I didn't answer right away as I quickly watched that memory on my inside screen.

"Okay, It's like this . . . I killed a guy. It was an accident but the brass didn't see it that way. That's why I'm no longer a homicide detective."

"Oh. I didn't know—I'm so sorry."

"Don't be."

Neither of us spoke and the Muzak suddenly seemed louder.

"Sure you don't want that drink?" I asked.

"No, thanks. Look, I know it's none of my business, but can you tell me a little more about it—the trouble, I mean?"

"I don't like to talk about it. I mean, sure, I had to kill men before while I was in Nam, but that's different. When one is by accident it does things and everything turns upside down. I was working homicide—saw a lot of death. I know killing does to you. You change. The person who says otherwise is lying. But when it's an accident, the emotional attitude you form later varies greatly among individuals." I paused and took another swig.

"Anyway, some guys keep their blame alive. That's me. I always feared the worst consequence for myself. That's why I quit, not because they forced me out. No matter what you may hear, that's the straight scoop."

Another awkward moment followed as we both sat quietly. I rattled the ice in my glass and decided to continue. "I was always envious of family and church-oriented people. When I thought about retirement, somewhere in the back of my mind was a house with a white picket fence, a loving wife, two kids, a dog, and a nine-to-five job where no one wanted to kill me. I'd see myself getting some ice cream and sitting in the sun, listening to the ocean."

"So, what happened then?"

I signaled the bartender for another drink before I said, "I worked undercover, mostly. I thought I did pretty good too. But the Chicago Police Department never liked its disguised unit made up of guys like me, who looked and dressed like derelicts and muggers. Professional jealousy, I guess. I don't know."

I heard myself standing on a soap box and stopped for a moment. My tongue was definitely getting loose from the scotch.

"The spit-and-polish people neither trusts nor understands its undercover squad. They don't give a happy rat's ass how effective those guys are. Weird people, especially when they're effective, are a threat to the establishment"

"I don't understand."

"Well, it's simple. When push comes to shove, you need certain people to have your back. When they don't, people like me take the fall: Duane Carlizzio and Jessie Waters were the kind of small-time dirt bags that made life a little tougher for everybody. They'd rob anything that wasn't nailed down, burglarize any house or business they thought might be empty, get drunk and choke down every drug they could get their hands on. It's a long story, but . . . bottom line—I wasted Carlizzio during a routine drug bust."

Betty's eyes widened. "But, the police shoot bad guys all the time—don't they?"

I grinned. "Miss, you've watched too much *Law and Order*. The reason you watch those contrived TV shows about law enforcement is that often the real story is so depressing, nobody would believe it. "Very seldom do cops shoot to kill."

She continued to stare at me.

"Anyway, I didn't need Internal Affairs crawling up my ass for the rest of my life. And, I didn't want to end up slouching sullenly on some shrink's couch, staring at a box of Kleenex, folding my arms defensively and talking about how I hated my mother and what a God-awful mess I made of my life. So I flipped my badge. If I hadn't, they would've just shoved me out eventually, like I was shit on their shoes. A cop in that position is guilty until proved innocent."

Her eyes ticked away from mine like a second hand going to the next hash mark, and then came back. "I'm sure you must have had a good reason to kill him."

"Yes."

We were both quiet. "Again, I know it's none of my business, but do you want my opinion?"

"No. I don't even know why we're having this little talk."

She cleared her throat. "I think you're too hard on yourself. You should quit stirring up the past so much. My mother told us, 'If it's not moving, don't poke it.'"

"Yeah, well. Easy for you to say."

"I'm sorry . . . so sorry I bothered you." She began to get up. "I'll just..."

"Wait, it's okay, take it easy." I paused a beat and took another swallow.

"Tell you what—no promises, but I'll see what I can do, alright?" I gave her my everything-under-control smile. She still didn't look convinced though. I guess it's tough for a has-been to look convincing. I handed her my card.

"I'll need a lot more info on your sister, though, and now is not the time or the place."

"Anything. What do you want?" She sat back, crossing her arms tightly against herself.

Hopefully she'll turn up; in fact I'm quite sure she will. But, I still have an office over on Wells. It's on my card. You come in there tomorrow morning, and we can talk without this drink in my hand. Know what I mean?"

Her eyes lit up. "Yes, of course. I'll take the morning off...the whole day if I need to. I have some sick days left. What time do you want me there?"

I gave it some thought as I looked at her. "I go to the gym early, so let's make it nine-thirty?"

"That's fine. What do you want me to bring?"

"A dust rag and a broom. No, just kidding. Bring pictures. Recent stuff of your sister—more than one, mind you —a bunch. Different shots from your collection—know what I mean?"

"Okay, sure. Anything else?"

"Yeah, her telephone records, bank statements, any credit card receipts, and be ready to answer a bunch of questions. I'll need her Social Security number too."

We both stood at the same time. "Thanks so much, Mr. Hawkins." She extended her hand and I shook it.

"This means so much to me. I'll see you in the morning."

"Cleve... call me Cleve. And I take it you have a way home?"

"Yes, I'm parked right over on Rush Street. I'll be fine."

She turned to leave, then stopped and faced me again. "I almost forgot, so tell me—how much do you charge?"

I hesitated as I thought about the rent before I said, "Don't worry about that right now, okay?"

When she left, I strolled back to the bar and got the scotch I ordered.

I thought I might regret taking the job, but I couldn't just walk away. I guess I figured I needed to pay off my conscience.

CHAPTER THREE

Waking up alone is a bitch.

I stirred about twenty minutes to seven within the bright tangible silence of my bedroom, but I was glad to be there.

Stretching my aching body, I made my way to the living room and parted the curtains. The sky was gray, and the wind was blowing in the parking lot; pieces of newspaper flapped and twisted through the air. The earmarks of a shitty day were brewing.

I knew my place was a mess. Dirty dishes stacked in the sink, a Cheerios box was upended on the counter, a soiled pillow on the couch in front of the television. An open, half-empty bag of Doritos was scattered on the coffee table. The bathroom was far from clean. Towels on the floor, inside the toilet was speckled and the lid was up. Home sweet home.

I was glad my meeting with Betty Rohrman was to be at my office, even though I knew *it* also needed cleaning.

I reached in the fridge and grabbed the container of Minute Maid and drank straight from the container while the coffee was perking and pondered my agreement with Betty the night before.

Call it crazy or whatever, but I had turned down plenty of other jobs recently, including one missing persons case. So, I was still questioning my motives. As a PI, I had handled scut work for bondsmen and liability lawyers, wives who wanted their unfaithful husbands bankrupted in divorce court, and cuckolds who wanted their wives and their lovers crucified. So, why this case?

The woman was attractive, true enough, and she had those damn beautiful legs—for which I have always been a sucker, but I'm sure that wasn't it. And then, there was Maureen. I knew I wasn't over her, and probably never would be.

So, why did I let this girl's story get to me? I think it was because of my nagging blue-colored cop's blood. And, although I hadn't told Betty, in so many words, I was plenty concerned about the possibility of a serial killer on the loose. Child molesters, pimps, dope dealers, and men who abuse women get no slack from me. In recent weeks, the entire missing girl thing ranked real high on my bad-shit-o-meter.

I took a shower and shaved carefully while the coffee bubbled in the old percolator I had salvaged out of my grandmother's things when she died. Funny, I always thought about that fine old lady when I made coffee. The thing always made such a soothing sound until it was finished perking.

As I drank a cup I considered breakfast. I really wanted a donut —a sourdough donut. Beats me why there's this thing with cops and donuts, yet people find them synonymous for some reason. Anyway, I wasn't going to have a donut today. Well--maybe later.

Shuffling to the front door, I retrieved the newspaper, and got the jug of milk from the fridge on the way back. Grabbing the box of Cheerios from the counter, I straddled a chair at the kitchen table poured the milk and chowed down. I savored my second cup of coffee as I eyed the bold headline on the front page of The Tribune.

"TWO MORE COOK COUNTY WOMEN MISSING"

The serial killer certainly was getting his share of ink. What had begun as the report of two young women's bodies discovered in an abandoned warehouse on the southwest side had grown considerably in recent days. The first report had been on the inside of the second page, four or five months ago in April. Now, two more women had disappeared, this time from the DePaul University area. The headline was bold type, and included headshots of the women just below the fold on the front page. I suspected however, that this report did not include Betty Rohrman's sister, Chelsea.

It was a little after eight when I left the apartment with a thumping head, but clear eye. It was still windy and overhead, the sky had turned to the color of gunmetal; lightning broke across it in brilliant spider-web lines as I drove over to the American Fitness gym located on the second floor of the old Nautical Maritime Building on Clark Street.

I set my duffle down and flashed my membership card for Jessica, who was working the desk. Even the regular clients, like myself, had to sign in., which I thought was BS.

Jess is a young woman with a big chest and a small sweater who I love to watch. Apparently, she had come straight from her own workout, wearing lavender leotards, pink knit leg warmers, a headband and white sneakers. Pointing her ample chest at me she said, "Morning, Cleve," as she slid the clipboard over to me and smiled.

"Our machine is on the fritz. Just sign in, handsome."

"Morning, bountiful . . . I mean beautiful."

She giggled as I scribbled my signature. "That machine thing seems to happen a lot. Tell your old man I said he needs to get a new one." She shook her head as if there were a horsefly on it. Her husband, Junior, was an okay guy, but he had to be careful not to drag his knuckles when he walked. And he was cheap.

Jessica always looked pretty good, with her corn-silk hair and eyes a darker blue than the bluest sky, but she went overboard with layers of foundation, blush, rouge, mascara, eye-liner, lipstick, and a daily drenching of a perfume that, when mixed with her tobacco smoke, reminded me of the smell of a cat's neglected sandbox.

The place wasn't busy for a Friday morning, in fact there were only two other men working out. One, lifting weights, looked like a steroidasaurus. The other, a silver-haired gent, appeared exhausted and ready to fall off the treadmill.

I rarely miss my gym time, no matter how I feel. Continuing my workouts saved my ass when I left the department and found myself getting lazy. I was still overdoing the scotch and had adopted an "I don't-give-a-shit" attitude, so it was in my best interest to continue at the gym.

Anyway, I launched into a circuit on the machines. Starting off with my upper body, shoulders, chest, triceps, and then onto back and biceps. As usual, I jumped from one exercise to the next, giving myself no rest or downtime. I finished off working my legs and lower back. Counting off two minutes on the clock, I repeated the circuit two more times. Using heavy weights, I took twelve to fourteen reps on most exercise. On the last cycle, I felt fatigued but strong. I showered and changed clothes.

Ordinarily, I tucked my Glock into a belt holster in the small of my back, and, because I'm slightly paranoid, a little .25 auto in an ankle holster, but that day I had them packed inside my gym bag. I'd feel naked if I didn't have my tools with me.

My office is on Wells Street, near what has become known as the Old Town section on the near north side. I know it's not much of a layout, but it suits my needs. My ex- girlfriend, Maureen, kidded me, saying it would be an ideal spot for a VD clinic or a public exterminator. I hadn't been there in a month or so, but kept up the rent just in case I decided to get an attitude adjustment and go back to work.

A middle-aged black guy, the street calls Deckle, was perched on my stoop puffing a cigarette when I parked at the curb. He wore his everyday, grimy Sox ball cap, cruddy jeans, mis-matched running shoes, and a hooded sweatshirt of indeterminate color. Stained thermal underwear was visible at the neck of the sweatshirt, and he had what looked like a week-old- stubble.

The way Deckle tells it, years ago, a gangbanger's gun butt had reshaped his nose. I actually think he'd fallen flat on his face in a drunken stupor. He's a homeless, hundred-and-twenty- pound ferret, who has problems, but is a useful gopher, and an excellent snitch. They say Deckle could steal the stink off shit and not get the smell on his hands. I believe it.

I locked up the car and watched him, as he took a long pull on a half-pint bottle. His Adam's apple bobbed up and down like a yo-yo as he chugged about half of it down. When he spotted me, he jumped up like an invalid woken from an afternoon nap and gave me a face full of guilt, before he tucked the bottle in his coat pocket.

The cigarette he was puffing on was crooked; he'd probably picked it up on the street. It waggled up and down in the corner of his mouth as he spoke.

"Well . . . if it ain't Fearless Fosdick. Hey, Cleve--where ya' been, my man?" He slowly dragged his fingertips through his eye sockets. "Ain't seen you in one helluva long time." He had that dumb glazed look of a man who had conditioned himself to go through life with absolutely nothing. I couldn't help wondering where he'd slept last night.

"Hey, Deck! This is my office, remember? Business, strictly business here, my friend. How about you? Haven't seen any troublemakers hanging around my door, have you?"

"No, but I do move around, my man. You know how it is. I coulda' missed a lot. Why? You spectin' some trouble hereabouts?"

"Not really, just wondering.."

He was right on my heels as I went up the steps. "Mind if I come in?"

"Not right now, Deck. I've got a client on the way—she should be here pretty quick. Maybe we can bullshit a little bit later- okay?"

"Right on, my man. Right on." He gave me a shaky thumbs up and jerked his head when the cigarette burned his lip.

I turned the key in the lock and went inside, hoping he wouldn't traipse in behind me, as he was prone to do. The lock snicked into place behind me and I stepped over a pile of mail laying under the mail slot and opened a window. The office is a ten by twelve space with a desk, a file cabinet, and a couple of stuffed arm chairs for clients. There's an old-fashioned iron radiator with broken controls and a stamp-sized bathroom with a toilet and sink.

Closed for nearly a month the place reeked of foul air. The smell of old and nasty, like the stale odor of cigar smoke, hit my nostrils. I opened the other window and retrieved a can of Glade from the bottom drawer of the file cabinet. Spraying it generously, I checked for anything out of place as I went.

A spider made its way down a large web on the window; dust was thick on the sills. I picked up the red plastic milk crate that I'd left on one of the chairs. It held my baseball mitt, a bat, and some tennis balls.

A bunch of files was still piled on the desk, right where I'd left them, and a Christmas Cactus sat on a small table in the corner, near death, from lack of water. The coffee cup rings on my desk reminded me that I needed to start a pot. The Mr. Coffee couldn't begin to brew a cup like my percolator at home but it worked. I threw the mold-filled coffee filter in the wastebasket, rinsed the pot, then measured the coffee into a new filter and poured bathroom water into the reservoir. Joe DiMaggio would be proud.

I took off my jacket, picked up the mail, and sat at my desk to go through it.

There was a phone bill, the light bill, a correspondence course offering to teach me Tai-Kwon-doo at home in my spare time. Also, an invitation to take a Disney cruise, an advertisement for a socket set from Sears, and an invitation to join the triple A motor club. There were no checks. Big surprise.

I spent the next half hour on the phone with hospital emergency rooms and the Cook County Medical Examiner's Office asking if anyone named Chelsea Rohrman, or fitting her description, had been admitted, living or dead, but came up empty and glad of it.

I tried to tidy things up a bit more, but the timing couldn't have been closer; at exactly nine-twenty, Betty Rohrman strolled in.

"Good morning, Mr. Hawkins."

"Morning, Betty—and, it's Cleve—okay? Mister Hawkins passed away almost twenty-three years ago. Have a seat." I pointed to one of the client's chairs.

She sat in front of my desk and opened a large brown purse on her crossed knees. "Are you aware that a very seedy-looking man is sitting on your front steps?"

"Yeah, I know he's not exactly GQ material, but he's a harmless friend of mine, no problem. His name's Deckle."

She looked me over like a weight-guesser at a fair. "If you say so." She faked a shudder with her shoulders.

I noticed she had dark circles under her eyes and her nose looked a bit red from crying. She was wearing a green blouse, designer jeans and tennis shoes. It was a shame she was hiding those legs. Fumbling around in her purse, she retrieved a pack of Mistys, tapped one out of the pack, and put it between her lips.

"I've been meaning to give these up," she said rather sheepishly. The unlit cigarette bobbed up and down in her mouth as she spoke. I picked up my silver desk lighter and held it to her cigarette. "You don't have to smoke that one, you know."

"Mmmm. Thank you," she said as she inhaled.

I watched her sit back blowing a slow stream of smoke, somewhat relaxed in the chair. She had changed in some way since yesterday at the bar. More nonchalant, I guess. She remained quiet and concentrated on the cigarette, bringing the ash to a point.

"Let me get you a cup of coffee—my special blend—cold water and Maxwell

House." I smiled, but she didn't think it was funny, I guess.

"Sure, that would be great, thank you, I . . ." She paused, and I felt her eyes on me--casing my every move. "My, but we are so polite this morning," she finally said, as she sat her bag on the floor next to the chair.

I shrugged and winked. "We try."

When the coffee was ready, I poured a cup for each of us. She took the steaming cup from my hands and, at the same time, looked for a place to tap the ash off her cigarette. I filled a Styrofoam cup with water and put it on the corner of the desk

"Sorry, no ashtrays here." I smiled. "You take cream or sugar?"

"No, thank you, black is fine." She stared at me over her coffee mug and I was reminded of last night's meeting—awkward and tense. Sometimes the silence says it all. She exhaled a stream of smoke and stared at the cigarette.

"So, Betty—did you bring some stuff for me-- those pictures and the rest of the information I asked for?"

"Yes. I've got the things right here." She sat her coffee on my desk and picked up the brown bag, which was about the size of a briefcase. Reaching inside, she pulled out a brown 8x10 inch envelope and handed it over. It was a bit heavy—had a little heft to it.

"Good, thanks."

"Everything's in there." She took another drag of her cigarette and then dropped it in the cup. "I got Chelsea's Social Security Number from Mom, but I don't have her driver's license, and we don't think she had any credit cards. Mom says all Chelsea's cards were maxed out a long time ago. A copy of her birth certificate is there, though." She began to wring her hands while I examined the pictures.

Most of them appeared to be taken with family in group-shots at the beach, picnics, church, and so on. There were school pictures covering her elementary and high school days. In one, her sister's hair was done up in pigtails. Her eyes were vacant and her small mouth was set in a thin, unemotional line. No joy, no sadness, no nothing at all.

In another, Chelsea's hair was tied back in a ponytail, and she wore amber sunglasses with Day-Glo frames and a silver one-piece bathing suit at a beach.

What looked like her yearbook picture, was a typical glamour shot of sorts, and probably the best one of the bunch as far as I could see. She was smiling and looked younger than her years, as though perhaps she hadn't outgrown her baby fat. She looked like a girl who had been loved and who believed the world was a good place where the joy of young womanhood waited for her with each sunrise.

"Chelsea's a pretty girl," I remarked. "Do you have something more recent?

I mean besides the graduation picture?"

"No, not really. Oh, wait-- of course I do—silly me. I have one from two years ago, right here." She pulled her wallet out of her bag and handed me a headshot of her sister. It looked like one of those taken at JC Penny's as part of a package deal. No question, it was a more recent picture. Her dark hair was pulled back loosely behind her neck and her brown eyes appeared to be moist. Her strong facial features, including high cheekbones, were striking. I continued to look through the pictures while Betty lit another cigarette.

I leaned back in my swivel chair. "So—tell me about Chelsea. What's she like?"

Betty sighed, giving it the weight of the world. "I guess you'd say my sister is like smoke. When we try to catch her, she evaporates. She's very confusing, difficult to understand. When we were kids, she could be sweet and sensitive, unafraid to show her affection to our mother and me, and a moment later, she'd be bratty and selfish, making demands of the entire family." She paused and stared at her feet for a moment.

"Sometimes . . . sometimes, I think the only reason she stays close to the family now is to borrow money from us. But, she's really a quiet girl, you know—doesn't do drugs as far as we know, and she's not a weirdo."

"Weirdo?"

"Yeah." She smiled. "Like this girl at my job who has a safety pin in her nose, a platinum screw through one eyebrow and an I-bolt in both ears. We call her 'Nails'."

Smiling, I said, "I see. And your father? How did she get along with him?"

Betty's eyes suddenly took on a hard look. She squeezed her fingers, like she could ring the answer out of her hands. Disappointment or hate manifested itself in those eyes. Her face reddened and she began to let some tears go, but not a downpour. I stood, circled the desk and put one arm around her shoulders and stayed with her.

Betty had a faraway look in her eyes when she continued. "He was our stepfather, actually. Our real daddy died in Vietnam in 1971." She paused before she said, "You must understand my mom. She's really a saint. Oh, we weren't like Beaver Cleavers with a stay-at-home mom in pearls making us pies and pouring us milk after school. That isn't it. She's just a decent soul, with a wonderfully big heart that didn't deserve to be wrung like an old dishrag."

Betty struggled to get another cigarette out of the pack before she went on.

I returned to my chair. She lit up and exhaled a long plume of smoke.

"Our stepfather didn't deserve her. He's dead now—thank God. He was a short, potbellied and sour-faced man, who always seemed to have an unlit cigarette over one ear and a can of beer in his hand. He was a drunk that got mean and sometimes used my mom for a punching bag."

I was lost for words for a beat, but I said, "Fate, unfortunately, which might have been kind to your Mom in the past, was obviously pissed off for some reason and so . . . anyway, shit happens. Sorry," I murmured, "They oughta be able to make body armor for the soul. Your mom sounds like a strong woman, though."

"Yes, indeed she is. Don't be sorry, though. We're certainly not. The son-of-a-bitch died three years ago—Diabetes complications. You may think I'm cruel, but I really am glad he's gone. So's Mom, but she just won't admit it.

I tapped my fingers on the edge of my desk. "So how did your sister get along with him while he was alive?"

"Ha! How do you think? She hated his guts. Couldn't wait to get out on her own when she was barely seventeen." I noticed she was biting down on her lower lip with her upper teeth. Her eyes were wide and fixed on me-tears on her cheeks.

It was nothing new. I'd heard this story before. Betty blushed slowly but pervasively. "I think you get the point," she said.

"Yes, I understand."

She suddenly leaned forward. "I'm sorry, but what does all this have to do with the fact that my sister's missing? I mean, who cares about my stepfather? I told you my sister is a loose cannon when it comes to men. How much more do you need? I want you to do something about finding her."

"I know, and I will, Betty, but the more information I have to work with the better I can investigate her whereabouts. See what I mean?"

She shifted in the chair and sipped her coffee. "Nobody seems to care. I didn't even see anything about her disappearance on the ten o'clock news. That's the cops for you. Look, Cleve-- we'll pay you whatever you say, just help us, please?"

I sighed. "This is not about money, Betty. Sure I get paid, but I told you, we can discuss my fee later. Right now it's all about your sister. Now, we have some tools to work with in this business. People use credit cards, and credit histories list purchases, and people own cars and driver's licenses, and social security numbers, and all of these things are ideal for tracing a person. I'll look through her phone bills and talk to the utility companies, check with the DMV and that kind of thing. And listen, of course, I care. You wouldn't be sitting in that chair if you didn't believe me now, would you?"

She settled back and exhaled a puff of smoke. "No . . . I guess not."

"See, I've found that when I take the time to learn that much about someone, there's usually a reason for the interest that's not readily apparent to everyone. Please, just trust me and bear with me here. First of all, we don't know that your sister has met with foul play. Not at all. I need time to do some investigating, and I promise I'll stay in touch. I can reach you at this number you gave me, right?"

"Yes." She folded her arms. "I'm trying to understand . . . really, I am, but, we're really so afraid something's wrong." She bit down on her lower lip.

"Try not to worry so much. Let's assume that your sister is okay. Think positive. I'm going to get right on it. I've got to track her car through the DMV and talk to some people. Lots of people. I have contacts on both sides of the law, including some real dirt bags."

"Really?"

"Yes, but I just want you to realize some things here from the get-go. When you hire me I work for you. That means I'm on your side. My job doesn't mean working with what the cops dig up. So, if you don't want the cops then I'll try to live by that." I paused and watched her face for a reaction before continuing.

"That also means I don't have to be nice. I don't have to read the Miranda to a suspect, and I sure as hell don't have to wait for any lawyers. Now, I know you're scared, but try to realize that your fear is really an irrational emotion that sort of floats from place to place like a helium balloon that you touch with your fingertips. It'll be where you want to find it."

"Well, I'll try real hard, but it's so difficult." She blotted her eyes with Kleenex and stood to leave. "Thank you, Cleve. Please call me as soon as you know something, will you?"

Outside on the steps, as Betty and I shook hands and said goodbye, Deckle who was ambling along the curb, made a gross sound when he hocked up a goober and spit in the general direction of the curb.

Betty looked back at me with widened eyes. She shook her head before she got in her car and drove off.

That Damned Deckle.

CHAPTER FOUR

Bart felt a catch of lust in his throat. He gnawed at his lip. The thought of taking the new woman made him tingle, pulled at him, like a nicotine addict who'd gone too long between cigarettes.

His gaze darted everywhere, his mind a microprocessor clearinghouse of potential problems and what to do about them as he tailed her to her house in the suburb of Des Plaines. His ego was intact, while his predatory senses were always alert—a lone wolf who knew which prey was weak and vulnerable and which was dangerous. He was an animal and proud of it.

He had shadowed her for more than two weeks and knew she would be next. He thought he knew everything about her—at least everything he needed to know. Where she worked as a legal secretary and where she lived. She didn't appear to have a boyfriend. Not many visitors either. Several times he'd watched as she used the front door key, which she foolishly kept hidden under the welcome mat. Welcome indeed. Bart grinned.

That day, she was wearing a cream-colored silk blouse, hip-clinging slacks, and low heels that lengthened her legs and tightened her ass at the same time.Her hips twitched sideways with each of her steps, like two bobcats fighting in a gunnysack. They were soft moves, the motion of the world right there in raspberry slacks, with the slender back tapering down to her waist, her heels clicking on the sidewalk, her shoulder-length hair swinging in a backbeat to the rhythm of her legs. Bart doted on that action now as he sat in his car, waiting.

His anxiety accelerated later on as he watched the young woman came home from work and used an automatic garage door opener to pull inside and close the door.

Parked just down the street, Bart would wait until all the lights went out in the house. He hated the wait; it was the worst part, but he knew it would be worth every second once she was his.

His patience paid off after midnight, when he saw the drapes being drawn in the front room. All the lights went out and the house was shrouded in darkness. On her way to bed, he assumed. It was as dark as a womb, and she was in there, alone

It was nearly one in the morning when Bart slipped on his latex gloves and reached for the .38 caliber Smith and Wesson, with a silencer. It was wrapped in a towel, and tucked under the front seat. He scanned the area and neighboring homes before slipping the ski mask over his head. It was time.

He popped the trunk, slid from behind the wheel and got out. His boots barely made a sound when they touched the pavement. His eyes swept the entire area once more, before he loped toward the house with the gun held down at his side. Reaching the doorstep, he crouched down and put his ear to the door. He heard the humming of the air-conditioning, and that was all.

Adrenaline surged through his body as Bart located the key under the mat and slipped inside through the front door. He stood as still as a statue, allowing his eyes to adjust to the dark. He listened for a moment, until he was satisfied that all was clear, then tucked the gun inside his belt and pulled the hypodermic needle from his jacket pocket. He slowly made his way to what he knew to be the woman's bedroom door which was slightly ajar. A portable television sat on a dresser at the foot of the bed. Canned audience laughter accompanied the jittery blips that flashed sporadically on the bed and bedroom wall.

Lisa Idone awoke from her restless, dream-filled sleep, to see the frightful image of a man wearing a ski mask hovering over her. Bart stood there, backlit by a grainy light that seeped around the bathroom door-- a faceless silhouette with shoulders like mountain slopes. When he jabbed the gun into her forehead, Lisa's eyes widened and panic exploded in her face. Shards of it wedged in her throat, making her gasp for breath. Bart saw the muscles in her arms and legs lock up and she started to scream. He smacked her across the face and slapped his hand over her mouth.

"No, no. Shut up! Don't move and don't scream, bitch. I will kill you."

Bart jabbed the needle into her neck and watched her eyes as they slowly closed. When he was sure she was out, he snatched up the bedspread, rolled her body up in it and threw her over his shoulder. He pulled the bedroom door closed behind him and paused briefly, before he made his way to the front door. He heard a dog bark in the distance, but satisfied that all was clear, he let himself out, sprinted to his Volvo, flipped the lid up, dumped the body in the trunk, and drove away.

Thirty-eight miles outside of Des Plaines, the road shrank from four lanes to two, and shadowy hills sprouted up. The landscape became nothing but forest, while, the road straightened out, like a tunnel through trees that were twisted like weeds competing for light and air. It was as if they had transplanted themselves a hundred years before on abandoned land. A half-hour later, Bart was driving on an asphalt ribbon that wound through a wide flat area of greenery half the size of a football field. It was Lewis Lisecki's driveway.

Using the opener, he pulled the Volvo inside the three-car garage, where he parked next to Lewis's Mercedes. He closed the door, grabbed his gun from under the seat, and got out, then followed a narrow stairway out to the backyard. The property was manicured, filled with plenty of natural flora: scrub oak and maple trees, monkey flowers and renegade grass. Bart walked to the edge of the veranda and spat in the shrubs before entering the house through a back door.

Lewis sat at his desk, smoking a cigar, pretending to ignore any intrusion.

His tri-level house had an interior that screamed money. The den, situated off of the living room living room, boasted a cathedral ceiling. It was elegant, with comfortable furniture and chandeliers. Matching chairs faced an immense flat-screen television, centered to perfection in a mahogany entertainment center. The windows were draped with white shears, and an orange, brown, and cream, hand-crocheted afghan was precisely folded and arranged over the back of the champagne-colored couch.

Bart stood in silence after he entered the den, where he saw Lewis, and hovered nearby, waiting to be acknowledged. His hands were folded in front of him, in a pose of respect--ready to step, fetch, and kiss his friend's ass.

"Yo, Lew! Red dog has got somethin' for ya." He knew Lewis was aware of his presence, but insisted on playing his usual head games by feigning ignorance. To Bart, it was like getting ice water thrown in his face. The man pissed him off when he acted so arrogant, not letting on what he was thinking or how he felt. Bart didn't see why he should be expected to read the professor's mind.

"Oh, there you are, Bartholomew. Come right in. Want a beer?"

Bart sniggered. "Does a bear shit in the woods? Ha. Ha. Hell yeah, man"

"Help yourself," Lewis murmured as he sipped the cocktail that sat on his desk.

He was bald, unflappable and soft-spoken. Screwed at birth, he had been given a dumpy fat boy's body to live inside, one with flaccid arms and a short neck, duck feet, and bad eyesight so that he had to wear thick, round glasses that made him look like a goldfish staring out of a bowl.

"I sure as hell will," said Bart. "Want me to get you another *Grey Goose* while I'm at it?"

"No. I'm all set, thanks." He slid back in his chair and watched as Bart, wrapped his fist around the neck of the bottle and took a long swig of beer.

"Did you see the papers?" Lewis asked. "The heat is really on, my friend."

Bart took another swig and burped. "No, I ain't read the paper today.

Why? What's goin' on?"

Lewis glared at him as he ground his cigar in an ashtray and sighed heavily.

"Bartholomew, do you suppose someday you might consider conducting a conversation without scratching your balls?"

"Ahhh! Get off my back, will ya', Lew? You know, sometimes dealin' with you is like jerkin' off with sandpaper." He chugged the rest of the beer and headed to the fridge for another. Lewis followed his every move.

Bart opened another beer and said, "Hey, here's one for ya' boss. What's black and brown and looks good on a lawyer?"

Lewis glared with his "don't-fuck-with-me" look, which Bart fielded with an incorrigible grin.

"Give up? A Doberman. Ha. Ha. Ha."

Lewis sighed. "As I was saying, Bartholomew, the situation is getting too hot. I don't think you are tuned in at all, anymore."

"And what does that mean, exactly?" countered Bart.

"Meaning. . . we have to lay low for a while after tonight. The papers are full of it every day now, pictures and all, must I make it any clearer? And you can bet the police are beginning to put some pieces together. We need to cool our heels and do without for a while. That's it, you understand?"

Bart laughed. "I told you, Lew, don't sweat it. They ain't got shit."

Lewis got up and walked past a stuffed chair located near the front windows. He nudged the drapes aside and peered out, into the night, then drew them closed.

"No, I suppose you are right, but we can't possibly know that for sure, now can we?" He lit another cigar and studied Bart. "And we sure as hell don't need to help them, do we?"

"Help them?" Bart's brow wrinkled. "What in the hell do you mean by that?"

"Well, for instance, you need to do something with that red hair of yours."

Lewis spoke with what's known as New England Lockjaw— an affliction of women, for the most part, but men are sometimes stricken with it, and it usually occurs in social functions when the speaker's teeth are clenched, and enunciation is accomplished by moving only the lips.

"My hair? What do you' mean?"

Lewis watched him rub the back of his neck, like he was checking to see if he needed a haircut.

"I don't know. Change the color, for one thing. Dye it. That red hair stands out like red on the penis of a dog. It's got to go."

"Say what? Hell no! Look here, Lew—there's a lot of red-headed dudes running around. Why should I fuck with mine?"

"Please don't ask something so stupid, Bartholomew. Surely you know the answer to that ...and your hair needs to be cut, too. This is 2010, not 1974. As it is, you blend in with the general populace about as well as a rhinoceros in a petting zoo."

Bart's ass cheeks clenched like a boxer's fist. He almost laughed, but said, "Nobody's got their eyes on me so far, partner. You think I'm the only redheaded fucker on the planet? I don't think the color of my damned hair looks suspicious, but I'll cut it shorter—okay? Damn! You're always looking for the dark lining in a silver cloud, Professor."

"Please, just listen to me on this, I . . ."

"Oh, shit! Comes down to it, you should shove that rug back further on your fat head, instead of wearing it like an overseas cap. Jesus-- all that green you got, and that thing looks like it came from K-Mart."

"Just trust me, it will be for the best, believe me," said Lewis. We must be extremely careful. That's all I'm saying. Now then... you have a treat for us tonight?" He cracked a smile for the first time since Bart had arrived.

"Sure do," said Bart. "Got 'er in the trunk—all bundled up and waiting for you.

She's dying to get out, you might say." He paused. " Ha, Ha--get it?"

"Ahh, yes," Lewis sighed. "Your sense of humor does amuse me now and then." His thoughts were elsewhere, and his heart was beating so fast he felt faint. "I must say, I haven't been this anxious in a very long time, Bartholomew."

Bart sniggered. "Got that old Viagra kickin' in, do ya?" He fussed with a pimple on his Adam's Apple as he spoke.

A stern look clouded Lewis's face. "Enough! I'll dim these lights. Why don't you, go and fetch our new friend. Take her right downstairs of course. I'll be along directly." He took out a handkerchief and mopped the beads of sweat from his brow.

"Is she beautiful?"

"Hell yeah. I would never let you down, boss . . . you know that. I owe you big time and I ain't forgettin' it."

"I certainly hope not. Our arrangement incorporates zero fuck-ups, my friend, and don't you must start listening to me. By the way, I gave you enough money last time to switch vehicles—did you take care of that?"

Bart scrunched his eyes closed and smacked his forehead with the heel of his hand. "Aw shit! Sorry, Lew. I forgot about that different car thing."

"See what I mean, Bartholomew? You don't listen," he growled. "Do you realize how few Volvos there are on the road? You need to get another vehicle right away.

I trust you still have the funds I gave you?"

"Yeah, sure. I'll do that tomorrow, for sure—first thing." Bart stared at Lewis to see if he was really pissed, reading his face, his eyes, although he knew it was nearly impossible. Lewis was a man who believed he knew everything and had to have complete control. He was always one or two steps ahead of the rest of the world, in his opinion.

His voice sounded shaky and he glared as his faced reddened. "Bartholomew--get that new vehicle immediately. You make me angry with this cavalier attitude of yours. The smallest details can end up causing insurmountable problems when not handled properly."

"Don't you think I know that shit? Jesus, you remind me enough."

Despite his arrogant, street-punk posture, Bart always attempted to show patience with Lewis. He figured putting up with his bullshit went with the territory. People living his lifestyle had to be patient as well as cold-blooded. Bart swallowed the last of his beer and burped again. "Okay, so I'll meet you down there."

. . .

Lisa was conscious. She thrashed and moaned as Bart dragged her out of the trunk. "Mmmmff. Mmmmff." He hoisted her over his shoulder, unconcerned about her noisemaking; nobody would hear her. The duct tape still covered her mouth, and the nearest neighbor was almost a quarter mile away. Taking his time, he re-entered the house and headed down the marble steps leading to the basement.

The room looked new, like it had been built recently , or at least, remodeled. It was decorated quite tastefully, the way many woman might have done their bedrooms if they had the money. There was a genuine brass bed, an Antique white dresser with brass handles and flowery wallpaper. Plush Berber carpeting covered the floor, and a dressing table displaying a silver brush, comb and mirror sat near the bed.

There were no windows.

Several U-shaped hooks were anchored into the walls, and long, chrome chains dangled from each of them. An assortment of leather accessories--whips, black boots, masks, nipple pinchers, and other bondage paraphernalia was showcased in a mahogany cabinet situated on the opposite wall. .

When Bart tossed Lisa on the bed, her eyelids fluttered as though the fluorescent lights in the room were short-circuiting. A flash of anger suddenly disappeared from her eyes, replaced by the crush of confusion and fear. "Mmmmff" The left side of her face was swollen and bruised from the slap Bart had given her earlier. Blood oozed from the corner of her mouth and she was covered in sweat. Her muffled breathing was labored; her chest rose and fell uncontrollably.

As he unrolled her body from the bedspread, her pink nightie, rode high on her thighs, and Bart got an instant erection. He cuffed her wrists to the sturdy brass poles on each side of the headboard and removed the duct tape from her ankles, because Lewis always wanted the legs free to direct as the action dictated.

Lewis crept downstairs wearing nothing but a white T-shirt and boxers. About thirty pounds of unnecessary gut spilled over the waistband. By the time he arrived, Bart had everything secured and the overhead lights were dimmed. The camera, sitting atop a tripod was on.

The two men stood side by side and admired the exquisite paleness of their new victim's body—her beautifully shaped hips, legs and breasts, the pink nipples and the dark thatch of pubic hair, that was partially shaved and shaped. Bart's breathing was heavy; he felt his erection throb.

"Good work, my friend," Lewis breathed. "She's perfect." His words caught in his throat. "Simply perfect."

Lisa's eyes were filled with terror. Her body wriggled, bolted, shook. She moaned, and thrashed up and down on the bed. "Mmmmff. Mmmmff."

"Shut up, bitch!" Bart barked as he backhanded her across the face. Holding his gun with one hand, he grabbed a handful of her hair with the other, then wrenched her head straight back and locked his eyes on hers. Shoving the muzzle against her forehead, he growled, "Listen, sister—you can make this easy or real fuckin' hard—don't be stupid now, calm your ass down." He grinned. "Enjoy."

He stuffed the gun back inside his belt, and his eyes glazed over as he slid both hands inside Lisa's nightie. He felt her body's heat against his palms, her breasts felt soft and warm and he fondled them like a juggler with several balls.

"You won't need this," he grunted as he ripped the skimpy

covering from her body. Completely naked, she made a desperate attempt to break free by suddenly whip-lashing her body up and down. "Mmmmff. Mmmmff. Mmmmff."

Beads of sweat broke out on Lewis's chest and he swiped the moisture off his face with the handkerchief he had wadded up in his hand. Gripping Bart's arm, and in a quivering, yet calm voice, he murmured, "take it easy, Bartholomew." He was enjoying the panic in the woman's eyes. "We don't want to spoil this for the young lady, do we?"

He traced the tips of his fingers along her cheek. "She's so wonderfully young—and yes, so beautiful." He nudged Bart aside. "Pay my friend no attention, Sweetie. I'll make you feel better now." He leaned down and suckled her nipples as he ran his hands up and down her wriggling body.

Glancing over his shoulder, he said, "A shame you had to tape her mouth." He stared into her eyes and said, "I'd like so much to kiss you, my lovely." Realizing he could wait no longer, he dropped his boxers and stepped out of them. Delirious with lust, he slowly stroked his erection.

Climbing onto the bed, Lewis slipped on a condom and shoved Lisa's legs apart. He kneeled at the ready, but she kicked and flailed, so he couldn't penetrate her. With her head flying from side to side, she continued to protest. "Nuuuh! Nuuuh! Nuuuh!

Seeing the fear and loathing in her eyes only enhanced the man's raging excitement, and he continued to stroke his erection in anticipation.

He gritted his teeth. "Hold her fucking legs, Bartholomew. This pretty little thing is not cooperating. Feisty though . . . You know I love that."

Bart grabbed the girl's legs and forced them apart while Lewis's erection stood straight out. He moved out of the way as Lewis guided himself in with one hand while squeezing one of her breasts with the other.

When he entered her, Lisa's hips jumped as if a powerful electric shock had zapped her. Her muffled sobs were loud and continuous despite the tape covering her mouth. Lewis slobbered on her neck and delighted in probing inside her vagina again and again, until less than a moment later, with a loud gasp, he finished and rolled his trembling body off of her. "Oh, sweet Jesus, that was the best, you sweet thing,"

Bart had dropped his jeans and was jacking off. He wanted to slice the girl's throat more than anything else. He could smell the blood and taste the power. Backing away, he stroked himself as he watched Lewis's assault. Leaning a shoulder against the wall for a moment, he slid down to a seated position on the floor and stared until Lewis withdrew his phallus and removed the condom with a resounding *snap!* His breathing was raspy and labored as he gazed at Bart through slitted eyes. He scotched his fat body off the bed and retrieved his boxers.

He croaked, "Now then, she's all yours, Bartholomew. I commend you on your choice this time." He was still breathing hard when he headed for the stairs, then turned and said, "It's a pity we cannot keep her for another round. However, as I said, it's the end of this until further notice, my friend. Be sure and clean things up when you're done." He continued to leave and said, over his shoulder, "Go out the back way, and don't forget to turn off the camera and lights."

CHAPTER FIVE

Most of the time, Deckle had the thinking processes of a squirrel with rabies, and little or no conscience regarding hygiene. He needed a shave, a shower and less alcohol when he stumbled into my office three days later.

I was just enjoying my third cup of coffee and perusing the *Sun Times* when he came about 9:30 and straddled the only hard-backed chair I had. It sat in the corner where I wish he had left it.

"Morning, Cleve." He cleared his throat and grinned like a butcher's dog. I could smell the booze from where he sat, six feet away.

"Morning, Deck." I glanced back at the paper and paused, allowing him time to finish wiggling around on the chair. "How's it going?" I grinned. "You've been into the hooch, this morning, my man?"

"Naw--not yet," he lied. "I just thought maybe you had something for me to do today, is all, so I come by early." He leaned back and almost fell ass over end but righted himself. "Ooops! Yeah,

I knew you'd prob'ly be in today, it being Monday and all--now that you're back that is. You *are* back to stay, aintcha?"

"I don't know, Deck, we'll see."

I needed to talk to my old partner, Kris Branoff who was a D3 now. A Detective three, now in charge of all the other homicide detectives, he had moved up in the ranks since I'd left. I punched in his number.

Deckle said, "I could go get you some of them donuts and then . . ."

I stuck a finger in the air and shook my head. "On the phone now, Deck?"

Cradling the phone between my ear and shoulder, I leaned back in my chair. Good old landline phones. I've got my smart phone, but still prefer the old-fashioned real phone I keep in my office and at the apartment. I waited, and in the background, I heard other cops talking, phones ringing, typewriters tapping and a bit of male laughter.

Deckle nervously tapped his foot on the floor to let me know he was anxious. I ignored him and gazed out the window at the intersection where a crew of construction workers were setting up some scaffolding around what used to be The First National Bank building. It had been vacant for close to a year, and now the rumor was that a computer sales and fix-it shop was going in. There goes the neighborhood, I thought.

I hadn't had breakfast yet and my stomach was begging. Holding for Branoff, , my eyes shifted over to Deckle for a moment and I said, "Why don't you have a cup of Joe while I finish making some calls, Deck? No, better yet ..."

I went in my pocket and found the smallest bill I had, which was a twenty. "Go ahead, run over to the bakery and get a half-dozen?" Deckle rocked up on his feet in a flash. "Yeah, my man, Cleve, I can do that. What kind you want today? What kind, huh?" He reached for the money with a trembling hand.

"Ah, I don't care. Get me three jelly and three of whatever you want. I'll need the change when you get back though--right?"

"Oh, yeah, sure. You know me, Cleve, I'm always good with

change. Heh. Heh. Heh. Yes-sir-rebob."

"Okay, well--get going, my gut's growlin'."

He scooted out the door and I continued to wait. I hate being put on hold. It's such bullshit. However urgent a thing is, there comes a point where there are no more places to go. So, the urgency burns out, and you sit there like you've got all the time in the world, while the world rolls on around you. Another two or three minutes went by before the receptionist, came back on the line.

"Cleve, you still there?"

"Yes, Brandy--go ahead."

"Well, Detective Branoff said he'll have to call you back, he's tied up for a while. You know how that is, Slick."

"Yeah, okay. That's alright. Just tell him I'll be stopping by this morning and hopefully, I'll catch him then. Thanks."

"Okay, Cleve, I'll tell him. Bye bye."

I realized I needed to talk to Betty Rohrman's mother, too, so I dialed the number Betty had given me with her sister's picture. It rang twice.

"Hello?"

"Good Morning, Mrs. Rohrman?"

"Yes."

"My name is Cleve Hawkins. Betty, gave me your number. She was in the office to see me about your daughter, Chelsea."

"What? Sorry, who are you again?"

"Cleve Hawkins, Ma'am--private investigator. "Have you heard from Chelsea at all in the last few days?"

"Heaven help me, no I haven't. I remember now though, Betty told me about you. You're the cop."

"No, Ma'am, I used to be an officer. I do private investigation now. Listen, I can certainly understand your concern over Chelsea. Would it be okay if I stopped by later today so we can talk about it."

There was a spot of dead air before she finally said, "Yes. I 'm not going anywhere. Betty told me you might call. You're not a cop, eh?"

"No, Ma'am. I'll be out later today then, if it's okay?"

"Yes, I guess that will be okay. Betty told you where we live. I just need you to find Chelsea for me." She hung up without saying anything else.

I thought about my plans to visit the police department and see Branoff, before I went out to her house. I wanted to see what homicide had on this serial killer the papers were headlining lately.

And then, just like that-- there she was: Maureen. Right there, in the front of my mind, despite everything else that I should be wrestling with. Strange, how some things haunt a man. I knew Maureen still worked at the station, but I hoped I wouldn't run into her for some reason. Crazy, I guess.

I sat there staring at the phone, when Deckle came back with the donuts.

"I got you three strawberry, Cleve."

"That all they had was strawberry?" I shook my head. "No raspberry?

He sat the box on my desk and I grabbed a donut.
"Nope, they had blueberry too, but I know you used to like strawberry, so..."

I waved him off. "It's okay, Deck. There's no such thing as a bad donut. Fugeeddaboudit."

He hunched over his coffee as if it were a small fire, keeping him warm.

Sipping it, he said "Ugh. It's cold now and it needs more sugar, too. Ya' know, Cleve . . . you really need a microwave in here."

"Yeah, Deck. I'll have to remember that. Grab a donut."

I knew the welcome mat wasn't out for me at the headquarters. That would be true even when I showed my private investigator ID. Then there was Maureen. Damn, I thought, as I looked up and caught Deckle smiling, showing me his near-toothless condition.

"So, you got some more runnin' for me to do, Cleve?" He talked with his mouth full and it wasn't pretty.

I put out my hand. "My change?"

"Oh, yeah. Man, I almos' forgot." He handed the change to me in a wad of bills and coins. "So, if you ain't got nuthin' for me today, can you spot me a coupla' bucks and I'll work it off for you later--

you know I will, Cleve."

"Ah, yeah, sure." I sorted out the money and handed him a fin. "Just see me next time I'm here. I might have something for you then, alright, Deck?"

"Yes, sir." He quickly stuffed another donut in his mouth and was still chewing when he zipped out the door. "Thanks, see ya, Cleve."

I put on my jacket, turned off the lights and locked up. After I donned my Cubs cap I was on my way to see Branoff. I hadn't been by the station in months and wondered how I'd be received. Private detectives never get the same respect as real cops, and it's easy for some to forget I was one of them. "I'm here to see Branoff," I said when I got to headquarters on the south side a half-hour later.

The desk sergeant wasn't impressed with my ID. Smitty's was his name and he looked like Ernest Borgnine, with the crew cut, skin the color of fresh ham and king sized eyeballs. At six feet four, he weighed at least 280, but he was more thick than fat. He seemed to smile--for whatever reason. I smiled right back. Friendly.

"It'll be awhile, Hawkins, I can tell you that,"

I studied his eyes and saw the dumb glazed look of a guy who had conditioned himself to go through life pissed off. No wonder he was no longer riding in a patrol car.

Anyway, I figured I'd cool my heels in the duty room since there would likely be a wait. I took a chair from the corner, twirled it around, and relaxed, letting my arms dangle over the back as I looked through windows that needed washing. The sports section of the Tribune was laying there, so I looked through it while I waited.

The room was shiny glass and polished wood. Cops and civilian workers came and went, in and out, and I got the kind of hostile looks and blank stares usually reserved for drug dealers hanging around grade schools.

About thirty five minutes into my wait, Kris Branoff called the desk. He came out with his new partner Phil Andrews who I knew used to work Vice.

"Hey, Hawk, how's the hammer hangin'?" Kris smiled and

extended a hearty handshake. Branoff was six feet two inches tall and weighed at least two hundred and thirty pounds. A former college football hero, he was blond, handsome-- I guess--but, his eyebrows look like they've been fed steroids. Rugged and well-dressed, a guy who looked as though he just walked out of an L.L. Bean catalog: white shirt and tie, khaki pants and suspenders. To his credit, Kris could see through bullshit the way Superman could see through steel.

"Sorry about the wait, buddy. The girls said you called earlier. I've been as busy as a whore in prison with a fistful of pardons.." He turned to Andrews. "You know Phil here, don'tcha?"

"Yeah, sure." We shook hands.

Andrews, formerly a detective with narcotics and vice, was so huge he was hard to miss: six seven or eight, maybe two hundred and sixty pounds, with over-the-ears blond hair, and gold-rimmed glasses. He looked like a tight end for The Bears. He was dressed in a dark sport coat over a black golf shirt because they made him look smaller, I figured.

"Come on in, Hawk. I'll have Maureen bring us some coffee."

"Sounds good," I said as I watched him wave his hand over the security pad, He held the door open and we followed him inside. As we passed Maureen's desk, my heart pushed into my throat, feeling larger than a clenched fist.

Maureen is tall, exceptionally lovely, and not yet forty. The way her blond hair curved around her swan neck turned most guys to mush. She had stunning blue eyes and long, beautiful legs. That day, she was wearing a black summer suit with a very short skirt and a white open-collared blouse. A simple gold chain adorned her neck. She tried to hide a smile as we passed by.

"Hey, Mo," said Branoff, "would you get us some coffee? And, look who stopped by--Cleve Hawkins."

Maureen smiled faintly and nodded. She stared at me without expression, in a way that made me feel uncomfortable. I felt myself flush. "Cleve--how have you been?"

"Fine, thanks, Mo. I grinned as we locked eyes. *What the hell was I supposed to say?*

Branoff closed his door and we got down to business. Slumping in his chair, he exhaled and looked around at the piles of files stacked on the floor around his desk. Andrews stood to the left and behind him with his meaty hands shoved in his pockets.

"So, what's up, Hawk?"

"Well, I've got a new client--young gal--says her sister has gone missing. I know you guys are up to your asses in alligators on these missing girls right now, but I wanted to see what you had on my girl--if anything."

"Her name?" said Andrews. His voice was deep and flat, making the kind of throbbing purr that powerful engines make.

"Chelsea Rohrman. Her sister, Betty is my client."

"The name's not ringing any bells," said Branoff. "Nothing on her yet, that's for sure. We've identified the two that were found on the south side. You probably heard about them."

"Yeah, who hasn't?"

Branoff pawed through some notes on his desk. "Yeah--one was Gwen Saffner, caucasian, twenty-five years old, graduated in 2010 from Loyola College, was not employed. The other was a hooker with a street name of Pearly. Haven't got her real ID yet. Both of them were raped, tongues cut out and throats slit. Bad shit."

Branoff stared at me with a look that drew lines in his face and made it appear rigid. It was obvious that he was frustrated and pissed with the situation.

"We believe six to eight women are missing so far. All young, late teens, early twenties. Most of 'em, college students. Only the two have been found, though." He paused as his eyes locked on mine. "The one you're talking about could make it nine, Hawk. For chrissakes, I hope not. All of these women were reported missing in the last eight weeks. We think we're in the middle of what could be one of the worst kidnapping and killing sprees in Chicago's history."

I fell back in my chair. "Jesus, Kris. Any leads?"

Andrews remained quiet and guarded. Branoff shook his head. "We're nowhere, so far, Hawk. This case is about as easy as opening a can of peas with your fingers. You know how it is. We're doing all we can as fast as we can--got a task force set up, but we need a break of some kind. Phil has the book right there on his desk.

Andrews held up a blue three-ring binder that I knew was the murder book. As the lead homicide detective, he filed all the reports, witness statements, and relevant evidence he accumulated in that one binder. I could see that there weren't many pages yet in the book, but more would be added as the case developed.

"We'll let you make notes, Hawkins," he said as he handed it to me. "The medical examiner's prelims are in here. You can read it here at the station and make notes, but you can't make copies. You know . . . that's the way it is."

I said, "Just so everyone understands, what we now have is a two-way flow of information, right? None of us has a problem with that?"

"Hawkins," Andrews said, "I'm looking for the killer, so long as you don't do anything that interferes with my case, help yourself. If you find something that helps us out, so much the better."

I pulled Chelsea's most recent picture out of my inside pocket and handed it to Kris. "Here's the woman I'm looking for."

Branoff studied it briefly and passed it to Andrews.

Andrews said, "The shit sheets are heating up, too. The TV people are okay, but compared to the newspaper people, they're mongrels at a dog show. Some of them would have attained asshole status in any part of the world. I've even heard somebody is saying there's probably more than one killer. What the hell . . .?"

Branoff turned his chair, and, with his back to me, studied the wall of respect behind him. Pictures of the family, awards and so on. After a suitable pause he swiveled back and looked hard at me.

"Nuts don't come in bunches. Only grapes do. We need some tips. So far, the people I've talked to would have trouble finding Lassie in a cat show."

"I knew that was all I was going to get, so I stood. "Well, I guess I'll leave you two alone so you can get back to the grind. You'll let me know if anything comes up on the Rohrman girl, eh? I'll do the same."

"Yeah, for sure, Hawk. Good to see you back at it." Branoff stood and shook my hand. "I'll assign a contact officer to you...most likely, Andrews, and you'll be briefed. They'll give you copies of all reports, transcripts and witness statements if you need them. I'd appreciate hearing anything you find out, too. We can use the help, Dick Tracy." He forced a smile.

"You got it, and hey . . . don't let the press give you too much shit."

"You know I won't, Cleve. I'll give them something, alright. You know how it is, though. You can be going along working the case as best as you can, but then something happens and the case isn't what you thought it was anymore. Suddenly, the way you see everything is different, as if your world has changed color. We'll keep up a good front, anyway."

I said, "Remember, partner . . . wonderful things can happen when you plant seeds of distrust in a garden of assholes."

"Indeed," he said as we shook hands.

I passed Maureen's desk on the way out. "Nice seeing you again, Mo" I said as I tipped my Cubs cap.

She smiled and slipped me a note as she said, "Yes...be careful out there, Cleve."

As soon as I got behind the wheel of my car, I cranked it up and read her note that I had scrunched up in my hand. It said, "Call me."

CHAPTER SIX

Florence Rohrman had a low, grainy voice, like that of my third grade teacher in a nightmare. One of those people whose telephone voice exactly matched her in person. She was wearing a yellow polka-dotted dress when I got to her house in Lombard.

Her daughter, Betty had told me Florence was fifty-six years old, but she looked much older. She was breathing like someone with emphysema and tried to steady herself as she pointed to a chair. "Have a seat."

The furnishings were meager to say the least, and I immediately noticed thr senior pictures of Betty and her sister, Chelsea, displayed on the wall behind a sofa that should have seen the back door of Goodwill years ago. I smiled my friendly neighborhood detective smile and thanked Florence.

Reaching for a Pall Mall, she tore the pack open to get the last one.

"Why don't you go ahead and tell me everything you can about

Chelsea, Ma'am."

She still wasn't sure about me and folded her arms across her chest as if she'd grown cold. We sat quietly for a moment before she lit the cigarette, raised her head and blew out a stream of smoke.

"So, you were a cop or something?"

"Or something."

"Thrown off the force for drinking?"

"No."

"Police brutality?"

"No."

"Then, how come you're not a cop now?"

I hesitated, then sighed and said, "It's a long story."

"You must have seen too many bad things in the world, eh, Mr. Hawkins."

"I have. And to be honest, I've contributed my share to the world's problems."

"Have you?"

"Maybe not on purpose."

"Tell me a good deed, you've done on purpose"

Florence caught me off guard. "Oh, I don't know offhand . . . I've seen good deeds . . . It's not a bad world, Ma'am, and I don't mean to suggest it is. For all the bad things I've seen, I've also seen the most extraordinary acts of courage, kindness, honesty and love."

"Well, our family is pretty torn up. We're not The Waltons by any means."

I saw her reading my reaction, trying to figure out if I believed her, I guess.

"Chelsea was a fat kid with a terrible overbite. That bastard husband of mine made fun of her. Can you imagine that? Anyway, we handled the overbite with braces and by the time she was fifteen she'd trimmed down to look like Barbie. Problem was, Chelsea was like smoke--hard to hang on to." She stared off into the kitchen as she spoke. "She still is."

"That must have been hard for her, though."

"To put it mildly," she said. "Nothing has ever worked right for her." She was in between cigarettes and her hands flopped restlessly in her lap. Sobbing once, she stuck a knuckle in her mouth and turned away.

"She always did like the boys," she continued. "Well, of course they chased her, plenty. It seems like she was always getting her heart broken, though...you know what I mean?"

I nodded and started taking notes on a small pad I carry.

"I couldn't convince her to stay home. She wasn't interested in college, like her sister." Florence pulled a wadded tissue from the pocket of her housedress and blew her nose.

"Finally, Chelsea left home as soon as she turned seventeen--lived with some guy we'd never met before. You know, a young wise-guy from school. It was a shame, because then the old man up and died on me. Hell, she would have been happy here, I think, with him out of the way."

"Yes, Betty was telling me her stepfather was a drinker."

She nodded. "Absolutely."

"I have to ask you this, Florence, is Chelsea a drinker, too?"

"No, not really. Oh, she likes to have a good time, alright. What young girl doesn't? But she isn't a drunk by a long shot."

She opened a new pack of Pall Malls and lit another cigarette.

"Does she have her own car, Ma'am?"

"Yeah, that old red Toyota. It's paid off, as far as I know."

"I don't suppose you have the license number do you?"

She shook her head. "No, I wish I did."

"That's okay, I'll be able to get that."

"How about work. She must have a job?"

"Well, I'm not so sure. She's had a few of them. The last I knew, she was working for some company called Edelman's over on the west side. I don't know the exact address."

I was still writing when I said, "How about credit cards?"

"Ha! It's funny you should ask. Chelsea has had a Target card and a Discover, but she maxed them out a long time ago. Last year, I think it was. I still get the threatening letters every week from both outfits."

"I see. Well, I'll need copies of those letters, if you don't mind."

"Sure. You can have them all, if you want."

We let the silence hang for a moment while I made more notes. Florence coughed and cleared her throat.

"Betty said she believes in you, Mr. Hawkins. Please be honest with me, do you think you'll be able to find Chelsea? I mean, I reported it to the police and all, but I understand a lot of people go missing and they never find them."

There was a crack in her voice as she continued. "All I know is what I see on TV and in the movies. None of the criminals in those shows seem very smart and they are always getting caught by the good guys, even though they don't really seem much smarter than the bad guys."

I looked into her wet eyes. I'd seen the same eyes so many times. "Listen, Florence, we don't know that Chelsea is really missing, yet. But I'll be honest with you, it does seem that way, and if God forbid, she doesn't show up, any candid cop will tell you that if we don't grab the bad guys during the commission of the crime,

there's a good chance we won't catch them at all. When we do nail them it's often through informers or because they trip up and turn the key on themselves. But I intend to do my best. We'll find her, you can depend on that."

She nodded, rolling her eyes like that was all a load of crap.

"Now, you indicated that Chelsea likes to have a good time. Can you tell me where she liked to hang out? Friends? Bars? You know."

"Oh, I don't know, really. She's been on her own so long. I only see her about once a month--if that. According to bits and pieces I've picked up though, she liked The Hideout on Clark Street, and I understand she went to happy hour like it was mass, at a place called Ernie's on Halstead Street. I've seen that one--it's a dump, believe me."

"Okay." I reached for one of my business cards and wrote my cell number on the back. I stood and passed it to her. "Well, that should be enough for now. If you'll give me those letters from the credit card companies, I'll go and get started. Please stay in touch and let me know if you hear anything at all, and I will do the same."

When I left the Rohrman house, the sky was clear and struggling to be blue, and I felt as though I could breathe again.

Florence called out as I was on my way to the car:

"I don't care that you're not a cop, anymore, or why . . . just bring my little girl home, please?"

I waved as I opened the car door, and even though I had my doubts, I yelled back, "We'll find her, Ma'am." But, I was really beginning to wonder if she would be alive when we did.

CHAPTER SEVEN

I learned a long time ago that it's better to ask for forgiveness than permission but I was on the fence. While I grabbed a burger and coffee for lunch at Mickey D's, I looked at the slip of paper that said, "call me." I could smell Maureen's favorite perfume on it.

I waited until I got back to my apartment before I called her and we agreed to get together for a drink, and possibly dinner. I'm not sure why, but I was nervous and assailed by doubt. It had been a long time since we'd been together.

After showering and shaving, I brewed a pot of coffee, then dressed to impress in a black turtleneck, crisp dark Levi's and my tan sport jacket. No scotch. Freshly caffeinated and smelling of after shave, I went to pick her up. I didn't think I should wear my Cubs cap.

Her place was on the near-north side, an older, affluent area in the city, only a couple of miles from her work. I rang the doorbell, and a moment later I heard footfalls, then the porch light flicked on and I caught chords of background music as the door opened.

"Hello, stranger," she said.

"Hi, Mo. You look great."

"What did you expect?"

"Nothing less, believe me."

She wore a black sheath dress with sheer black stockings and high-heeled pumps. A chunky necklace of black onyx with small diamonds rested on her chest. I remember when I gave it to her for Christmas. I leaned in and kissed her lightly on the lips. She smelled so damned good I wanted more but decided to act my age.

"You don't look half bad yourself." She looked at me as though she might be going to buy me.

"Thanks, it's the other half that's a real mess," I said as I took her hand and led her to my car.

"I'm glad you haven't lost your sense of humor, Cleve. Where are we going--not too far, I hope. I'm starving."

"I thought we'd go to *Geja's Cafe* on Armitage just for old times sake. You remember the fondue place?"

"The romantic place, you mean?" She grinned. We made small talk for the rest of the drive; it was stumble-and-awkward time for both of us, but more than cordial. We skirted along the lakeshore where in the early evening, when the temperature drops, seniors come to watch the sunset, and families come to feed the ducks and play children's games.

We didn't have to wait long for a table at *Geja's* and the waiter brought menus with our drinks. We toasted with a Grey Goose gimlet for her and Dewars scotch on the rocks for me. The drinks shimmered in the glow of the table's candle. Mo's eyes sparkled.

She leaned in and put her hand on top of mine and gripped it with amazing strength. "Thank you," she whispered.

"For . . . ?"

"Calling. I wondered if I'd ever see you again."

"You must know I could never let that happen. We've got history, right?"

"Yes. History is the story that survives." She paused. "How are you doing, Cleve? Really, I mean--I want facts, nothing but."

"Ah--I'm hanging in there, but I'm getting the feeling I'm going to be x-ed from the Citizen of the Year Award by the Chicago police."

"Why? Something go wrong the other day in Branoff's office?"

"No, not at all. I'm working on a new missing person case, is all that was about."

She looked quizzical. Her eyes narrowed and she let out a long breath, her lower lip protruding in a lovely pout. She moved her hand back. "Let's not talk business. Have fun with your life before you turn old and feeble." She couldn't hold back a slight giggle.

"Hmmmm. I'm looking forward to my feebletude," I countered. "Okay--no business tonight." I picked up my scotch, drank most of it and rattled the ice in the glass. "Another round?"

"I've barely started mine." She squinted at me and took another dainty sip.

"And I knew I wouldn't get a real answer, you goof." She glanced at my glass. "Not having any problems with that stuff, are you?"

"Nah. I laid off pretty much after one shitty night that almost cost me everything."

"What happened--mind if I ask?"

"No big deal. A little tiff in a bar." I paused. "Maybe later, okay?"

"Sure." She paused and fiddled with her napkin. "You're a good man, Cleve. Good men don't need to say anything. But, you realize that you are a control freak." She had a half smile on her face as she spoke. "You get pissed off at people who don't toe your line, people who don't follow your script, people who ask questions you don't want to answer."

"Yeah, there's that," I said with a smirk. "Sometimes, I'm not thinking straight. Actually, telling people what I think of them is not difficult, because they already know it and are probably surprised I haven't said it sooner."

She nodded. "You just need a mental enema. A testosterone overflow is part of the problem, I think." She smiled at me, her eyes flickering over my face. "Do you know what a real man's example of group therapy is? Answer: World War Two."

I couldn't help but grin. "Is that right?"

The waiter came back with another scotch and I started to wave him off.

"No, no, Cleve. Let's order, do you mind? I'm hungry," she said, as she glanced at me and the menu at the same time.

"Sure. Okay, let's do it. Fondue is the name of the game here, remember?"

"Oh, I know. I just want to look. It's been a while." She put her hand over mine and looked at the menu a moment longer. "Why don't we just get a Premium Fondue Dinner for two?"

I shrugged. "Sounds great." I nodded an okay to the waiter who was still there.

There was a pregnant lull, and for a moment I found myself studying the colorful pattern of the booze bottles stacked behind the bar. I listened to the soft human sound of the half-full bar and thought about my evenings alone.

Suddenly, loud applause erupted, and we turned to see a young guy on bended knee at the far end of the bar. A beautiful young girl sat on one of the barstools, with her hands over her mouth. The guy had evidently just proposed and she had accepted. This was not an uncommon sighting at *Geja's Cafe.* Maureen and I looked into each other's eyes for a split-second and then quietly laughed. She squeezed my hand..

We caught up with each other's lives for a while as we had dinner, and I must admit, I felt more comfortable as the night wore on. I actually had thoughts of what may be in store for us later on.

Later, while we stood outside on the sidewalk, in front of her place, I watched the blinking light of an airplane passing overhead. The nighttime view was spectacular. There were broken clouds high in the sky, a bright moon, and a beautiful starlight. Perfect.

Then the stars and the moon seemed to disappear, replaced by the darkness of my silhouette, and I was kissing her, my hand cradling the back of her head, then her neck. I felt raindrops, but didn't give a damn.

My heart danced when Mo wrapped her arms around my neck.

She smelled of lavender and good soap. Our movements were so easy, I thought. Our heads turning at just the right angle, our arms going around each other with no wasted motion, like pieces in a puzzle someone was sliding together.

"Know how long I've wanted to hold you like this?" she whispered. She was kissing me then, clinging, working at it and I went along, letting it all happen again, letting her brush her mouth over my cheek and lay her head on my shoulder.

"I didn't know if I'd have to hit you over the head and jump on you or what, in order to get you to hold me," she whispered.

"I wanted you too. Why couldn't you know that?" I murmured.

"You could have called me anytime, Mister Hawkins," she whispered.

"Yeah, but . . ." She placed her fingertips on my lips. "Let's get together again, sometime soon," she said. Her beautiful blue eyes were wide open. I felt my heart sink as she turned, blew me a kiss, and disappeared into her house. Even with heavy heart, I couldn't help studying her backside until she was gone.

I sighed, walked back to my Explorer, and drove for ten minutes in a light rain to my apartment. The night enveloped me, the darkness broken only by the lights on the dash. When I turned off the ignition, I sat in the car for a moment to get my bearings.

I finally went inside and up the stairs to my place, an apartment in an older brick building on Surf Street. I've got four rooms, and a bath, with a compact kitchen at one end of my living room. An oversized leather chair faces my flat screen television. *What else could a man want?*

I went to the fridge where I knew I still had about four bottles of Old Style left. Cracking one open, I took a long pull and it felt great going down, burning the back of my throat with its cold bite.

I couldn't help but focus on the evening's events, and compared them to my outings in the past, before Maureen: Dating other women, I discovered they had more euphemisms for lovemaking than Eskimos have words for snow. And they rarely use masculine nouns or pronouns when describing their love life. "I'm dating someone, I'm seeing someone, I've met someone, and I date other people," and on and on. Whereas a guy will just ask another guy, "Hey...Joe, you fuckin' anybody?"

I had dozed off watching TV, when the phone rang. I checked my watch. It was three in the morning. I watched that phone like a cobra, before I picked it up.

CHAPTER EIGHT

When the phone rings at three in the morning, it can't be good news, but I didn't hesitate to pick it up.

"This better be good," I said.

"Why are you still up at this hour?" Maureen asked.

"You're joking, right?" I grinned.

"No. I'm sorry, I just couldn't sleep."

"I'm having a little trouble myself--must be something in the water at *Geja's* place."

"Yeah...must be. Listen, I wanted you to know--well-- I had to tell you--I had a wonderful time tonight . . . well last night now."

"Yeah, me too."

There was a long beat of silence before she spoke again. Rather than try to help her out, I just shut up and listened. "Please understand I did want to invite you in, but--well--please stay in touch, Cleve."

"I plan on it, Mo. I really do. I'll let you go, though, okay?"

"Yeah, sure. Well, goodnight."

"Morning, you mean. Goodnight, Mo." I heard her giggle a little before she hung up.

In the quiet that followed, I pondered the entire situation, rolling our evening over in my head. As we used to say in school, "Getting laid is no big deal, but not getting laid is a very big deal. I knew she needed more healing time so remaining horny would be a problem--my problem, at least for now.

I reflected on past relationships I'd had before Maureen and I began dating. Sally Burke was a good one. She was attractive, had a cute South Carolina accent, didn't hate Yankees, loved sex and Jim Beam, was poorer than me, and had always wanted to marry a cop. I don't know if she ever realized her goal but, as it turned out, she wasn't the one. I fell asleep on the couch watching re-runs of Lucy.

. . .

The next day, events kicked into overdrive. The promise of an early spring had turned to overcast skies and spitting rain. It was after three in the afternoon and I had a late lunch. A half-eaten burrito lay on my desk, sitting on oil-stained paper.

I was waiting until it was close to happy hour at the bars, specifically, Ernie's on Halstead where Chelsea Rohrman hung out, according to her mother. I'd finished reading The Tribune's coverage of the serial killings and scrutinized some mail. I also looked over the threatening letters to Chelsea from credit card companies and made notes on purchases. I shoved my own bills aside, figuring I'd deal with them later. I knew the rent was due-- I damn sure didn't need a reminder.

I swiveled my chair around, rested my feet up on the windowsill, and watched the rain. The wind was blowing in the parking lot and small trees across the street whipped back and forth.

I needed to get started, but I don't work well with a lot of scientific clues. Since nearly all the crimes I've looked into were human, it figured that all the clues I came up with would be human.

I stood and stuck my .38 in the holster behind my right hip. It was a bit chilly, so I slipped into my bomber jacket and grabbed my

Cubs cap. I'd just turned the key to lock my desk when Betty Rohrman strolled in.

"Good afternoon, Mr. Hawkins."

I smiled. "Please--I thought we were on a first name basis, Betty. It's Cleve."

"Yes, okay--sorry. Am I interrupting anything?"

"No, not really-- have a seat."

She drifted across the room and took it upon herself to close the blinds. She sat in my client's chair and when she crossed her legs, she showed me a flash of thigh. I don't think it was on purpose, but a leg man notices.

Her hair was up in a bun, and she wore thin horn-rimmed glasses and a little business suit that was way too short for any real librarian to wear. She paused and looked around . "Your office is exactly the way I expected," she said.

"Yeah, I'm saving up for a neon sign of a smoking gun."

She smiled but then suddenly sat very erect, her knees together and neck held high. She took out a pack of Misty menthols, and looked around for an ashtray. She lit a cigarette, half-heartedly, and fanned away the smoke. I reached in my drawer and retrieved an ashtray. "Sorry about the cup last time."

"Thanks. I understand you were out to see my mother."

"Yes. She's a fine lady."

"Hmmmm. My parents," she said, and shook her head. "My step-father was a psychotic; people who got too close to him suffered because they did not--could not--understand the sheer uncontrolled malevolence of the bastard. And as for my mother-- well, there were times when I would rather have eaten worms in a root cellar than go to a restaurant with both of them. Did she give you anything that will help you find Chelsea?"

"Ahhhh--yeah, I got a couple of things I can use."

"Like what?" She lowered her eyes.

"Well, as a matter of fact, I'm on my way right now to check out a spot your sister used to frequent. Who knows what I may find there. Maybe some small bit of information. You might be surprised at how those small things can become really big, important clues.

The blood of investigation is just that--clues."

I skirted around the desk, sat on the edge of it, and looked down at the top of her head. "Listen, Betty. Sometimes the smallest mistake can trip up the bad guys. You'd be surprised. Ever heard of Watergate?"

"Yes, in school. Why?"

"Well, the Watergate guys weren't nickle-and-dime second story idiots. They had worked for the CIA and FBI. The reason they got busted was because they taped back a spring lock on an office door by wrapping the tape horizontally around the lock rather than vertically. A wanna-be-cop security guard spotted the tape and removed it but didn't report it. One of the burglars came back and taped the door open a second time. The security guard made his rounds again, saw the fresh tape and called the Washington police. The burglars were still in the building when the cops arrived."

"Oh, I see. Well, anyway, I quit my job yesterday morning at the insurance company."

"What?" I circled back around and retrieved my Cubs cap from the top of the filing cabinet; I tilted it back on my head. "Why's that?"

She shook her head from side to side. "Because, I was fed up with the boss. I have been for some time, and now with Chelsea missing, I just can't concentrate, especially with that bastard, Jenkins, hanging all over me."

"You mean, your boss is sexually harassing you?"

"Yeah---well, no--not really. It's just that-- well, I sort of blew up and called him an unprincipled asshole, an utterly cynical bastard, and a monumental prick." She stared at her feet which she clicked together, back and forth, like Dorothy. "I believe that was the last thing I said."

"Hmmmm. I see. Well, I don't know your circumstances there, of course, but you may want to reconsider--I mean the way the job situation is right now and so forth. I know it's difficult, but try not to worry so much about your sister. I realize that's easy to say, but I am working on that. You can't help things by quitting your job. In fact, truthfully, it's better if you stay busy. I'll bet your mom could use some help, financially, too, couldn't she?"

"Yes," she murmured.

There was a long moment of silence before Betty drummed her fingers on the edge of my desk and spoke.

"So . . . You think maybe I should go back and apologize for my profanity, rephrase the sentence in Proper English, and ask him if he'll work on those problems. Is that right?" Sarcastic, I thought.

"I would."

She stayed seated for another moment, then stood to leave.

"Just call me the minute you hear anything--alright, Cleve? Please?"

"Of course. You know I will," I said as I shook her hand. Her heels echoed loudly in the hallway as she left.

The rain pattered on the brim of my ball cap as I jumped in the car and headed for Ernie's on Halstead. Happy Hour would get under way, soon. Maybe I would run into some of Chelsea's friends. I had the radio turned low to a jazz program on WBEZ, Stan Getz played horn during my twenty-five minute drive. I was feeling good, figured I looked rakish in my Cubs cap and leather bomber jacket. It had stopped raining and the sun peeked through leftover clouds.

A half-dozen cars were parked at odd attitudes around Ernie's tiny parking lot when I got to the bar. I crept around and parked by easing nose-first into a slot, shut it down and locked up.

The bar's windows were tinted, so that patrons could see who was coming in from the parking lot without being seen themselves.

The joint was owned by Ernie Jurnic. I knew him. He was a snake in a suit, who was nothing, if not an expert in how to break the rules. I was quite sure he hadn't changed. I had my beefs with him when I was a rookie in uniform. He could sell cheap drinks, he said, because he avoided high overhead. He avoided costs by not fixing anything. The pool table used to have grooves that would roll a ball through a thirty-degree arc into a corner pocket. The overhead fans hadn't moved in years. I wondered if Jurnic would be around.

Ernie's looked like hundreds of other bars, a country ballad on the jukebox, workingmen sitting around drinking Budweiser, some college students and secretary types were perched at the bar. I had to wonder why in the hell Chelsea Rohrman found the place so appealing. I felt I fit in about as well as a cat at a dog pound.

The man behind the bar was in his late sixties, short and stout with sloping shoulders and no neck. He was bald as a cue ball, with shaggy steel gray hair ringing the sides of his head and sprouting in fantastic tufts from his ears. A cloud of curly chest hair spilled out of the V of his plaid shirt.

I noticed one of the waitresses wore a tight open-collared shirt with Garth Brooks's likeness plastered across it, and tight jeans that hugged her wide hips and disappeared into the tops of red, high-heeled, looking-for-trouble cowboy boots. She was chewing gum and had a butterfly tattoo just visible on the swell of her left breast.

"Can I help you, sir?" she asked in a tone that meant, "What the hell do you want?" She was as perky as a chickadee but I was assuming dumber. She said, "You look like a cop, and I wish you'd please quit staring at my tits."

The bartender put six long-necked bottles of Pabst Blue Ribbon on her tray, Then, he rang up the bill, put that on the tray, and she left me and charged back toward the big round table in the corner. I caught snatches of conversations and the sounds of a cell phone playing a symphony of downloaded tunes. I'm still proud of the fact that my phone simply rings when someone calls me.

I dropped on a stool and the bartender wiped his way over.

"What can I get you, friend?"

"Ernie Jurnic here?"

He coughed before answering, turning his head away, not bothering to cover his mouth. Spit flew down the bar. He had an expression on his face that suggested he hadn't had a proper bowel movement in too long. "Ernie's dead," he said, recovering.

"Dead?"

"Yeah. Choked on a fuckin' bratwurst at a Bears game last winter."

"You gotta be kidding me."

The guy shrugged, started to smile, thought better of it, and shrugged again. Coughed. "His time was up," he said, running his rag in a circle. "You a friend of his?"

"Jesus Christ, no. I'm looking for a customer of yours. At least I'm told she's a regular."

"Yeah? You a cop?"

"Nope."

He looked around. Happy Hour had begun and I could see he was itching to take care of business, but he leaned in and said, "Who're you looking for?"

"A young girl by the name of Chelsea. Chelsea Rohrman to be exact. She liked to make your happy hour, I understand."

He turned and walked over to another girl working with him behind the bar. He said something to her, she nodded and came my way. She was a young one with a short skirt and very short blond hair. She wore a T-shirt that read *Save Gas, Fart in a Jar.* "You lookin' for Chelsea?"

Her voice was like fingernails on a chalkboard and she folded her arms, defensively.

"Yes. You know her, I take it?"

"Yeah, most all of us know her in this place. She's a fixture, you might say." Chelsea, by her account, was a precocious, snotty little bitch, who everybody liked, because she was bright and beautiful.

"What's your name, Miss?"

"Barb. Who's asking?"

"My name's Hawkins."

The waitress stayed on the move as she talked. I watched her lean over the bar to pick up empty bottles. She rolled her eyes, looking as if she had had years of experience. "What do you want with her? You a cop, Hawkins?"

"No, I'm not a cop, but I need to talk to her."

"Well, you're outta' luck. I work everyday except Sunday and I'm telling' ya', she ain't been in."

"When was the last time you saw her...can you remember?"

"Ah, I don't know. Say, why all the questions if you ain't a cop?"

"Okay, her family thinks she's gone missing. They haven't heard from her in over a week. Understand?"

She paused a minute and turned a bit serious. "Yeah, . . . a week ago, huh?" She stared at the ceiling as if it would tell her what she wanted to know. "Yeah, I do remember something, now that I think about it. She was having a bunch of drinks with some guy. Yeah, that's right. Yeah, they were sitting over there at the bar when I came to work. That was around five on Saturday. I think she left with him too." She sniggered as she said it.

"Really? Are you sure about that, Barb?"

"About what? Her leaving with a guy, you mean? Yeah. She left with the guy, alright-- but that wasn't so strange. What the hell-- Chelsea hung out with lots of guys."

A joker sitting two stools down craned his neck and said, "Yeah, I saw that dude with Chelsea, too. He was a young guy who wore his red hair like a big throwback afro that reminded me of a young Michael Jackson. Quite strange, since the dude was white."

I picked up my glass of beer, moved down the bar and stood next to him. "What did you say, friend?"

"Huh? Oh, I said, I saw the guy with Chelsea."

"Your Name?"

"Jesus Christ."

"I doubt it," I said.

"What's my name matter, you wanna' know what that guy looked like?" He wiped his nose with the heel of his hand and sipped his draught.

No shit, I thought, but I didn't answer at first. After a moment I got right in his face. "Yeah, go ahead. What did he look like?"

"Well, let's see . . . I remember he had lots of pea-size freckles all over his face." He made a small circle with his thumb and forefinger to show me. "And his hair was bright red and shaggy. Yeah, he had long red hair. He was wearing a Red Sox baseball cap, but I could tell his hair was long. Red, too, well orange anyway-- that's how I remember. Why? You a cop or somethin?"

"No--not a cop, and that's really good that you remembered." I took out my ID. Listen, I'm a private detective and I'm trying to find Chelsea. I've got some cop friends downtown. Would you mind coming down there and taking a look at some mug shots?"

"Nah. I don't want nothin' ta do with the cops, man."

"You won't even have to talk to a cop. I just need you to look at some pictures...see if you can spot the guy you saw her with."

He studied me for a moment, swallowed the rest of his beer. Then, after setting his empty mug on the bar with a resounding thud, he said, "Tell you what, Dick Tracy--you buy me a beer and I'll think about it, how's that?"

CHAPTER NINE

Manny Dubiel 's nose was alcohol-red. He wore faded jeans with a rip in the knee, mud-smeared Nike sneakers, and a wife-beater shirt that said *"Eat Shit and Have a Crappy Day."* He was around thirty-five, had a four-day beard, and the beginnings of a beer belly hanging over his belt.

When he approached me in Ernie's, he had been accompanied by a woman with a low tooth count who had her arm draped over his shoulder, and didn't want him to leave. She favored Ernest Borgnine's sister and I wondered if I was making a mistake trusting Dubiel's reliability, but figured it would be worth the gamble. I didn't want to lose this lead. For the price of a couple of Miller drafts, I convinced Manny to come with me to police headquarters for the purpose of looking at mug shots. I didn't have much so far, but maybe if I tugged on this thread hard enough, the whole thing would unravel.

I called Detective Kris Branoff who said he was fired up to go home, but would have his partner Phil Andrews stick around and wait for us.

Dubiel was a talker. We drove in my car and he never shut his mouth for the entire trip. He was well-versed in the rudimentary techniques of bullshitting, and trying to have a meaningful conversation with him was like petting a porcupine.

When he paused, and took the Camel cigarette out of his mouth, I noticed the end was all soggy and mulched.

"I'd appreciate your not smoking in my car, Manny."

"Yeah, okay," he said and kept talking. Then, he lit up and found a comfortable spot for his elbows to rest on the back of the seat. "So--if I identify this guy, is there any reward?"

"I don't think so, Manny. There usually isn't. You're being a good citizen, that should be all that matters, buddy."

"No shit? That doesn't seem right though, does it?"

I didn't reply. After a brief pause, he took off in a completely different direction, and I began to put this experience down to my usual bad luck of getting in a supermarket checkout line where the cashier was the village idiot.

He asked, "Do you know how to blind a redneck driver?"

"No."

"Put a windshield in front of his face. Ha! Ha!"

I had my fill of his mind-numbing jokes long before we got on Michigan Avenue, but his face lit with an idiot's grin as he continued to seek my acceptance of his talent.

"Hey, Dick Tracy, you hear the one about the dumb wop walks into a pizzeria and says to the guy, 'I want a whole pizza.' And the guy says, 'You want it cut into eight pieces or twelve?' And the dumb wop says, 'Let's make it twelve, I'm really hungry. Ha! Ha!"

"Dial it down, Manny," I finally said. "You're giving me a headache."

I was happy when we reached headquarters, parked, and went inside to the investigations division. Phil Andrews was seated at a desk, a cell phone stuck to his head. When he saw us, he clapped the phone shut and I introduced him to Dubiel. Then, Andrews took us in the back where access to the database was located.

"Have a seat, guys." He loosened his tie. "Now, Mr. Dubiel--I want to ..."

"Manny. My name is Manny--you can call me that. I like it better than that Mister stuff. You'll make me feel like you're getting ready to book me or something Ha! Ha!"

Andrews shrugged and glanced at me. "Okay--Manny--we have thousands of faces in our system. So I need some info to put in here first off, so we can narrow it down. Understand?"

"Yeah, I get that." He still looked as if he was waiting to be cuffed.

"So, tell me what you know about this individual you saw leaving Ernie's bar."

Manny looked like a kid that just discovered there was no Santa Claus. He stared at Andrews, his face knotted with disapproval. "I'm not going to get in any trouble doing this, am I?" Andrews looked my way and rolled his eyes.

"Of course not. Go ahead, Manny," I coaxed. "Tell Detective Andrews what the guy looked like."

"Yeah. Well, like I told Dick Tracy here, the guy that left with Chelsea had bright red hair--real shaggy, you know? Well, really orange hair. Sort of like that Carrot Top guy you seen on TV, ya' know. And he had a lot of spots--like freckles all over his face."

"That's it?" Andrews said. "Anything else?"

"No. Not really. Oh, wait a sec, he had big-assed ears, too."

"Okay. Anything else? How tall would you say he was?"

"I don't know. Maybe about as tall as you."

"So ,a little over six foot?"

"Yeah, I guess so."

"Okay, anything else?"

"No, that's about it. I wasn't really checking the guy out or anything, ya' know? He was busy making Chelsea giggle. His back was turned to me--know what I mean?"

"Okay. Give me a few minutes here." Andrews did his thing on the computer, and soon we were looking at mug shots of some mighty ugly citizens. Manny studied the pictures as we looked over his shoulders. Andrews kept advancing the screens.

Forty-five minutes later, Manny Dubiel was still looking through the database when Phil Andrews stood up.

"Can I get you a cup of coffee, Cleve?"

"Yeah, I could use a cup. How about you, Manny?"

"Huh? I didn't hear you. What did you say?" He was picking at a pair of ripe pimples on the peak of his Adam's apple as he stared at the monitor.

"Coffee. You want a cup?"

"Okay, sure. But I'm getting' tired of this. I can't believe so damned many dudes have red hair and turd spots on their faces. I don't think the man is in your computer. I've been looking a long time, don't ya' think?"

"Okay, just a little longer, Manny, alright? We need to be sure."

"Jesus! Yeah. Okay, I guess." He leaned back, his hands folded over his beer belly, stretching his shirt into a tight mound. He was a somber Manny now--much different than his earlier mouthy demeanor.

Another twenty minutes or so passed and I had just finished my coffee when I saw it. A Jolt! A small one--the smallest of tells on Manny's face. It was there though, a slight widening in the eyes. He recovered in less than a second and shouted, "There! There he is! That's the dude, right there!"

He tap, tap, tapped on the monitor screen. Andrews and I both leaned in to get a closer look. The man had a long, horse-like face, splotches of freckles and red hair just as Manny had said. An obligatory diamond earring sparkled from his left lobe.

"That's the guy, huh?" said Andrews.

Manny rolled his chair back. "Yup, that's the dude that left with Chelsea."

Andrews slid his chair over, in front of the computer. "Hmmm. Charles Bartholomew Hodgkins. You sure that's him, eh?" Andrews asked. "I need you to check him out real close now, Manny."

"Yup. I'd bet my mother's gold teeth on it." He jabbed his finger at the screen. "This is the guy I told you about. Trust me. See them spots all over his face. His hair is shorter in this picture, but it don't snow me. It's him alright." He threw his hands in the air. "Yes!"

"Okay, Manny. Why don't you go with Mister Hawkins here to the waiting area out front?" He looked at me. "Take Manny out front, then come back, okay, Hawk?"

"Hawk? Is that what they call you? Hawk? Ha! Ha! I like that." He nudged me in the ribs with his elbow. "Better than Dick Tracy, ain't it?"

I walked him out to the lobby. "You wait right here, Manny. Have a seat on that bench over there, I'll be right back."

"Yeah, okay. I done good, didn't I, huh?"

"Yeah, Manny, you did real good."

I started to walk away and he yelled, "This is gonna cost you another beer,

Tracy." He laughed. " I mean Hawk."

"Yeah. You just wait right here, okay?"

"Yeah . . . Okay, but I'm getting hungry, too," he mumbled. I went back and Andrews buzzed me in.

"So what do we have on this guy, Phil?"

He typed something into the computer before he answered.

"I don't know but it looks like you've got yourself a real prize here. Quite a sheet on Red. He was charged with assault in 1999, petty theft 2001, assault again--this time with a deadly weapon in 2003, indecent exposure same year. He spent three years of a five year stretch in Menard Correctional for armed robbery and broke parole. Ha!" He looked at Cleve and smirked. "Judge Philbin spanked his hands for being in a bar. That'll teach him, eh? Let's see--then, he was pulled in as a rape suspect in 2009. It says he beat that one because the victim recanted. He's not registered as a sex offender. I guess that's it."

"Jesus! That's quite a sheet. Maybe I'll get lucky with this asshole."

"I hope so," said Andrews. "But, look here--his last known address was an apartment in Cabrini housing, that was back in 2003, for chrissakes, while he was still on parole."

"Evil doesn't have a zip code, we know that Phil.."

Yeah, well, evidently after that he went off the grid. Seems like this guy leaves shit prints on everything he touches. Watch your back and good fucking luck, pal. We'll let you know if we find anymore on him and you keep us updated, right?

"For sure. Tell Kris I appreciate the help, too. Thanks, Phil."

I gathered up Manny and left. I was going to tell him he should get something to eat and go home, but on further consideration, I realized that would be like trying to teach a pig to sing; it wastes your time and annoys the pig. So, I dropped him off at Ernie's and gave him ten bucks for his beer, then headed for my place. On the way I ran through an Arby's and got three roast beef sandwiches and some curly fries. I held off eating until I got home in order to wash everything down with a cold Old Style, from the fridge.

I turned on the TV, sat on the couch, kicked off my shoes and thought about Chelsea in the hands of the red-headed guy. At least I caught a break, and I hoped he was the key, but worried that I would be way too late.

Tomorrow I would talk to Branoff about an APB. We had to find that guy. As I ate the sandwiches, I thought about calling Maureen, but that's all it was--a thought. I went to bed; it felt a lot better than the couch, but it took me a long time to find sleep.

. . .

Next morning, I called Branoff but he had left word that he couldn't see me until one o'clock in the afternoon. Meanwhile, I'd sent Deckle out to pick up sliders and fries for lunch. We had just polished them off when Kris called:

"I took care of the APB on your suspect, but I think you'll want to get in on something else that came up this morning."

"Oh--what's that?"

"Another possible lead on your missing girl, what's her name . . . Rohrman?"

"Yes. Chelsea Rohrman."

"It's a beautiful day, I thought you might like to take a drive in the country."

"What? Are you serious? Why?"

"Out in Aladdin, two teen boys went off the beaten path, exploring the forest for adventure and God knows what the hell, when they heard horseflies buzzing and seen them clustering on the ground and rising suddenly in the air. One of the boys found a long stick, and began pushing shit around. Long story short-- we've got bodies in shallow graves out there in the woods.

"Oh, shit!" It felt like my heart dropped out of my ass.

"Yeah. I got a call about an hour ago, and the proverbial shit has hit the fan here as you can imagine."

"You said bodies...how many?"

"I don't know, two so far, and forensics is still digging. I figured you might like to ride with me. I hope I'm wrong about your girl, but--well-- are you with me?"

"Hell, yes. Give me ten minutes. I'll be there before you get your coat on."

"Good. Andrews will be riding with us. See ya', and oh--the media has already got this shit on the wire. Don't drag ass, Hawk."

CHAPTER TEN

I knew the truth, had known it from the first day. To echo the words of Florence Rohrman: "something has happened to my daughter. Something bad."

I didn't believe that beautiful girl, with that smile, just decided to run away and not tell anyone. Nor, did I really think she took off on her own and was savvy enough to never use her cell phone or ATM or credit cards.

So far the police had made no actual mention of a serial killer, although that must have been on the minds of people living in and around Chicago. Their knowledge of law enforcement was derived from a lifetime of watching TV shows in which all cases get solved. The well-groomed actors find a hair or a footprint or a skin flake, they put it under a microscope, and presto, the answer comes to light before the hour mark. But that isn't reality. Reality was better found on the news. The cops in Colorado for example, still haven't found the killer of that little beauty queen, JonBenet Ramsey.

Elizabeth Smart, a pretty fourteen-year-old girl, had been abducted from her bedroom late one night. The media had been all over that kidnapping, the whole world transfixed, all eyes watching as the police and FBI agents and all those crime scene "experts" combed Elizabeth's Salt Lake City home in search of the truth--and yet for more than nine months, no one thought to check out a crazy homeless man with a God complex who'd worked in the house, even though Elizabeth's sister had seen him that night. If you'd put that on CSI or Law and Order, the viewer would toss the remote across the room, claiming it was "unrealistic."

My thoughts dwelled on this as we rode out to the crime scene. Branoff drove, with Andrews in the passenger seat. I had plenty of room to spread out in the back of the Crown Vic. Andrews draped one arm over the front seat and zoomed in on me.

"So, do you think your guy from the bar gave you good dope on the mug shot?"

"Ah, I don't know. He got pretty excited when he spotted the guy, didn't he? Seems legit okay, but Manny Dubiel's a little flaky. I don't think he's the brightest bulb in the chandelier to begin with."

"I think he might just be a lush looking for attention, and I agree, he has got some loose shingles."

I laughed. "Yeah, we can't go by his IQ. If the guy was any dumber, you'd have to water him twice a week."

"That sounds promising then," said Branoff, sarcastically.

The April sky was blue and bright, but the lifeless trees were black from an early-morning rain. Soon, we were out in the country cruising past cornfields, cows in pastures, and signs on trees that said JESUS SAVES. Fallen branches and logs filled the scruffy forest like petrified bones. The sun struggled to shine through the clouds, and the air was crisp.

We drove northeast to get to the outskirts of the small burg called Aladdin, watching the tattered spring earth roll by. The land was inundated by creeks and drainage ditches, broad fields showing the remnants of last year's corn and soybean crops.

When we arrived at the scene, the site was a jumble of sheriff's squads, highway patrol cars, ambulances, fire trucks, civilian vehicles and four-wheelers. A helicopter and one light airplane could be seen circling above the area like mechanized vultures.

Yellow crime-scene tape vibrated in the wind.

"This is gonna be a friggin' media free-for-all," said Andrews.

We got out and I put on my sunglasses. Branoff shielded his eyes from the sun's glare with one hand. The air was foul. Tiny beads of sweat broke out on my forehead and upper lip. I took a deep nervous breath, and could feel the dampness under my arms. People never get used to this shit.

The paramedics were zipping up the body bag on the remains of a female who had been buried in a remote section of a dense wooded area. She was white. It was impossible to tell too much more about her. Birds and animals had been feasting on her, and she almost didn't look human anymore. She didn't have a face; the skin and tissue had been eaten away. Red ants were crawling on the outside of the bag, the two men averted their faces when they picked up the bag and set it on the gurney, then one of them bent over and puked in the weeds. At times, all the masks and Vicks Vapo-rub in the world don't help.

The wind shifted out of the south, and the odor struck my nostrils, making my throat clench. We walked into the trees where there was a clearing of sorts. I wanted to puke, myself. They say, the day it doesn't bother you is the day you should quit.

At the edge of the clearing, someone had pierced the ground with a shovel and replaced the divits, creating a broken pattern that made me think of a root-bound plant in a cracked flowerpot.

"So, how did these kids actually find the body, Kris?"

"Wasn't very difficult. Like I said, God knows why, but they were deep in these woods when they spotted the flies. When they got closer, one of them started messing around by shoving the dirt with a stick. Then the smell grew stronger and he poked something soft, he said, that made him drop the stick and step back. They thought at first that it was a dead animal. I guess one kid's eyes started watering, not from the smell, but from what he thought they were about to see. They stumbled backward, away from the thing that was buried, but they couldn't look away from the hole the digging had created. In the dirt, all they could see was a sneaker attached to a foot."

"Jesus Christ! So then they ran like hell and called in on a cell, I take it?"

"Yeah . . . 911. I was told that the initial findings by forensics showed the body was that of a young girl or woman. She was fully dressed and had been covered over by no more than a foot of dirt. Blond and about five and a half feet tall, she wore the kind of sneakers a kid might, but because of the heat and the dampness in the ground, plus the piles of red ants that had been pushed into the depression with her, the decomposition was so advanced that it was impossible to figure her age.

Branoff had a mask over his face when he crouched over the empty grave of a recovered body. He leaned forward with his elbows on his knees. He didn't turn around, but I could see the rigidity in his back and the blood rising in his neck like the mercury in a thermometer. "Why does this shit always seem so shocking?" He looked down for a moment and rubbed his forehead with his fingertips.. Then he looked up. "No matter how many times I witness this shit, I'm jolted. It's just crazy, I tell you."

I caught myself hyperventilating and tried to slow down my breathing cycle. Running a hand back through my hair and then back across my mouth. In fact, minutes went by before I forced my heartbeat down by taking huge gulps of air.

I looked over to where the forensics people were still digging. Five bodies had already been exhumed and lay atop mounds of dirt. I wondered how many more and if Chelsea Rohrman was one of them.

Branoff stood and took me off to the side. "The last victim was discovered late this morning by the team doing an extensive crime scene examination of the area. We've got a fuckin' graveyard here, Hawk." He cleared his throat and spit off to the side. "They think that's it, thank God. You know they'll be out here all night though, and for however long it takes to be sure. I hope like hell that your girl isn't here."

I pulled Chelsea's picture out of my jacket. "I'm going to check before they bag the rest of them up."

"Sure. That's why I figured you'd want to be here. What we

know so far though, is that none of the victims have any ID on them and I have to be honest with you, Hawk, the bodies are so far gone that we'll probably have to rely on DNA in order to track them." He paused and shook his head. "Of course, your girl has been missing less then ten days, supposedly, so maybe you'll be able to ID her, if she's here."

"Damn . . . I hope she's not."

"Yeah, I know what you mean."

Branoff was at my side as I watched them finishing up with each victim. I gritted my teeth and hoped that none of them would look like Chelsea's picture.

As we checked the fourth victim, my heart sank. I double checked the picture with what was left of the woman's face. A forensics guy I know by the name of Hank Ketchum, gently brushed the dirt off her chalk- white face. I studied the vacant eyes that were still wide open with fear. I stared at her and felt as if the ground was tilting under my feet. There was no doubt---victim number four was Chelsea Rohrman. *Fatal Beauty.*

I hesitated to notify her mother or sister, Betty. Not yet. I knew I needed to wait until after the Medical Examiner, Bill Farnsworth, confirmed his findings. I hoped he would put a rush on the results for victim number four, listed on the tag as no name-- not even a John Doe . . .just a female corpse with a number.

. . .

These things take time, but Branoff and I had coffee two days later and met with Farnsworth, at the city morgue. He was a short man with a pugnacious face, a brisk manner and a tic. Every few seconds, his entire head dipped slightly to his left.

We all agreed, there was little doubt that all the girls had been abducted and murdered, or held, in the same place by the same killer or killers.

"Your particular vic was shot in the head at very close range," said Farnsworth, "but with no defensive wounds on her body and nothing under her nails. I rushed a tox screen and I'm operating under the theory that the victim was drugged and raped before she was shot."

"Jesus!" I murmured.

"Yeah, whoever did this made her suffer. The young woman was mush inside. Approximate date of death is hard to say, but she was in the ground at least six to eight days. Age-- I'd say between twenty-two and twenty-five."

"Evidence of rape?" Kris asked.

"No doubt," said Bill. "Abrasions and contusions around the vagina, also the rectum. So he sodomized her to boot. No traces of bodily fluids, in other words the perp used a rubber."

'So, what's the actual cause of death?" I asked.

"Well, she was shot, of course. But was she asphyxiated beforehand? Could be. I doubt that, but lack of powder burns on the skin tells us something was placed over her head during the killing. There are no ligature marks on her wrists or ankles, but, she was bound up with the duct tape for a long time, maybe tortured. Her stomach was empty, but we did find alcohol--enough to suggest a lot of drinking prior to death."

"How in the hell did he manage to grab her?" I asked.

"She was probably abducted while she was drunk, I'd say. Her first tox screen was clear though, which tells us she wasn't a prostitute. I suspect she was grabbed off the street or lured into a captive situation. Maybe she met a guy on the internet. You know how many young women are out there now flirting with guys just itching to tear them apart?"

"More than we know or want, that's for damned sure," said Branoff.

Farnsworth scratched the back of his neck as though a mosquito had just bit him. "Here's what I think. At a certain level of fear, the capillaries pop, and blood issues from the pores with a person's sweat. This girl suffered real bad. She was scared shitless."

"Damn. How about prints?"

"Zero. Either rainwater or mud ruined anything that might have been there, unfortunately. We're still checking the DNA. I'll notify you, Branoff. You can give those results to Hawk. I no can do, as you know, Cleve." He smiled and winked. "Serves you right for quitting."

The long day fell on me like an anvil. When I got home, late that night, I took a long drink of Johnnie Walker. Standing in the kitchen under the light fixture, I was unable to take the glass from my mouth; my shadow was like a puddle of ink around my feet. I drank until the glass was almost empty, wishing I could melt and seep through the cracks in the floor and disappear.

I had never agreed with the idea of capital punishment, primarily because its application is arbitrary and selective, but that night I had to agree and the killer or killers of Chelsea Rohrman and those other girls belonged in a special category and deserved the needle. Now, I'd find the killer--and if I could, I'd shoot the bastard and take a nap after I did it.

Now, the hard part. I'd have to have Florence Rohrman ID her daughter's body.

CHAPTER ELEVEN

When the Medical Examiner drew the dark-colored curtain aside, Chelsea Rohrman's corpse was on display in the glass window for her mother, Florence and sister, Betty to identify. The body was covered with a sheet which the ME slowly pulled away to show Chelsea's face.

Florence moaned and collapsed. Betty and I caught her before she fell all the way down to the floor. Betty nodded in lieu of her mother's affirmation. "My God, it's her." she screamed. "Chelsea!"

I helped with her mother. "It's Chelsea, alright. It's my sister." She sobbed uncontrollably and I collected Florence in my arms and took her to a nearby wooden bench where I held her in my arms. You never get used to this part and I felt the tears well up in my eyes. At that moment in time, I wanted to confront the killer and make him accountable, not simply for his crimes but for his existence, even though I had learned long ago not to stray too far through the webs of my soul.

The usual portrayal of a P I's life is romantic, a noir trip into a world of intrigue, with wealthy female clients dressed in veils and overweight bad guys sweating under a fan in a bar in the Caribbean. The real world of the PI could be compared to shit running through a sewer.

Real life is a bitch and there always will be a dirty side to deal with. I often wonder if some people are made differently, born without a conscience, their sole purpose in life to destroy everything good in the world. A cop's heart bleeds for the victims and their families. Anyone who thinks differently knows nothing and has no heart of their own.

After they calmed down a bit, I walked out with Betty and her mother. It was raining softly while I tried to comfort them in the only way I knew how. "I'm really sorry, but we're going to get the man who did this--I promise you that. It may take a while--but we will get him."

"Really?" said Florence. "Will that bring my daughter back?" She looked at me as though she were coming out of a trance . . . her voice, little more than a whisper. She was still hyperventilating as she tried to continue. "You know as well as I do, Mr. Hawkins, these people never get caught, so please don't promise us anything today. It doesn't become you." Tears of frustration spilled out of her eyes and rolled down her face.

Betty had one arm draped around her mother's shoulders as we talked. She inhaled on a cigarette with the other hand and let the smoke drift out of her mouth, as she eyed me and shook her head with disgust.

"You said you'd find Chelsea. You promised us--remember? You shouldn't make those kind of promises." She paused, looked at her mother, and pulled her close. "I don't blame Mom. She's right, and you know it. I'm sorry, but you are a huge disappointment, Cleve Hawkins. Detective? Not at all. What I think is that you couldn't find your own dick if you had a string tied to it."

I didn't reply. I couldn't-- and looking at the two women I felt as useless as a human being could. I slowly pawed the ground with one foot and cleared my throat.

"I'm so sorry, I just . . ."

Betty interrupted and tugged at my arm. "Sorry for that. I

apologize for the way I say things. My best friend tells me I have the sophistication of an elephant falling down a staircase. But you have to understand--you failed us, and now look. Can you honestly blame us for being angry and hurt?"

"No. Not at all, Betty."

Florence looked into my eyes; she was searching for reasons, and perhaps, answers. Her face became empty of expression, as though she had lost track in our conversation.

"What is it you really do, Mr. Hawkins? You're not a cop. Are you even qualified to search for missing people?" She began to sob again and I felt helpless.

"Ma'am, I'm a licensed PI in Illinois, but I have to be honest with you, a private investigator's license has the legal value of a dog's tag. I chase down bail skips for a couple of bondsmen, so I have some powers that cops don't have. Yes--I find people, and I've been a homicide cop. As a PI, I can even cross state lines and break down doors without warrants. Cops can't do that. I can cuff people and hold them in custody indefinitely. Now, as an ex-cop, I also have access to police records and so on, and finding Chelsea was priority--you must believe me. I am truly sorry for your loss."

"But none of what you say helped, and you didn't find Chelsea before it was too late."

"Actually, Ma'am, we have identified a suspect."

"Oh, and when did this come about?" Betty's voice was loaded with sarcasm.

"A few days ago. I haven't been able to work on the information because everything is coming apart at once, but I promise you, I'm on it. There's an All Points Bulletin out for the suspect as we speak."

Telling them anything at all was not helping. I might as well have been speaking to the wind, and I felt like shit.

We walked slowly to Betty's car and I helped with her mother as they got in. I put my hands on the door and leaned in.

"There is one thing you can do for me if you would, Betty; I need permission to go in Chelsea's apartment. You told me you had a key. I want to get that from you as soon as possible."

"Yes, I suppose. Anything to help." She began to fumble around inside her purse and then handed me the key. "You have the address I gave you, right?"

"Yes, of course," I said as I held the key. "I'll get this back to you as soon as possible. The police will want to search Chelsea's place, too. I'll tell them I have this key and got it from you."

"Won't do any good," what can you find in her apartment?" said Florence. "You think the madman that killed my baby will be there?"

I started to reply, but couldn't find my voice.

They drove off and for the first time in years, a tear formed in my eye. It would have run down my cheek if I hadn't quickly brushed it away.

I walked to my car remembering what Betty told me about her sister that first day, when I met her at Redhead's bar. Chelsea had promised her, the last time they spoke, she would not become the mistress of any man old enough to be her father, no matter how much money he had or how great a lake front apartment he offered to rent for her. She would borrow from her mother only in an emergency, and pay back all she owed as soon as she could. She'd pay off her credit cards as soon as possible, before they threatened to take her mom's house. She further promised to stay off cigarettes and avoid Absolut vodka, which caused her to embarrass herself in public. She would not automatically be impressed with BMW-driving assholes. Dreams. Promises. None of them mattered anymore.

When we parted that day, the rain had stopped, but the sky was still overcast and dark enough to look like the end of the world.

The next morning, I took a long hot shower and shaved. It was hard to look at myself in the mirror. I got dressed, made another pot of coffee, then loaded the so-called old-fashioned .38 caliber Smith and Wesson that I'd grown quite fond of.

Holding a gun feels great. On television, the average person always acts indignent when the gun is first handed to them. They make a face and say, "I don't want that thing!" But the truth is, to a cop at least, having a gun in your hand feels not only good, but right and even natural. I picked up the gun and clutched the grip of it the way a child holds his or her blankie. I would be armed from here on, until we found Chelsea's killer. I was damned sure he'd have one.

The rain had done its magic, it had blown out overnight. The sky overhead was bright, cloudless and blue. Even with springtime weather only a few weeks old, there was already a hint of green everywhere. I went to the house on Elmwood where Chelsea had rented an apartment.

It was a white-stone turn-of-the-century Victorian with a sweeping porch that disappeared around one end. It needed paint, a new roof and some yard work. The windows were dingy and the gutters were choked with leaves.

I needed to caution the owner, Bertha Quinn, about my presence and the reason for going into one of her apartments. I rang the bell five times before she opened the door.

"What? What is it?" she questioned, her eyes filmed with sleep.

She had a figure like a garbage can atop two bowling pins. Appearing to be in her late forties, she was dressed in a frilly blouse and a pant suit with big buttons. A graying mass of hair was piled on top of her head and her face was as round as a muskmelon. For whatever reason, she seemed to be wearing huge amounts of perfume that could knock down an elephant. A cigarette dangled from her lips.

I flashed my badge and said, "Hello, Mrs. Quinn?"

"Yeah. Oh! The police? What do you want? Wait--I didn't call for no police. Go away." Her voice was husky and her manner compact--efficient. She started to close the door.

Smiling, I said, "Ma'am, my name is Cleve Hawkins, and you look like a good judge of character. Do I really look like I will go away?"

She rubbed her sausage fingers over her third chin. She had the manic look and manner of a woman who might have spent her life inside a bar. She drew on the cigarette and coughed a hacking, irritating cough that reddened her face and caused her watermelon breasts to gyrate.

"I said I didn't call no cops-- so, what do you want, anyway?" She crossed her arms and studied me.

"I'm sure you heard about the unfortunate death of your tenant, Miss Rohrman?"

"Oh, yes. Isn't that terrible. Did you catch the guy who did it yet?"

"No, Ma'am. We are still investigating. I need to get into her apartment and have a look around. I've got the key and the family's permission."

"Hmmmm--and who are you, again?" I couldn't help but notice, her breath was stale and her hair smelled like an ashtray.

"Cleve Hawkins, I'm a private investigator, working with the police."

I watched her eyes dart around, looking over my shoulder and back to me again.

"Well, okay, I guess. Come on in. That girl's place is at the top of the stairs. Or it was. Now I gotta find another renter. First door on the right. Hey, are a whole bunch of you guys gonna be snooping up there?"

"Some more officers will be by, I'm sure, Ma'am." I glanced at my watch as she followed me up the stairs.

"It don't surprise me none that the girl got killed."

"Oh--and why is that?" I asked as I unlocked the door. Bertha was so close, I felt her breath on the back of my neck.

"Ha! Let's just say she had a lot of boyfriends coming and going. Trashy-looking--you know the type. She was way too loose, if you ask me."

"Yes, Ma'am." I stepped inside and looked back at her. I'll be alright now, if you'll just allow me . . . "

"Well, yeah-- sure. What do I care? Go ahead and do your thing. I'll be downstairs."

After I heard her footsteps finish thumping down the stairs I began to look around. I wasn't even sure what I was looking for, but maybe there would be something--anything to point me in the right direction. The room was in semi-darkness, and the air was thick with the perfume of stale pizza.

In the kitchen, someone had left a half-eaten specialty pizza in a grease-stained box on the counter. The pizza had congealed into a solid mass and sat next to a saucer filled with cigarette ashes. The counter was also littered with fast-food wrappers, empty soda cans, food-encrusted plates, and cheap dented pots. A bottle of Miller beer had been left open.

Pictures on the walls were of the discount-store variety, framed prints of Picasso and one of a monkey drinking some kind of Italian wine. The living room floor was bare, scarred wood, and the furniture minimal. There was a lumpy secondhand couch and two folding chairs with Marrs Funeral Home's name engraved on the back. A rickety end table had been placed between the two folding chairs. A thirteen-inch portable TV sat atop a cheap brass stand, by the only living room window.

It seemed to be obvious that Chelsea had left in a hurry. A dirty fork lay on the floor, along with a glass. I walked around and searched for signs of a struggle but saw none. No telltale smears of blood or bullet holes. No scuffed heel marks on the floor.

I checked the phone for a voice mail service, but the line was dead. So few landlines left these days. I wondered if Chelsea had a cell phone. *Her sister said she talked to her every other day, didn't she? Yes.*

A suitcase lay open on the unmade sofa bed. It was half filled with jeans, sweatshirts, socks and under things. I checked a chest of drawers, finding mainly clothes. There was a collection of maybe thirty CDs of singers and groups. She had magazines that told about the private lives of celebrities. One was open to a page of Hollywood weight loss tips.

Dirty laundry was strewn on the floor in the bathroom. The medicine chest was empty except for a bottle of Bayer aspirin, a few band-aids and a box of Midol.

When I was finished nearly an hour later, I went downstairs where Mrs. Quinn came out of her apartment to meet me. With hand on hip and cigarette in hand, she said, "Well--did you find anything?"

"I'm sorry, I'm not free to say, Ma'am. Tell me--did Miss

Rohrman have a car that you know of?"

"Sure. A Pontiac. One of them Firebirds. An old one." She took a deep drag on the cigarette which wore it down to the filter. Blue smoke filtered out her nose, and she flicked the butt away. She continued, "I wish she had of moved it before she left, too. It's parked alongside the house--just before the alley."

"Okay, well, thank you for your time, I'll be going now. We'll get back to you if we need anything further."

"Yeah, okay."

She called out after I was down the steps: "Hey--see what you guys can do about getting that piece of junk hauled out of here will you?"

I walked around the side of the house and checked out the car which was covered with tree sap and dust. It was locked, but I peered inside and saw feminine stuff everywhere. There was a box of tissues with flowers all over it, and a dead lipstick in the recess of the console, right next to a pink Teddy bear sitting upright in the passenger seat. The floor of the car was piled with trash--Styrofoam food containers, paper cups and flattened Misty Menthol cigarette packs. The ashtray was overflowing with butts. I needed to get inside the car. Maybe all those butts weren't Chelsea's, and who knew what else might be in there. In the trunk?

Before I walked away, I took down the plate number and read the bumper sticker that said: *"Don't like my driving? Call 1-800-BITE-ME."*

My cell phone vibrated just as I got behind the wheel of my car. It was Maureen. I wanted to answer, but thought I'd wait until my mood changed for the better--if that was possible. I needed to talk to Branoff. Maybe they got a hit from the APB mug shot. But then, he would have called, wouldn't he?

CHAPTER TWELVE

I was hungry, but I needed sympathy and understanding far more than I needed my ham and eggs. Saturday morning I dressed in a pair of gray sweats, laced up my Nike running shoes, and went by the gym. I took along some street clothes in my gym bag. After working out, I stopped for breakfast at the diner.

Dixie's Diner was bustling at nine in the morning. During the week, plenty of young professionals and grizzled retirees occupied the tables, reading fresh copies of The Sun Times or the Tribune on their I Phones. It was always packed on Saturday, but the pace seemed slower in every way.

Still in a somber mood, I took comfort in the diner activity. The pouring of coffee, orders barked back to the chef, and the clang of silverware were better than my solitary kitchen. The inside of Dixie's was warm and peaceful, something out of the Saturday Evening Post. I ordered and watched the people eat breakfast and drink coffee in vinyl booths.

I nursed two cups of coffee and about ten minutes after I ordered, my waitress came and slid a warm plate in front of me.

American Fries with onions and two over easy with sausage links--rye toast. No donuts. My mind wandered as I ate.

I felt like I had failed the Rohrmans, even though I knew I couldn't have prevented Chelsea's death. She was most likely dead within twenty-four hours of disappearing--but still, the entire thing haunted me. And, the images of scotch on the rocks were looming larger. With tonight being Saturday night, I realized I was

in danger of getting drunk, because I wanted to tie one on in the worst way. The thought of a drink had been haunting me and that scotch last night had not helped. In fact, serious drinking kept lingering in my head, but I'd kept trying to keep it in my denial file. I pictured that shiny row of bottles behind the bar at Ernie's place and realized I needed to talk to somebody before I screwed up. I finished eating and stepped outside where I flipped open my cell and called Maureen.

"Hi," she answered.

"Hi, yourself, stranger."

"Nah. It hasn't been that long. I was wondering if you'd mind me stopping by?"

"When?"

"Anytime, but I was thinking around one or so, if that's okay."

"Oh--sorry, Cleve, I've got all kinds of errands to take care of today. It's my catch-up day, you know? Why don't you just drop by around seven or so tonight? Can you manage that?"

Bad news. I didn't want to hear that, but it was better than nothing to look forward to. Maybe better than anything. "Yeah, sure. Want me to bring something? How about some Chardonnay?"

"No, thanks. I'm all set. Just bring yourself, gumshoe." There was a brief pause before she said, "I've missed you."

"Same here, Mo. See you tonight."

I decided to go home and do without a drink. Kicking back on the couch, I watched some PGA golf and then the Cubs game until the seventh inning. We were losing, which was nothing new, but when Vince Vaughn sang "Take Me Out To The Ballgame," I dozed off.

When I woke, the sun had slipped behind the trees and my

living room was dim with shadows. I sat up and tried to rub the sleep out of my face. It was five-thirty.

Grabbing a Pepsi from the fridge, I headed for the bathroom and took care of the three S's, then dressed to kill and headed for Maureen's place. I felt bare without my Cub's cap on my head and naked without my gun.

When I got there, Mo had a glass of wine sitting on the coffee table. I held her in my arms and kissed her as if I hadn't seen her in years.

"Wow! You must have really missed me, huh?" she whispered.

We stood head to head, my forehead against hers, and I stared into those gorgeous blue eyes. "You got that right. I have been thinking about you a lot."

She slowly backed off and holding my hands in hers said, "How about a scotch?"

Funny. I avoided booze all day, but, somehow I felt safe having a drink with Mo. It's crazy, but I knew I would be okay.

"Yeah, okay--sounds good."

I sat on the couch and watched her pour the scotch over some ice, and we clinked glasses after she snuggled up to me. She was wearing a black turtleneck and designer jeans-- no shoes or socks.

"You look great, tonight," I said.

She placed her drink on the table, picked up her pack of Virginia Slims and lit one. "Thanks a lot," she said as she blew her smoke at me and took a sip of wine. My scotch tasted great, and I studied her closely now. Her breathing had deepened, but her face was smooth, untroubled.

"How have you been?" she asked.

"Really? The ultimate fucking lousy."

"What?" She giggled. "Why? What's going on? I called you yesterday afternoon--you got the call, I assume, but no call back."

"Huh? No. I must have accidentally deleted it or something--sorry."

"Well--what's up? You look down in the dumps." She kissed me on the cheek and I felt her hot breath on my neck. "It doesn't bode well for a fun night, you know. So spit it out, Detective."

I took another taste of scotch. "Have you ever seen someone cause a disastrous accident by driving so slowly that others are forced to pass them on a hill or a curve? That person causing the accident rarely looks in their rearview mirror and is seldom held accountable?"

She edged over closer and draped her arm around my shoulders. "I'm not following you. What do you mean?"

"The Rohrman girl. It was my job to find her before she got butchered by some sick sonofabitch. I guess I didn't take the whole thing seriously enough. I don't know--I just figured she was off on a binge or something. Anyway, as you probably know, she's one of the seven women they found out in Aladdin."

"No, I didn't. Of course I was aware of the find, but I didn't know your girl was one of them. Oh, Cleve . . . I'm so sorry. I'll bet the family is crushed."

"Crushed? That's not the word for it. And they're pissed at me for not finding her soon enough. I feel like shit."

She rubbed the back of my neck and kissed me on the cheek again.

"You can't blame yourself for that. Sounds like it's time for you to move on; nothing you can do about it now."

"Yeah, I know I should, but this one eats at me. I'm determined to find the bastard who did this, no matter what."

There was silence for a beat until she said, "Not that it's important, but are you getting' paid for any of this?"

"What? I don't know. I was going to, I suppose, but now . . . I would never ask those people for anything. Look, Mo--when we split, I lost some of myself, and I started drinking. This morning, I had the urge to get wasted. I'm just plain fucked up."

She smiled and began to rub her fingers along the inside of my thigh.

"You'll be alright. I know you, big guy."

"I don't know, I feel like . . ."

"Shhhh," she put a finger to her lips. "Follow me," she said, as she tugged at my belt. "We'll try to un-fuck you."

We stood awkwardly, facing each other, and we seemed to run

out of small talk. She blushed slowly but pervasively, then pulled her turtleneck out of her jeans and said, "Well, I'll break the ice." Pulling the sweater over her head, she threw it aside, then unhooked her bra, slipped it off, and let it drop to the floor. "Okay?" She held out her hands, and I took them. She put my hands on her breasts, and I caressed them, feeling her nipples harden.

Reaching out, she unbuttoned my shirt, then ran her hands over my chest.

"You feel the same, Cleve."

"You, too."

She pressed her breasts against my chest, and we kissed while she slipped my shirt off. Still kissing, she undid her jeans and pulled them with her panties down her thighs. I knew her ass was wonderful, but I had missed it so much and groaned as I held a cheek in each hand.

She directed my hand down and between her legs. I felt her pubic hair, then the lips of her pussy, which were moist and I heard myself gasp.

She eased back and sat on the bed, pulling off her jeans and panties. Completely naked now, she looked at me and smiled, "Is this really happening again?"

"My God, Mo, you're so damned beautiful."

She suddenly reached out and cupping the back of my head, she stood and kissed me. Kissed me hard, and I knew that special kiss. It was the prelude. Despite what was happening in the world, my body began to sing. The kiss grew hungrier. She moved closer, pressed against me. My eyes rolled back and I moaned.

"I love you," she whispered.

I picked her up and eased her back onto the bed. With her laying on the quilt, legs over the foot of the bed, I bent down and kissed her breasts and then her stomach. I knelt and ran my tongue along the soft inside of her thighs, first one, then the other. Mo spread her legs so I could continue on my path.. I continued with small, wet kisses everywhere, and purposefully let her feel my hot breath on her clit. I kissed it--just a small one, before I flicked it with my tongue. She arched her back, and moaned as I put my hands under her ass and pushed my face deeper between her legs. I worked my tongue around and around in circles on her clit, at the same time running two fingers inside of her wet pussy. Her breathing was ragged and she continued to moan as I reached up and caressed her breasts, before I stood and slowly undid my belt and jeans.

She lay on the bed, breathing hard, then slid back to put her head on the pillow and watch me undress. My rock-hard dick jutted straight out. She watched every move I made as I came toward her, and when I was in reaching distance, she took my hands in hers.

I kneeled between her legs and kissed her her breasts. I murmured, "Okay?"

She whispered, "Oh, yes." I lowered myself and she guided me inside. She gasped when I slid in; her wetness enveloping me.

We kissed and held each other, caressing, moving as if we had all the time in the world. Our slow rhythm continued for what seemed like such a brief time before I picked up the pace and used long strokes, faster and faster until we both exploded at the same time.

We stayed that way--locked together, kissing and caressing.

Suddenly, she took a deep breath and said, "Oh my God!" and began gyrating her hips. Seconds later, she had another orgasm. I loved the feeling of her pulsating and squeezing me inside of her.

Laying, on our sides, she was behind with her arm wrapped around me and her legs entwined with mine. Like nesting spoons. She kissed my neck and whispered, "Going to sleep?"

"No. just dreaming."

"Me, too." She hugged me tighter and ran her feet over my calves.

"I like that."

"I know."

I turned over and we wrapped our arms around each other.

After a while, she whispered in my ear. "Is there any worse fate than loving and not being loved in turn?"

"I don't think so."

We lay there, saying nothing--until she finally spoke. "If the color gray could be used to describe an emotional condition, it would be a life without affection or human warmth. You agree?"

"Of course. Why didn't we make it work before, Mo?"

She snuggled closer, and said, "I'm not sure, but I don't care about the past. The past is nothing more than a decaying memory."

She pranced off to take a shower, and I lay there trying to avoid thoughts of the past few days and my next move to find a killer.

CHAPTER THIRTEEN

Cockroaches don't like sunlight, but from time to time, Lewis ventured out at night. He frequented a strip-joint called Chest Candy, which aggressively catered to strippers, transvestites and aspiring nymphomaniacs.

There were times when he missed having a normal relationship, but they were rare. Joanie Vidross had been the latest in a long line of trysts he'd managed before hooking up with Bart.

Those experiences never lasted long, and he never had a real heart-throb, a girlfriend, or a full-fledged mistress--they were all just sport fucks of short duration. In fact, somewhere in the back of his mind, the professor knew he was incapable of any real relationship with a woman, and his encounters were simply targets of opportunity--the town sluts, women who ran afoul of the law, desperately lonely divorcees, and barmaids who needed a little extra cash. They were all easy targets for the professor, or Phillip, the name he went by while on the prowl.

But tonight, Lewis stayed home. Bart would be along directly, and they needed to talk. Lewis was having difficulty sleeping, patricularly after the burial site was discovered.

With the bodies unearthed in the hinterlands of Aladdin, the police would definitely turn up the heat. And not just the city cops--now the State boys would be involved, because the location was in the country. Maybe, the FBI would get involved, too.

Lewis was once again questioning his judgment in taking Bart into his confidence as a partner. The man had balls, of that there was no doubt--but he was, after all, an ex-con, and had obviously been slipshod in some manner, or the bodies of the women would not have been found. I believe it's time to get rid of my red-headed friend before the roof caves in, he thought.

While he waited for Bart, Lewis sat at his desk in the den, and tried to read a thesis written by one of his students. It related to theological influences of Scientology and the church.

He was still dressed from a day's work at the university, wearing a crisp white shirt, button-down, all cotton, pinpoint, with a small, dark silk bow tie. His tan looked like it had been induced with chemicals or acquired in a salon. A sixty-year-old model, Lewis thought at times, when admiring himself in the mirror. He wore his reading glasses, which bestowed upon him a look of extreme intelligence and wisdom.

Bored with the thesis, he slowly opened his bottom drawer and retrieved his collection of sexual paraphernalia--toys for twats as they're known in the trade. Lighting a cigar, he leaned back in his swivel chair and fondled the toys, smiling as he remembered their use in the past-- as well as potential use in the future. He was much too tense to linger with such thoughts for long however, and dumped them back in the drawer after a few moments. Remaining seated at his desk, he stared into space. Yes . . . Bartholomew definitely has to go. Ignorant asshole, Lewis thought. He believes he's wise because he isn't dead.

Years before, Lewis had been a presiding judge in Cook County. He kept a lot of important people in his pocket. He was known to bend the law from time to time, but where Bart was concerned it was a multiple fracture. First, he called in favors, so that Bart got his original three-year sentence for assault with a deadly weapon, reduced to a year plus probation. Then, when Bart stopped reporting to his probation officer, Lewis again smoothed things over before he vacated the bench and began to teach at the university.

The inmates at Menard Correctional Facility had called Bart Hodgkins, "Red." He was released after nearly two years, thanks to Judge Lewis Lisecki, and regularly neglected to shave, bathe, or change clothes. He stayed high on pills and pot in addition to frequenting the bars when he could afford it.

Hodgkins had another woman in the trunk of his car when he rolled into the winding drive at Lewis's house that night. He had found her at the Trailways Bus Depot hours before. A runaway.

She was a square-shouldered young girl of medium height, probably not yet twenty-one, with black hair and large, dark eyes, who wore two fake diamond studs in her ears. There were dark circles under her eyes and her nose was red, from crying. She wore a skimpy green blouse and faded jeans. Her mouth, hands and ankles were wrapped with duct tape.

She would be one of three surprises for the professor who thought he was simply stopping by to talk. Lewis would be so happy with the second and third surprises, too. Bart had shaved his head-- the red hair gone; he was bald. The fact that he got rid of the Volvo, and was driving an old Chrysler Imperial would bring a smile to Lewis's face too, he hoped. Lots of trunk room in that baby.

It was midnight when he slammed the car door and opened the trunk to check on his latest victim before he went in the house. The girl looked wretched with tears filling her eyes. The cords stood out in her neck as she squirmed and strained against her bindings. Her shoulders jumped and her back arched. Bart closed the trunk.

His gaze was glassy-eyed, from smoking some dandy Hawaiian Gold and he had also downed three Bennies and a Xanax to make him mellow. When the professor wanted to talk, Bart knew the bullshit would be fly and piss him off. As usual, Bart was in low gear with his dims on--as crazy as a shithouse rat. He looked like hell.

His denim jacket had grease stains on the sleeves and his jeans had battery acid holes front and back. He had stopped along the road to take a leak and his fly was wide open.

Once inside, he went to the den and rubbing his shiny scalp said, "Hey, Professor! Lookee here, I decided you were right. I cut all of it off. See? Now, I'm fuckin' bald. How do you like it? I agree with you, why attract attention? No asshole takes an accordion band to a deer hunt, right? Ha! Ha!"

Lewis stood. Bartholomew, I just don't . . ."

"And, you ready? And . . . I've got a nice little surprise for you out in the trunk of my new car" He sniggered and snuffed snots through his nose, as he strolled over and poked Lewis in the shoulder with his fist.

Lewis backed away. He held his cigar out in front of him, the ash so long it was about to fall off. He turned, to Bart, and he clenched his jaw like a bad actor, as he tried to hiss his tough-guy words. His respiration was suddenly shallow, his palms moist and his skin felt like it was crawling with centipedes. One of his eyes bulged from his head, like a prosthesis that didn't fit the socket. His voice was calm enough when he spoke, but the line of his mouth tightened, and it was obvious he struggled to control his anger. Control was everything, and he slowly removed the reading glasses and stuck one stem in his mouth and sighed.

"That's a pity," he said. "You look terrible, and I don't recall telling you to find another whore." To Bart, he sounded like a tire going flat. "In fact, I distinctly told you we had to behave for a while until things cool down. Do you recall that conversation, my friend? And, why must I constantly remind you to stop referring to me as professor or judge? You see, that's your problem . . . you don't listen well, I know you've been around, Bartholomew. You don't like cops, you're a wiseass, and you think you're smarter than everyone else. That's the profile of ninety-eight percent of the men inside the system." He paused and glared at Bart.

"I know you don't like women, and the reason for that is they don't like you. While, I, on the other hand, can find all the whores I need *without your help*."

"Huh? What the fuck is this shit all about? I just . . ."

"Shut up and listen, you moron. I'm exceedingly happy that you have rid yourself of the red mop you were sporting, when last we met, however--your eyebrows are still red. Is that smart? No. Have you considered coloring them? No, of course not. And the most serious infraction on your part is that you have gone against my wishes, bringing another whore out here."

"What? What do you mean? I done everything you told me."

Lewis paced and worked his way over to his desk. "Did I, or did I not, tell you that we had to lay low for a while? Obviously you don't read the papers or watch any television, or you would know that the authorities have discovered the burial site of the women."

Bart continued to sway and grin. "Yeah, but I couldn't pass up the chance at this one. She was so easy to take. I think she wants me-- and I figured I'd surprise you. Jesus! Talk about an ungrateful prick, Lew."

Lewis lunged forward and stood inches from Bart's face. "But . . . you did all this despite knowing about the police finding the bodies, did you not?"

"Yeah, so what. I know about that shit. I told you...they got nothing on us. If you're gonna be all bent out of shape, fuck it--I won't get another one--alright?" He paused, then threw his arm around Lewis's shoulders. "Let's have a little fun, though. C'mon. She's waiting for us."

"No! You are too careless. If you don't care about yourself, that's one thing, but I cannot allow you to bring me down with you, Bartholomew. Are we clear?" Lewis jabbed the new cigar out in the ashtray and burned his fingers. "Ouch! Dammit all. See, you have turned my life upside down with your foolhardy exploits."

Bart flopped down in one of the over-stuffed arm chairs. "I'm fine now. His voice drifted off as he said, "We're good here." He was all wide-eyed and flushed when he stared at Lewis. "A firm ass-chewin' does it every time with me, Lewis. Got a beer?"

"No. No more drinking. In fact, I want you to go home. I mean go directly home. No nonsense."

"Wait! I come out here to surprise you, done everything you told me. Got my hair chopped, so now I look like a fuckin' bald-assed Chihuahua. Traded cars, just like you told me. You didn't even see that yet. And, now I'm just supposed to take this bitch I got in my trunk and go home?"

He stood with his hands on his hips. "Your serious? Sure, you don't give a shit. I do all the killin' not you. You can't dirty your itsy bitsy, little girl hands to do shit, can you? I should be the one who's pissed, Professor." That's right--professor, Professor, Professor. There, tough shit you don't like me callin' you that."

Lewis glared. "Yeah, I suppose I am proud of you for cutting your hair." "Perhaps I should call in a few of your colleagues for a group hug. Maybe join hands for a rousing rendition of "Kumbaya?" He lowered his voice, "Your parents should have used a better form of birth control, Bartholomew."

Bart jumped up, grabbed Lewis by the front of his shirt, and yanked. His eyes were burning with hatred. "I don't think that's funny, Judge. How'd you like me to turn your ass into a hat?" He stared into a trembling Lewis's eyes.

"You think I'm going down by myself? I know the fuckin' stakes are high; one measly fuckup and we'll be on our way to the big house for the rest of our lives. Maybe even get the needle. So, I just ain't lettin' that happen-- because my luck, I'd probably be locked in a ten-by-ten with a monstrous-looking' black gay weight lifter who'd screw my skinny ass till I walk like Sandy Bullock." He jerked on the shirt and was so close his spit sprayed Lewis's face.

Lewis cringed and tried to pull away. "Alright--alright, my friend. Easy now, I was only foolin' with you." All the color seemed to be leeched out of his eyes except for the pupils, that looked like the burnt tips of wood matches.

"I've done stuff I wouldn't tell a corpse," Bart growled. "Don't fuck with me so much, okay?" He shoved Lewis away, dusted the shirt off with his fingertips, and smiled. "You should be more thankful, is all. If it wasn't for these whores I bring here, we'd both be dating Mary Palm and her five daughters."

Lewis backed away some more as if Bart was contagious. "That's another thing, my friend. My mother said a person should put on their manners every morning the way they put on their clothes. You, my friend have no manners whatsoever." He retreated back to his desk. "Now then-- were you intimate with this girl?"

Bart shrugged. "You mean did I fuck her?"

Lewis sighed. He gave a faint, embarrassed laugh, as if one of his students had said something awkward in class.

"Nah, that was part of my surprise for you. I wanted you to be first--honest."

"Where are you taking care of this?" Lewis asked. He emptied the ashtray in the wastepaper basket and lit another a cigar.

"Chicken shit. Ha! Se what I mean. Bart do this, Bartholomew do that. Don't sweat it, Professor. I'll handle everything, and don't worry, I'll get in touch before I grab another one."

He hiked his jeans up and headed for the back door. "I still think you should be more fuckin' grateful though. Anyway, you won't be seeing me for a while. Sleep easy, Judge. I'm outa here."

"That's what I want to hear," said Lewis. "Be careful, Bartholomew, and for God's sake, do something about coloring those eyebrows."

"Yeah, later, Professor."

Seconds later, Bart gunned the engine of his '89 Chrysler and backed out. Lewis parted the drapes and watched Bart reach the end of the driveway and then screech his tires, leaving long black worms of skid marks as he aimed the car down the road.

He had a fantastic Benzedrine and Xanax buzz working when he pulled into the two-track nearly five miles from Lewis's place. Going in, he found deep ruts and hilly mounds and at one point heard he heard his muffler and tailpipe scrape the ground. Dense forest grew on both sides and scratched the sides of the car.

There was no place to turn around and he realized he would have to back out, but that would be okay. He'd done it before.

After he stopped and got out, he popped the trunk and hauled the moaning young woman out. Stumbling through the saplings and brush, he was about fifty yards in when he tossed her body between two pines. He cocked his .22 automatic outfitted with a suppressor, and popped a round into her forehead, leaving a hole no bigger than the circumference of an eraser on a wood pencil. She lay on the ground in a heap, like a puppet whose strings had been released by a puppeteer. The animals will take care of her, he thought.

Bart stomped back to his Chrysler sedan that had RustOleum polka-dotting the door and hood. Back on the road, and content with his handiwork, he checked the clock on the dash. It was just one-fifteen. He had finished off the quart of Schlitz on the passenger seat, but needed another drink and figured if he hurried, he'd be in time for last call at the Golden Pony in Lombard. His foot smashed down hard on the accelerator.

The Xanax began to take its toll. Bart squeezed his eyes open and closed in an effort to stay awake. Ten minutes later, he found himself squinting to be sure he really saw the flashing blue lights in his rearview mirror.

"Oh, shit! Fuckin' cops." *Need to get rid of the gun.*

While he cranked the window down, the front of his car wandered back and forth like a drunken sailor, crisscrossing the white lines, but he managed to toss the gun out the window and straighten the wheels at the same time, before the State Police pulled him over.

CHAPTER FOURTEEN

Whoever said no news is good news was full of shit. Three days had passed and I still hadn't heard anything from downtown about Chelsea's car. I told Branoff I wanted permission to be on hand when they took it to the pound. I needed to look around inside, even though I knew the cops would get first dibs on the search.

I knew I should forget about the whole thing for that matter; I really had no stake in it anymore, now that we knew Chelsea was dead. But, I couldn't just walk away. I never have and never will. Besides, I figured I owed the Rohrman family big time.

I got back from the gym Thursday morning and found Deckle waiting on the steps. His expression was extra hangdog.

"Hey, Deck--what's going on?"

He stumbled getting up, and shuffled in behind me after I opened the door.

"Hey, Cleve. You know there ought'a be a law against those fuckin' big street-sweeper machine things."

I went about starting a pot of coffee and said, "Oh--why's that, Deck?"

"One of the damned things almost ran over me."

I poured the water in the reservoir and glanced at his face. He was serious.

"Almost ran over you? How did that happen?"

"Assholes. There I was checking the gutter for loose change-- minding my own business, ya know? And I hear that sweeping machine coming up behind me. So I kept walking cuz' he wasn't that close and then--and then, I saw a coupla dimes, ya know?"

"Yeah."

"So, I bend down to pick them up and I see more coin just a few feet ahead, ya know?"

"Yeah." I knew what was coming, but I let him ramble on.

"Next thing I know, the asshole driving that thing comes right up on me. He would'a bumped me in the ass if I hadn't jumped up on the curb."

"Boy--close call, huh? I don't blame you for being pissed, Deck."

"Yeah, I'm lucky, I guess--whew, I sure am."

"Hey, it'll be okay. Why don't you go to Jerry's Bakery and get some donuts to go with this coffee? Here's a ten. Get us half-dozen mixed and keep the change."

"Sure thing, Cleve." He grinned. "Thanks, buddy, be right back."

A few minutes later, the phone jingled.

"Hawk?"

"Yeah?"

"Branoff here. I've got good news and bad news, pal."

"Good to hear from you, Kris. What've you got?"

"Bad news is, I still don't have a release on that Rohrman car. Seems the mother is holding it up for some reason. And, that APB hasn't turned up squat, but--and this is a big but, my friend . . . the good news is we got a guy in custody that looks a lot like the mug shot Manny Dubiel fingered. We think he's our guy."

"No shit!"

"I kid you not. This guy is bald--looks like he recently shaved his head, and he fits the rest of the bill-- freckles and all. Still has red eyebrows. The deputies tell me he seems to be a couple of smokes short of a pack."

"What did they pick him up for?"

"DWI. He was shit-faced when the state boys pulled him over, just outside Lombard. Speeding, twenty miles over and he was stoned on his ass. Blew an eight and they brought him in. Car's in the pound. They didn't find any open booze or pot. Empty beer bottles though. The boys found some Xanax in the glove box though. Not his either. There was a warrant out on him anyway, as you know, for violating probation. I guess he gave the cops a real hard time. It took both of them to get him down and put the cuffs on."

"Damned right. He didn't want to be pinched. He knows. That mother-fucker knows he's wanted for more than breaking probation and drunk driving.

"Yeah, we're running his prints right now. I don't know why that took so damned long either. Anyway, I talked to the Captain and he agrees--we're gonna give you a little Carte Blanche on this case . . . you can sit in while we question this idiot."

"Thanks, Kris. I owe you big time, buddy. You don't know, he might pop like a grenade with its pin pulled."

Deckle was back and I was glad.

"Yeah, I agree," Branoff continued. "Could be something here. Dangle easy, Cleve. We'll see you in a while then?"

"Damned right. I'm on my way." I looked over at Deck as I hung up and slipped into my bomber jacket. I grabbed my Cubs cap and said, "Deck, I have to lock up." Grabbing a couple of napkins off the filing cabinet, I added, "Give me a couple of the jelly--you take the rest. I'm in a hurry."

Deckle looked lost and confused as I left him standing outside my door with the open box of donuts. Down the road, I realized he had kept my change again.

By the time I got to the Cook County lock-up, they had our man sitting by himself in an interrogation room. Still in street clothes, he was slouched down in a straight-backed chair with one leg extended out and up on the table in front of him. He was cuffed.

Besides myself, Branoff, his partner, Andrews, and the assistant district attorney, Carl Schneider, were on hand. Three straight-back chairs were available and I took one before Andrews could. He looked a little pissed as he strolled out to get another chair.

Branoff and the assistant DA sat across from the suspect who had a face like an Irish wolfhound: long and homely with fiercely intent eyes. A lot of cons had rabbit eyes, but not this one, I thought. He leered at us.

Branoff shoved the guy's leg off the table. "Get your fucking leg off my table and sit up, asshole."

The man smirked and took his time adjusting his position.

Over the years, I had interviewed enough witnesses to know when one was winging it. His body language and attitude weren't going to help him, but he didn't seem to care, one way or the other. Killers come in all sizes and shapes, rich and poor, humble and arrogant, regretful and cold to the bone. Usually they will just try to cover their own asses, a practice also favored by law enforcement pros.

Branoff read him his rights, and said, "You're Bartholomew Michael Hodgkins--that right?"

"What about it?"

"Nothing. Just verifying that a piece of shit like you has a name, is all. You understand your rights as I've read them to you, Hodgkins?"

There was silence for a moment before he answered. "Yeah--I get it."

Branoff looked at his file and continued: "So, I see here that you don't believe in reporting to your probation officer. He hasn't heard from you in damn near six months. Mind you, I'm just ball-parking here, Bart, but I'd say you are in a world of hurt. You're going back to Menard Correctional where, I think you'll be a little jailhouse bitch."

"Fuck that and fuck you."

Branoff slowly perused the folder laying open in front of him. He glanced up at the man.

"You know why most criminals are criminals, Bart? It's because most of them majored in dumb. You fit right in--driving drunk for starters, but we got you for a lot more than that this time, big shot."

"That's the biggest bunch of bullshit I ever heard . .I ain't done nothing since I got out." He stared at the ceiling. "I'm clean."

"Of course you are. You've been mister squeaky clean," said Branoff. "Probably just your usual everyday crazy-with-a-gun sort of thing--right?"

"I got no gun. You can't pin nothing on me. Try again, pig."

Kris paused and flipped a page in his file, then looked back at the suspect.

"You've got crazy-assed eyes, my friend."

"Fuck you," he said. "You got a lying mouth, too."

I studied him carefully and had a feeling this guy would definitely qualify as the killer. His smile was confident, challenging and mysterious. His eyes didn't come off their distant focus, until he finally leaned in on the table and said, "Look, I was speedn' and had a few drinks is all. I'm gonna bail out of this motherfucker and you all can kiss my ass. By the way, I want my lawyer."

"You broke probation, asshole. You're not leaving here with or without a mouthpiece. By the way, what's this lawyer's name?"

Bart swallowed twice, his Adam's apple bobbing. "I ain't got one yet. You guys have to give me that defender guy. So, he's my lawyer. Get him in here." He waved his hands like a bad actor in a TV drama.

"Not so fast, Bartholomew," I said. "We need to talk about a young lady you were seen with. Name's Chelsea Rohrman. Name ring any bells for you?"

I watched Bart's face-- it twitched like a plumber's helper . . . Then he grinned and I wanted to knock his teeth down his throat..

"I don't know any Chelsea . . . Chelsea--whoever you just said."

"Yeah and you don't know any girls, do you, Bart?" Andrews injected.

"Maybe you're a fudge packer," I said as I glanced at the assistant D A.

"I bet this prick was in the bridal suite every night while he was in Menard," said Branoff.

"Yeah, maybe he really is a shirt lifter," I added "Probably can't even get it up unless you're whacking on a helpless woman, right? Is it because you're so short?"

"Fuck you!" Bart growled. Beads of moisture covered his forehead. He was rattled. "I want my lawyer right fuckin' now!"

"I bet my left-hand pinkie is bigger. I held it out, halfway curled into my palm." Bart glared at me with those insane-looking eyes.

Branoff took charge again, while the assistant District Attorney took notes. "How about Joan Vidross? She a friend of yours?"

"Who?"

"Vidross . . . Joan's the first name."

"Never heard of her," he mumbled.

"That's strange you say that, Bart--because her name's on the bottle of Xanax we found in the glove box of that piece of shit you were driving. That's a controlled substance, and it isn't yours. How do you explain that?"

Bart cleared his throat and slammed his cuffed wrists on the table. "I said I want my fuckin' lawyer. I ain't sayin' no more 'till I get him in here, neither."

"Sure, but meanwhile, what would you say if I told you we have a witness puts you with this Rohrman girl?"

"Bullshit! I found them pills, and I don't even know who you're talking about. You got nothing."

"Really?" Branoff paused. "You ever been to a bar over on Halstead, called Ernie's?"

Bart glared at him. "I said, I want my fuckin' lawyer. Get the shit outa your ears."

"Yeah, we'll get him right in here. Detective Andrews . . . would you please go find Max Berman. Tell him Mr. Hodgkins needs him as soon as possible."

"Yeah--right now!" said Bart. The cords stood out in his neck. His face was as red, and his dark eyes were narrow-- filled with venom.

A uniformed cop tapped on the door and came in. He handed

Branoff some papers. "Just got them back," he said.

"Okay, thanks, Cliff." Branoff studied the papers for a moment before he spoke again.

"Oh, by the way--you ever hear of the AFIS, Bart?"

"No, and I don't care." He appeared to be shell-shocked, suddenly--glazed eyes, vapid stare, weak voice.

"Well, I'm gonna tell you anyway. It's the Automated Fingerprint Identification System, or AFIS. A miracle of technology. A latent fingerprint can be faxed to a computer at a regional office and within a coupla' hours be matched with your print that's already on file." Branoff continued to study the papers and shook his head: "It's pretty common....."

"Bullshit! You can roll up them papers, put a coat of grease on 'em and shove 'em up your ass. I don't give a fuck--okay."

Branoff shook his head. "Loud, arrogant, stupid, foulmouthed," he said.

"You really think he's foulmouthed?" Andrews asked.

"Fucking A," said Branoff.

The Public defender entered the room. Max Berman was short and wide. Hamburgers four times a week had pushed him off the edge. His facial flesh was loose and pink, and his hair looked recently cut-- short and brushed to the side like a schoolboy's. His dark blue suit was long in the arms, small in the waist, and loose in the shoulders. A baby-fat man, in his early forties, with more chins than a Chinese phone book. He was known to be a first class prick, and I'd had my problems with him in the past when I was still in uniform.

Branoff and the DA stood up when he came in. "He's all yours, counselor," said Branoff. "Just so you know, we have a lineup scheduled for later this afternoon. We think your boy here can be identified-- no problem whatsoever."

"Just be sure you get your shit together, detectives. You come to conclusions without looking at the evidence. Then you find reasons to justify your shoddy conclusions. It's most likely shit and you know it, You guys spend your time fucking your fist, then blame us when they walk."

"Who are you, Johnny Cochran? We just have to chip away the bullshit," Branoff said. "Me, I'm knee-deep in it half of the time. I don't even mind the smell anymore."

"The truth shall set you free," said Berman.

"Jesus! Let me write that down," I said.

I had enough. The whole thing stank--and the whiff of trouble was only about to get more fragrant. I had a hunch, Manny Dubiel would finger this guy, Bart Hodgkins, in the lineup. But, meanwhile, I decided to try and find out about Joan Vidross. Why did Bart Hodgkins have her prescription bottle in his car the other night. Who was she?

CHAPTER FIFTEEN

I was trying to give up donuts so I stopped at the diner after my workout at the gym. I ate biscuits and gravy with a side of three over easy and hash-browns, chased it all with three cups of coffee, then headed back to the apartment.

After my shower, I donned my brown blazer, straightened my tie, and brushed the chips off my shoulders--a well-balanced detective has one on both shoulders. Feeling pretty good about nailing Bart Hodgkins, I was on my way out the door when the phone rang. It was Branoff.

He said he was sending two uniforms out in a blue and white and I c ould accompany them to Manny Dubiel's apartment. Manny hadn't answered his phone when headquarters tried numerous calls. The whole idea of course, was to have Manny attend the police line-up and ID Bart Hodgkins as the man last seen with Chelsea Rohrman.

I hoped for a decent day without rain, but when Branoff called, the sky had the color and texture of green gas and the trees throbbed with birds. In the east, the sun was a tiny red spark inside rain clouds.

The cops rode in the front, while I hunched over from the back seat and spoke through the screen. I knew one of the officers, a veteran sergeant, who never made detective. His name was Al Schneider. I had worked with him on a homicide case in which he made an on-the-spot contributing arrest. He was a short, barrel-chested man who spent his spare time doing bench presses. He had a square, dry prairie face, thinning sandy hair, a short nose under glassy blue eyes, and a brush-cut mustache. His cheeks were hollowed out, his eyes plump with fatigue.

The other guy was a tall and lanky rookie named Rumple. He was doing the driving.

"So they still couldn't get hold of Dubiel, eh?" I said.

"No," said Schneider. "His secretary says she kept getting the answering machine--tried a dozen times, different times of the day--no luck. This guy's pretty important to your case, I understand."

"Yeah. He's a prime witness, you might say. Actually, all we've got right now."

"You ever been to his place?" Rumple asked as he looked at me in the rearview.

"No, but it shouldn't be too hard to find. Just take Belmont Avenue all the way out. We got his phone number and address when he was down at the station looking at mug shots. Hasn't been that long ago--should be right. I wouldn't think he moved."

"Yeah, we heard your guy might ID the bastard they figure is good for killing those women they found out in the country."

"Word sure gets around fast down there, doesn't it? Television, telephone and tell a cop." I had to chuckle a bit. "Yeah, this guy, Dubiel, is key alright."

"We get the updates at morning muster. You remember those days, don't you, Hawkins?"

"Yes, but the fact is, most of these assholes never pay for their shit. In Chicago around two percent are punished," said Schneider. "I hope your man helps us nail this guy." He took his hat off when we were underway and turned sideways, facing me. "Way we used to handle it, bury your fist in their guts, leave them puking on their knees-- click off their light switch with a slapjack if they still wanted to play."

"Nah," said Rumple. "Just put a .45 slug in the forehead--save the state a bunch of money, I say."

"Yeah, in the old days, when they talked law and order, it meant Wyatt Earp leaving hair on the walls," said Schneider. "And speaking of .45s, I saw a thing on the Biography channel the other day--you guys heard of Audie Murphy, right?"

"Yeah--most decorated soldier of all time--short little shit--movie star, too--right?" I said.

"Never heard of him, said Rumple.

"Uh huh." Schneider twisted around a little more to get comfortable and continued: "According to his friends, Audie Murphy fashioned a bedroom out of his garage in the hills overlooking Los Angeles and slept separately from his wife, a loaded army-issue .45 under his pillow. After the war he became convinced that, before he could sleep a full night again, he would have to spend five days in peacetime for every day he had spent on the firing line. For him it meant twenty years of sleeplessness. Poor bastard."

"No shit?" said Rumple.

"Yeah-- I heard that a long time ago," I said.

"I'll bet any money, that guy Murphy was snortin' cocaine in order to stay up, though," said Rumple.

"I can believe that," said Schneider. "But, things were different back then. The ruling class does not make alcohol or nicotine, illegal. It makes cocaine illegal. Makes marijuana illegal. Makes legal the drugs of the powerless. The drugs it doesn't use, or is not addicted to." He paused. "It's the Golden Rule--whoever has the gold makes the rules."

We drove about fifteen minutes to the northwest side. In certain sections there were shuttered houses, trashed buildings, and cannibalized cars on blocks. At night on virtually every corner something bad was going down and gunfire was as common as lightning bugs.

In other areas, the houses were modest. Cars were economy

models. And like much of that part of Chicago, Manny Dubiel lived in an emerging immigrant neighborhood of multigenerational families. Lots of Italians, blacks and Eastern European cultures.

His apartment building was four stories tall, probably two or three small apartments on each floor. Ground-level brick was covered with gang graffiti. Windows were dark. No street traffic. Wind-blown trash banked against curbs and collected in doorways and weeds flourished on the side of the building where a few cars were parked.

Old men loitered on front stoops, a few children were playing on the sidewalk. We saw a cluster of young black men, crew cuts so severe they looked bald, their pants pushed down to the crotch, boxers showing, puffy gang jackets, bulky tennis shoes with no laces.

"Bums. They come out of the womb looking to start trouble They oughta start building baby prisons before the bastards can really hurt anybody," said Schneider.

We parked on the street, and Officer Rumple stayed behind the wheel while Schneider and I got out. A dog barked as we approached the front door. By the sound of it, he was a large breed.

The landlady answered the doorbell. She looked at Schneider, then me and said, "Police? Oh, my. Can I help you?" The dog, part German Shepard, I thought, was just behind her and kept barking.

She smacked the dog's snout. "Shhh. Quiet, Samson!"

The dog endured our presence for a beat and then turned tail and hurled himself back inside, galloping from one end of her apartment to the other with ears flapping and tongue flopping. The woman closed the inner door and blocked him off. She said her name was Caroline Mesa and she owned the building.

I inched forward and handed her my card. She studied it through some pink-rimmed glasses with rhinestones on them, which hung around her neck on what appeared to be a cut-down shoelace. Her eyes strayed to feast on Schneider.

"Why are you here? What do you want?"

She was seventy if she was a day, and had skin like an alligator. Her bleached blond hair was teased into a rat's nest. If it was a wig, she got swindled no matter what she paid. She wore orthopedic shoes, fishnet stockings, a tight spandex miniskirt, and a skimpy tank top that showed a lot of wrinkled cleavage. I was guessing she smoked three packs of cigarettes a day and slept in a tanning bed.

"Ma'am we need to go up and speak to one of your tenants, Mr. Dubiel-- Manuel Dubiel."

Her facial expression changed to not happy. "Okay, I suppose . . . go ahead--it's number 204-- but I don't think he's home." She oozed unpleasantness.

"Why do you say that?" Schneider asked.

She put her hand on her hip, striking an indignant pose. "Cuz, I see who comes and goes here, pretty much. Make it my business to. Besides, his rent was due five days ago, and he always pays on time. Nope. I don't think he made it home this time," she croaked. Then, placing a liver-spotted hand on my wrist, she whispered, "He has a problem with alkeehall." Her breathing rasped with excitement.

"Mind if we go up and check," said Schneider.

"Sure. You won't believe me, come on," she said, and tottered away. We followed her up to the second floor and she pointed to apartment number 204. The hall smelled of beer, cigarette smoke and disinfectant. Outdoor carpet was hard underfoot.

Schneider knocked. No answer. He knocked again and I stepped forward. "Manny--this is Cleve Hawkins. We need to speak to you." I paused. "Manny--open up."

No answer.

"See?" said, Caroline. "He's not there. And I can't let you in without a warrant, neither. I know my rights. I woulda' known if he came home, believe you me. My God, what did he do, anyhow?"

"Sorry, Ma'am, we're not free to discuss that," said Schneider. "We'll check elsewhere. Thanks for your time."

As we walked back downstairs, I said, "Listen, Mrs. Mesa, you have my card, if he shows up, would you please call. Or, you can call the police department, too. Ask for Detective Branoff."

Outside, I looked at my watch. It was almost two. I told Schneider, "Just drop me back at my place, Al, if you don't mind. When you get back, tell Branoff I'm checking a couple of Manny's hangouts. I'll call him. Tell him not to cancel the lineup just yet. I think I know where I can get a line on Dubiel."

"Want me and Rumple to come with?"

"Nah, these people see cops, they'll freeze up--you know how it is."

They dropped me off at my place where I jumped in my car and headed for Ernie's bar on Halstead.

I strolled in and sidled up to the end of the bar where I'd first met Manny. I looked at the row of men drinking at the bar, slumped on their stools, their silhouettes like warped clothespins on a line.

"Well, if it isn't Sam Spade."

I turned to find one of the women I talked with last time I was in, nearly a weeks earlier. Her name was Samantha. Today, she wore a pair of gold hoops that went nicely with her threadbare blue sweatshirt, well-worn knockoff designer jeans, and dirty New Balance sneakers. A good-looking woman, I thought, who probably had been much more attractive before the drinking got out of hand.

"Hi there, Samantha, isn't it?"

"That's right--well, Sam, anyway. So what are you doing back here, Detective Bullshit?"

I smiled. "Looking for a friend of mine, actually. You know that guy--Manny Dubiel?"

Before she could answer, the bartender suddenly appeared in front of me. I realized he wasn't the same guy who was working the bar last time--that was for damned sure.

"Hell are you?" he said. His voice matched his bulk. It was deep, and the words were half swallowed by a heavy chest. He looked the part of a career criminal--long ponytail, studs in his ears, all manner of facial hair, massive biceps, and a collection of cheap tattoos a prison artist had most likely sold him for cigarettes. Methodically he clenched and unclenched his fists as if he were practicing isometrics, and I wondered what his beef was. Everyone sat up a little straighter at the bar and leaned forward ever so slightly, waiting for my reply.

"Name's Hawkins. Cleve Hawkins." I flashed my ID. "You got a problem with that?"

His eyeballs were bloodshot and his hair appeared to have been groomed with salad tongs.

Another woman stepped in. "Hey, Pete . . . this guy's okay. He's a friend of Chelsea's . . . and Manny, too--right, Mister?"

"Right." I remembered her. She had been waitressing when I was in Ernie's last time when I first spoke to Manny. The young woman was slim and toned and spray-tanned to something resembling orange mud. She had big boobs, lots of curly auburn hair tipped with blond and her lips looked like they had been inflated with an air hose. Not bad looking if you like the face of say, Scarlett Johansson.

"You were my waitress, last time I was here." I smiled. "Barb-- right? We talked before Manny got involved."

"Yeah--pretty good memory, detective. I still wait tables sometimes. Just slow right now, as you can see, so I'm just relaxing." She suddenly paused and glared at me as if I was a maggot on a wedding cake. Edging closer, she lowered her voice. "You are such bad luck, my friend."

Meanwhile, realizing he may have been a prick, Pete shrugged and adopted the pose of a confused old man even though his eyes were as sharp as black marbles in snow. He put out his hand and gripped mine like it was the last cold beer in hell. "Okay, so, do you want a drink or not?" he said.

I waved him off. "No-- not today." I turned back to Barb.

"Bad luck, you say? Why's that?"

"Ha! First you come looking for Chelsea, and she ends up buried out in the woods in some Godforsaken fuckin' place. Now you come around checking on Manny and he's in Lutheran General Hospital in a coma."

"Coma?" I felt my jaw drop. "Why? I mean, what happened?"

"Accident. Pickup truck T-boned his car over on Wells and Division about four days ago. He's lucky to be alive, from what I heard. Poor bastard's head was caved in like a rotten pumpkin."

The silence that followed was as dark as the inside of a coffin. My coffin.

CHAPTER SIXTEEN

I smelled blood on Bart Hodgkins, a common shitbird felon with a five-page rap sheet. The part of me that is wolf sensed danger before any other animal in the woods had an inkling of it, yet I felt marinated in ignorance. It seemed like everywhere I turned there was a basket of snakes and I was beginning to feel jinxed. It was as though I had cuffs on my own wrists.

I needed to visit Manny Dubiel in the hospital. I was sure he was still in no condition to speak, much less ID anyone, anywhere; nevertheless, I figured I owed the man, big time. However, he was in ICU and after my visit, I felt certain that he would never regain consciousness. Not allowed to see him, I asked and a nurse who informed me, on the QT, that the prognosis was not good.

Branoff was as disappointed as I was over the Dubiel fiasco, but what could we do? Another dead end.

My main concern, now, was that somehow, Bart Hodgkins would make bail and slip out of our clutches. Although I couldn't imagine how a scumbag like him could come up with the money. The law really had nothing on him, except DUI--that, and possession of a controlled substance that wasn't his. Of course, there was the probation thing, but I had been around long enough to know that something like that wouldn't hold him for long if he had an aggressive lawyer.

I needed a drink. When I finished at the hospital in Park Ridge, and got back in the city, I stopped off at Butch McGuire's place on Division. I knew I was flirting with trouble by drinking, but I wanted to recharge my brain cells--think things through. Scotch would do the trick.

The place wasn't very busy at three in the afternoon. I perched at the end of the bar and ordered a Johnnie Walker splashed with soda, then after a couple of good swigs, I decided to call Branoff. He was busy of course, so I left word for him to call me back ASAP. I was hoping Maureen would answer his phone, but such was not the case.

When Branoff called me back on my cell, about thirty minutes and two drinks later, he sounded upbeat. He started before I could get a word in.

"Some good news, if you can believe it . . . Florence Rohrman has agreed to let us go through her daughter's Firebird. The impound yard never had it, come to find out, she paid to have it towed directly to her house and since we really had nothing tying the car to her daughter's killing, our hands were tied."

"Why in the hell was she being so tight about the search in the first place?"

"Just the way she was feeling at the time--grief and all that, according to the daughter, Betty. I know it sounds crazy, but the mother felt like, if we searched Chelsea's car, we'd be stepping on her grave somehow. It's private property and none of anyone's business what was in the car, or so Florence said. I was all set to get a fuckin' warrant before she gave her okay."

"So, you must have made it clear how important it was for us to check it out, eh?"

"Yeah, well--actually, no. Her daughter, Betty, convinced her mother it was best to let us in. She told me they'll allow you and one of my guys--nobody else. Evidently the mother and daughter both like you. I don't understand that part at all, Hawk. Ha! Ha!"

"See, you still fail to realize just what a sweet guy I am, Kris."

"Yeah, sure. Well get this . . . she wants a list of anything you guys take out of the car. Hell, she must think we're a bunch of idiots, but, anyway, I told her no problem."

"Yeah. So when can we have access?"

"Anytime, but be sure to make that list if you should luck out and want to remove anything. Call me when you're ready to go out; I'll get Jordan or one of the other guys to meet you out there. I'll pave the way with a phone call to her when you're ready. Deal?"

"Got it. It's getting a little late now, but I'll get out there tomorrow. Meanwhile, I'm wondering if you guys were able to do anything about that bottle of Xanax taken from Hodgkin's car. I'd like to track down the prescription and find the owner--that Joan Vidrow or whatever her name was."

"Vidross, yes" said, Branoff. "I'm ahead of you on that one, Hawk. We dusted the bottle when we went through the Chrysler Hodgkins was driving. We found his prints on the bottle, but have to get a subpoena to get info on the Vidross woman's pharmacy. Fuckin' HIPPA laws, you know. Talk about screwing around--I mean those people at the county building can beat around the bush until the bush dies of annoyance."

"So how do I get the address of this woman? Have you guys done anything with it yet?"

"No, Cleve. Jesus! I've been busier than a whore in prison with a fist-full of pardons. I've got my whole department working on this one case and I was just informed that another woman's body was found in the damned woods."

"No shit? Where?"

"Out near Rolling Hills. We're not even sure if it's the work of the same killer because this victim took a .22 slug in the head and she wasn't buried. Two fishermen found her off to the side a two-track. Jesus! I needed this like a third tit, ya' know?"

"Holy shit! You have got your hands full, haven't you?"

"Yeah, well, you know the old saying . . . 'When you're up to your ass in alligators, it's hard to remember that your main objective was to drain the swamp' Anyway, if you want to, you can go to the property section and check that pill bottle. You can't take it, but the prescription info will be with it in the box down there."

"That'll work."

"We just got it this afternoon. In fact, I had Andrews on the phone talking to Walgreens on Rush Street when you called earlier. I'd go with you, but I just can't bust free for the next day or so, understand?"

"Thanks, Kris. Who knows where the hell that could lead us, if we find out who this Joan character is and how she ties in with Hodgkins. And like I said, I'll get out there to see the car tomorrow. Call you in the morning. Meanwhile you can tell Jordan or whoever, we're checking out the car tomorrow afternoon."

"Sounds good. Hey . . .where in the hell are you, anyway? I'm hearing music and a lotta talking behind you. You in a fuckin' bar?"

I hesitated, then said, "Yeah. I stopped here at McGuire's. I'm fine though--don't sweat the small stuff, okay?"

"Right. See ya,' Hawk. Man, my brain hurts." He paused just a beat before he said, "Hey!"

"Yeah?"

"Listen up, Hawk . . . I'm sticking my neck out a hell of a ways for you on this deal. Just remember, I need to know everything. If anything breaks, I want to hear about it before God."

"Me--forget about you? How could you think that shit? Don't worry--whatever I know, you'll know, Kris. See you later."

A Doctor Jennings from Evanston wrote the prescription for Joan Vidross, whose last known address was on Washington Street in Elk Grove. I headed out that way the next morning.

She lived in a small, redbrick house on a narrow road, a few miles west of the city limits. Her nearest neighbor lived in a double-wide trailer half a mile closer to the state highway. The terrain was familiar. Fallow post winter fields, some trees, a few old barns, an occasional grocery store, an untidy yard with used tractor tires for sale.

The grass was overgrown and had gone to seed. A rusted bike and a washing machine with its top lid askew decorated the front yard. The house itself was a small cinder block rancher built on a slab. It looked to be more of an outbuilding than a home. An red Dodge pickup was parked haphazardly in the yard, and I parked on the edge of the road, and made my way up to the front door which was screened. The lower half was ripped and it rattled when I knocked. A small dog yapped its way through the house, followed by a woman with a light olive complexion. She was early forties, possibly, rather than mid and had jet black hair piled high up on her head. It was tied in a bun, a chignon, or something like that.

She had large watery green eyes that flashed anger, sensuality, and iciness with equal intensity. Medium height and lean, she looked good in bright red shorts-- pretty, in a rather severe and no-nonsense kind of way. She looked tired and a little ill at ease as she exhaled the smoke from a cigarette and pushed the screen door open just a bit.

"Can I help you?"

"I hope so. Are you Joan Vidross?"

"All depends. Who's askin'?" The dog continued to yap. I noticed a man standing in the background, lighting a cigarette.

I had my ID ready and flipped the holder open. "Name's Cleve Hawkins, and I wonder if I might ask you a few questions concerning a client of mine."

"Let me see that again." She took her time and scrutinized the ID like a jeweler checking a diamond. When she appeared to be satisfied she said, "You a cop?"

"No, Ma'am. Private investigator."

She shrugged. "Same thing, as far as I'm concerned. What do you want?"

"May I come in?"

She hesitated, then turned and said to the man. "Clyde--please lock that damned dog in the other room." She looked back at me. "Come.."

Lowering herself onto a black Naugahyde sofa, which hissed beneath her weight, she picked up the remote and pointed it at the TV. The picture got sucked into a white dot, then she drew a heavy sweater around herself, and tucked her bare legs beneath her.

Clyde remained standing by the kitchen door. About forty-five, potbellied, unshaven, and red-eyed, he wore scrotum-tight jeans, an awful Hawaiian shirt that looked like a gag gift, and black construction boots. His jaw pointed at the ceiling, looking at something up there. Probably just ignoring me.

I wasn't offered a seat; instead, Joan Vidross blew out a stream of smoke as she drilled holes through me with her eyes. "So, what's up?"

"Are you acquainted with a man named Bart Hodgkins?"

"Bart who?"

"Hodgkins--Bart, or Bartholomew, Hodgkins."

"No." She shook her head a little. I watched her eyes very closely; the name seemed to draw no reaction as she said, "Should I?"

"I'm not sure, Ms. Vidross, but it's very important that you tell me if you do, of course."

This seemed to puzzle her. "Who is he, and why do you think *I* would know him?"

Clyde strolled over to a La-Z-Boy and flopped down. "Yeah, what makes you think Joanie would know this guy, Ace?"

"Hodgkins was arrested a few nights ago for driving drunk. A prescription bottle of Xanax was found in the glove box of his vehicle. The bottle was Joan's"

"Mine? No way!"

"You do have a prescription for Xanax, do you not?"

"Yeah. So what? Lots'a people do."

Clyde leaned forward in his chair. "What are you getting at, pal?"

I ignored him and zeroed in on Vidross. "Well, let me put it this way, Ma'am-- are you missing a bottle of the pills?"

"No. Hell, no! I don't even take them that much--only when people piss me off . . .just like you're doin', right now."

She stood and folded her arms across her chest. "I can account for all of my drugs, mister."

"Certainly, and I don't mean to infer otherwise, Ms. Vidross."

"Well, it sure sounds like it to me. I want you to leave right now.

I want you to get the hell out of my house."

Clyde grunted somberly. He was suddenly on his feet, and I knew I needed to get control of the situation fast. When the shit starts to fly you don't want to be the fan.

"Let's just take it easy here, folks. Fact is, this man, Hodgkins is a possible suspect in the serial killings you've probably heard about. He may be a killer."

Joan exclaimed, "What?" then cupped her hands over her mouth and fell back on the couch. Clyde sat down.

"Yes. So, although I don't mean to upset you, I do need to know a couple of more things--then I'll go."

Joan nodded. "Go ahead."

"I don't want you to be offended with what I am going to ask you, Joan, but how long have you two folks been together?" I tilted my head to the side indicating Clyde.

"Why? What difference does that make?"

"Please, Ma'am, it's important. How long?"

Clyde answered. "Me and her's been practically engaged for nearly five months now." I noticed he had weathered skin from working in the sun, no doubt, and small eyes that kept glancing somewhere else. Had trouble maintaining eye contact.

Joan said, "Yes, that's right, five or six months, why?"

"Do you have any family members that would have had access to your prescription for Xanax?"

"No. Absolutely not. All my relatives live in Iowa. Des Moines."

"No children of your own? Teenagers?"

She shook her head, no. "No kids."

"How about you, Clyde? Anyone close who may have had access to the pills?"

"Nope." He grinned. "I'm a loner--well least ways I was till I met Joanie." Rolling a cigarette from one side of his mouth to the other, he sucked hard, then blew the smoke in twin plumes from his nostrils.

"Okay, one more question right now, Joan. Who did you date before you met Clyde, here?"

Her face turned to stone. "I'll have you know, I don't sleep around. You may have heard that condoms are in again because of disease. These days you have to boil people in order to sleep with them."

"I'm not saying you were intimate necessarily, but did you date anyone in particular?"

"Ha! Yeah, just one asshole. And I mean asshole, with a capitol A.

Kind a guy was an intellectual but reads the shopping guide on the toilet?"

"I see. Did you date him very long?"

"Nah. Maybe went out with him four or five times. Guy had bucks, you know?" She smirked as though she had a secret she wasn't telling. "Yeah, for a while it was a blast."

"And, where did you meet this man?"

"Oh, I was working at Northwestern, buffing floors and cleaning for this company that did the maintenance contract. Bullshit job, but I met him there one day when he was leaving. He's a science professor, name's Lisecki. Ha! He wouldn't need my pills though. He's rich enough, could buy his own drugstore chain, most likely."

"Lisecki? And his first name . . .?"

"Lewis. Like I said--an asshole, but it was fun for a while. Good old professor Lew."

Clyde glared at her.

On the way back to my car, I eyeballed the license plate on the pickup sitting and I wrote the number in my book before I pulled away.

I heard a nameless voice repeating an admonition that I had pushed aside, a premise that almost all investigative law enforcement officers never forget. Crime is about money, sex, or power. If you have the money, you can buy the sex and power. So follow the money.

CHAPTER SEVENTEEN

Joan Vidross was pissed--so furious, she was shaking. When Lewis answered the door at eight that night, she skirted right past him and headed for the liquor cabinet. Her purse hit the kitchen table like a cinder block.

With Clyde two steps behind her, she cut through Lewis's Better Homes and Gardens living room, the heels of her pink pumps click-clacked on the marble floor of the foyer, which was three stories high. Huge crystal chandeliers dangled like outrageous jewels overhead.

Joan looked as if she'd spent the night in the trunk of a car. Having put on make-up in a color scheme that indicated she might be colorblind, she looked like a five-dollar hand-job hooker.

Clyde was dressed to kill in his black T-shirt with the sleeves cut off to accommodate tattooed upper arms as thick as Virginia hams. His stomach hung over his belt like a sack of grain, and his cologne smelled like fermented pig piss.

Lewis gave a snort of laughter as they breezed past him.

"I'd say welcome, folks . . but I'm not sure." He kept his eye on

Joan as he strolled in the opposite direction, down a short hallway. Clyde followed him through to the den, where Lewis promptly walked over and stood behind his desk.

He had a nasty grin and a disgusted look in his eyes, as he removed his reading glasses. His head sank into his neck, and his jowls swelled out like the bottom of a deflated basketball.

"Well--go ahead and have a seat, Clyde," he said, motioning to a rather plush armchair. He casually opened the humidor on his desk and offered Clyde one of his cigars, then lit one for himself. "Long time, no see. Have you been staying out of trouble, my friend?"

Clyde made quite a spectacle of blowing his nose as he ambled over and grabbed the cigar. Then examining the tissue to see what had been expelled, he sat back down, studied the rather thin Havana, and said "Shit! I've smoked fatter joints than this!"

Lewis regretted his own intellect. After so many years as a judge and educator, he'd lost the capacity to be personally insulted. Virtually nothing provoked him. Emotions were risky. They distorted the senses, led to grave miscalculation and foolish impulses. Of course it would be great to punch Clyde so hard that he puked up blood, but it would also be counterproductive. He knew Clyde's past-- and the man's future, if and when, he dared get too far out of line-- just as he knew Bart's. Besides, Clyde would probably kick the shit out of him in a flash, if the chance ever presented itself. Lewis preferred to ignore the man's smart-assed remarks. But, what in the hell do they want here he wondered?

He stood up and paced the floor. "This is a pleasant surprise . . . what brings you two way out here tonight?"

"Have to ask her, I imagine." Clyde's face crinkled and made him look as if he'd just stepped in dog shit. "I'll just say this--I think you opened Pandora's box, took out a can of worms, and threw it at a hornet's nest when you pissed Joanie off."

"What is that supposed to mean, I just . . ."

Joan steamed into the room with two Old Style beers in her hands. She handed one to Clyde, then opened a new pack of Kools and tapped one out.

Lewis scurried back around his desk, picked up a silver table lighter and held it to her cigarette and Clyde's cigar. He studied Joan's face as she sat back and blew a slow stream of smoke, relaxed now in the forest-green cushions of the sofa.

She winked at Lewis, then paused briefly before she said, "Thanks," paused again and continued: "You know, you're a first class prick, Lew."

On his way back to the desk, Lewis wheeled around. "What?" Women never talked to him that way. He'd never tolerate that. In fact, he'd never had a wife to scold him about anything, including his weight, make sure his socks matched, or do something about the stains on his shirts.

"Jesus, Joan. I thought we were best of friends. And, after all I've done for you? How can you say that?" He moved back behind the desk and grinned. "Perhaps you should cut down on your Vitamin Bitch Pills."

Clyde said nothing. He tended to hang back a little from those around him, took in their moods and actions, then reacted accordingly. He was not a bad guy, once you got past the two-hundred pounds of anger and dysfunction. Leaning back in the chair, Clyde scuffed his boot heels across the Berber carpet and guzzled the beer, He chose to stay alert, and listen to these two animals snarl at one another.

"Ha! The yin and yang of Lewis Lisecki," quipped Joan. "Charming, handsome old gentleman on the outside, nasty old bastard on the inside." Her voice rose to an octave normally only heard from Minnie Mouse. "Bullshit! Men are kind to women for two reasons. Either they want in their pants or they have genuine balls and don't have to prove anything. You, my friend, are a typical strip-show creep, who wears silk ties and passes out twenties like gumdrops."

"Now, you listen here, I . . ."

"No--you listen, Lewis. I kissed your ass and said thank you a ton of times, and I meant it. So let's move on, okay? Funny--I thought we were through with each other until this afternoon, but of course I was wrong."

Lewis sniffed and struck a pose like a Shakespearean actor on stage. "What? What on earth do you mean, Joan?"

Clyde leaned forward in his chair. "Ha! Ha! Big shot. Now look what you did to her. She's pissed. Man, you're a regular knight in shining bullshit."

Lewis's eyes were dark and probing as he stared at Clyde. He grinned-- almost laughed. "That talk is most certainly uncalled for. You're poking your nose where it doesn't belong," he said.

"Anyway, reason I'm here," said Joan, "I sort of thought you might be interested, Lew . . . I had a visitor today. He looked a lot like a cop, but claimed he was a private eye."

"Really? And, exactly how does that information concern me?"

"You tell me." She paused and her eyes narrowed as she continued. "What in the hell did you do with the bottle of Xanax I left here by accident?"

Lewis tried to remain calm, but his throat felt tight. *That fuckin Bart!* This is just like my fuck up friend, he thought-- he's dished out another helping of shit onto a plate that's already overflowing. The danger seemed unreal and remote at the moment, but that was the worst kind of danger; the kind you cannot or will not meet head on. He suddenly had the strange sensation of being removed from his body, as if the world had receded and he was no longer a part of it.

"What?" He bleated. Nervousness washed over him like a spray of cold rain. "What did you say?" He was trying to sound brave, but his hands were clenched and his lip trembled. Without touching the cigar with his hands, he flicked his tongue somehow, cocked his head, and it slid to the right side of his mouth. He could not worry about this. He knew that a man's worst enemy was a functioning conscience.

"You heard me," said Joan. "I believe I left my prescription bottle of Xanax here. I wondered where the hell it was, but thought I lost it somewhere. Then, it occurred to me that I must have left the bottle here the last time we dated."

"Whoa, whoa, whoa," Lewis stood and wedged his hands to signal time out, like a football coach. In recent years when addressed with questions on dwelling in the devil's pocket, Lewis was adamant and it worked.

"So that's it, Joanie. Well, they are not here, and frankly, I'm surprised you would accuse me of keeping them in any event."

She studied his face which had turned the color of spackle. "You are surprised aren't you?" She searched his eyes. "Well, don't act like a virgin, Lew. Nothing is all black and white, you know. If you want black and white, go watch a Bogie and Becall flick." She took a swallow of beer, slow and contemplative. "Maybe I'm wrong."

"Well, you are wrong, Joan." Loosening his necktie vigorously, as if escaping a noose, he put his hands on his head, and squeezed lightly, as if testing a cantaloupe for ripeness. "I haven't seen your pills-- and I'm confident that I certainly would have noticed something like that. Honestly, I would have called you immediately, if I found them."

Clyde wore a savage grin. "Too hell with all this horseshit . . . hey, Lew-- you're a smart man--full of shit, maybe--but a smart man. Let me ask you something . . . let's say you clone yourself--and then have sex with yourself--is it incest or masturbation?"

"Shut up, Clyde," said Joan. "Good God. Men and their dicks. If you didn't have them, we'd have to sew one on, just to give you something to talk about."

Lewis smiled appreciatively.

Clyde shrugged as if he didn't care, but his cheeks turned red and his eyes narrowed. He sighed, and leaned forward, resting his forearms on his thighs, he let his hands dangle between his knees.

"I'm sick of you guys arguing," he said. "Might as well face it . . . the world is a sewer and we're all dodging shit." Taking a comb out of his pants pocket, he ran it through his hair, touching the waves with his fingers simultaneously, his knurled forehead furrowed as his eyes bored into Lewis's face. He wiped his mouth with the back of his hand, then wiped the back of his hand on his pants. With a grunt, he stood and headed out to the liquor cabinet. "I 'm needing some fuckin' joy juice."

"Anyway," said Joan. "This private dick said they picked up some asshole for drunk driving the other night. Turns out, that hophead had my bottle of pills in his glove box."

"So, what would that have to do with me?" Lewis asked, as he strolled back and stood behind his desk.

"Nothing, I suppose. I just didn't know. Maybe he's a friend of yours. Do you know a dude named Bart?"

Lewis shook his head. "No--I can't say as I do know anyone named Bart." He felt the blood rush from his legs. Soon, he lost all feeling below the waist. So crippled with terror, he expected his bladder to fail at any second.

"Well, I guess I'm sorry I accused you, Lewis. Anyway, this asshole, Bart, supposedly was the one got picked up with the pills in his car. Where in the hell did he find them? I wonder what I have to do in order to get them back from the cops?"

"Gee . . . I wouldn't know, Joan. I can understand your anxiety. He paused for a beat. "You could probably use one of those pills right now, I imagine, huh?"

"Well, I don't take them very often, to tell the truth, but it's just the idea somebody running around with my prescription, ya know?"

"Yes. I can certainly understand. I feel bad about it, Joan--I really do."

Clyde strolled back in. He was carrying three mixed drinks very carefully. "Here we go, guys. Rum and Cokes all around. You don't like Captain Morgan, professor--you're screwed, cuz that's what I got here."

"That will be fine, Clyde. Thank you," Lewis croaked. The wheels in his head were meshing with an idea. He was beyond shocked that Bart had been arrested--and when? The night he left here? He thought it over. Oh, shit! It would be tricky, but he realized he had to get the dumb sonofabitch out of jail before everything went to hell. His own life depended on it. Bart's mouth would kill them both.

"I've got an idea, Joan. See what you think of this. Let's find out what the bail is for this idiot and work on getting him out."

"What? Are you serious? Ha! I got no money for that shit. Let the bastard rot in there as far as I'm concerned."

"Then you can get your pills back, though."

"Fuck them pills."

"No, no, I'll pay the bail. You needn't worry about that. I'll make some calls--find out how much the bail is, and go from there." He looked at Clyde who was rubbing his nose fiercely, as if trying to dislodge a bumblebee as he moved to Joan's side and hovered like a dentist's assistant.

"You could go down there with the bail, Clyde. I'm sure drunk driving couldn't be that much and the court doesn't care who pays it. When I was on the bench, I handed out a lot of fines for drunks."

"Nah. I got no time for that crap, professor. I got other shit to do, ain't that right, Joanie?" Turning away, Joan smothered a laugh, then looked at him curiously. "What have you got to do, besides sit on your ass, cowboy?"

Lewis moved around his desk and stood a few feet from them. "I'd pay you for your time and gas of course."

"You would, eh?" Clyde grinned. "How much?"

"How about a two hundred, plus a tank of gas?"

"Shit! Two-hunnert bucks? Hell, yes." He checked his glass, rattling the ice. "And that's just for going down there and bailing the asshole out of the tank, right?"

"Correct. I'll get all the information and call you. You come by and get the money and go down there. I think you know where the lockup is. And by the way, you must tell them you are a friend of his. You cannot mention my name in any way. I'd rather not be involved, being an ex-judge and all. You understand? It might not look good."

"Well, yeah. That's fine. I'm this guy's friend, I get it. I would not hesitate to call this guy as a card-carrying shithead though, and I don't get why you're doing this--but, hell yes--I'll do er."

"Remember now . . . if anyone contacts me on this, I will deny I had anything to do with getting this man out of jail. You'll be on your own, and I am sure you don't want to be in that position. So, just do as I say and we'll be fine."

Lewis smiled and looked over at Joan. "I'm doing it for my good friend, Joan. What are friends for, after all?"

Joan shrugged. She smiled and said, "Sure. Okay, you honey-tongued spellbinder."

Lewis thought, Bart you are a dead man. D E A D--fish chum, rose fertilizer--worm food—just done.

CHAPTER EIGHTEEN

I felt like a juggler with a hundred balls in the air, I was going to drop one sooner or later. My need to rummage through Chelsea Rohrman's car as soon as possible was at the top of my list, but the information pertaining to the bottle of Xanax had my curiosity pumped more than dealing with the search of the car. Branoff told me the Firebird was parked out at the Rohrman place, and I figured on tackling that after lunch.

I had a nagging urge to speak to this Professor Lisecki, Joan Vidross told me about. She said he was an asshole, but through the years I've found that I'm partial to assholes, so I decided to pay him a visit at the college.

It was a decent Tuesday, with no clouds and a slight breeze that had started during the night and chased away the humidity. Lines of smoky pink were beginning to burn against the sky, and early morning commuters were making their way along the still mostly empty streets.

I left my place early and worked out for an hour. I had brought a change of clothes with me so I could shower and change at the gym, before heading out to the University.

On occasion, I run into a clown named Tokey Higgenbottom at the gym. He probably isn't over five and a half feet tall, but his neck is thick and corded with vein, his shoulders wide and sloping like a weightlifter. As big and white as a Frigidaire, and just about as intelligent, his arms are the size of a holiday hams.

Tinker Bell on steroids.

As luck would have it, he was checked in and had worked up a sweat by the time he sidled up and filled my ear with nonsequitur bullshit while I attempted to pump iron. I have no idea why he chose to pick on me; I mean the guy is okay, but in addition to being mouthy, he's a couple of sandwiches short of a picnic.

While I changed clothes, he sat cross-legged on the locker room floor, spieling Harvard's theory that Bill Gates was not only the Antichrist but the illegitimate child of Billy Graham and Betty White.

When I finally escaped, I was so hungry I could eat the ass-end of a donkey, so I stopped at the *Hometown Diner* on Ashland Avenue,, where I knew the food was A-plus.

A good breakfast joint, and a classic Chicago diner, the place had wonderful shiny aluminum walls. Some newer ones had a faux-stone facade that makes one long for aluminum. The interior had, however, changed very little at *Hometown*. There were still small juke-boxes at every table; a counter with spin stools; doughnuts under Batphone-style glass covers; signed, sun-faded autographed photos of local celebrities you've never heard of; a surly guy with hairy ears behind the cash register; and a waitress who called you "hon" and you loved her for it.

I downed three cups of coffee with a stack of pancakes, three over medium and sausage patties. No toast. After I finished eating and paid the check at the register, I hit the road, staring at the trays of donuts on the way out.

I learned that Lisecki worked at the Lincoln Park campus and headed that way. Rush hour traffic is a bitch at that time of day and you never really learn to swear until you learn to drive, but I took the Kennedy to Fullerton, then out to Sheffield and was there in good time. It was just eight o'clock, and I was hoping to catch the professor before he got wrapped up in a lecture or class of some sort. Probably a busy guy. I had to poke around for a few minutes before I found the administration offices and a parking space.

The receptionist was on the heavy side--thicker in the waist, heavier in the face. The nameplate on her desk said she was Ms. Esther Roude.

I figured her to be forty or more. She wore her straight auburn hair pulled back severely in a bun, but a strand had come loose and fell into her eyes. When she looked at me over her harlequin glasses, she blew the errant strand away. Appearing as a prim, nervous sort, it was evident that she took her job very seriously-- probably smoked--maybe secretly. Drank--but definitely on the sly. A small sack that said *Krispy Kreme* sat by her purse on top of the filing cabinet.

Her desktop was spotless. I'd always heard that a clean desk is a sign of a cluttered desk drawer. But everything was neat and tidy. She had a neat and tidy job, probably working for a neat and tidy man in a position of authority. She most likely knew her place, and was happy to stay in it.

"Morning, Ma'am." I opened my badge holder and gave her my card. "My name is Cleve Hawkins-- here to see Professor Lisecki."

A smug and serious look shadowed her face as she studied the card and said, "Do you have an appointment?"

"No, as a matter of fact, I don't, but, I was hoping he might see me before classes, if at all possible; it is important and it shouldn't take long."

"Police business?"

"Not exactly, but close enough." I smiled.

She hesitated, and cleared her throat, then said, "Well, if you'll have a seat, I will go and see if the professor will see you. He is a very busy man, you know." She had a notebook in one hand and a ballpoint in the other.

"Thank you, that would be great." I picked up a copy of *Psychology Today* and flipped through it. I glanced at an article about employers taking responsibility for psychiatric care for their employees. I smiled. By the time one of those big companies got around to referring one of its employees to a psychiatrist, the screaming meemies would have already set in and the patient would be receiving radio beams from Mars.

Ms. Roude was back faster than I expected, considering the circumstances.

"Mr. Hawkins, Professor Lisecki will see you now, however I'm to remind you he has a session at eight-forty-five. Will that be enough time?"

I tossed the magazine back on the pile as I stood and smiled for her again. "Yes, that will be fine, thank you." She ushered me to the professor's inner sanctum.

His office was about fifteen by fifteen, knotty pine paneled, with two six-foot windows facing north and staring directly into the second floor of an older building next door. Not much of a view. With a strain, he could see a glimpse of the river to the north-west. Sun streaks slashed across the room. There were stacks of paper everywhere and probably two or three hundred books, on a number of shelves.

The professor was watering his window plants with a hand-painted teakettle when we entered. He moseyed over to me, sort of bowlegged, as if he'd been on a horse all morning, or maybe he had hemorrhoids. He extended his hand as he studied my card. "Mr. Hawkins--that right?"

"Yes, Sir, Cleve Hawkins." It was a weak hand I shook, like that of a woman.

"Thank you, Ms Roude," he said, beaming. "That will be all for now. Would you mind closing the door on your way out?" He set the teakettle down on the window sill and fidgeted with his tie.

"Very impressive campus, from what I can see, professor. It's my first time out here."

"Yes, we're quite proud of it. Students describe our professors as personable and engaging, because they actually get to know them. More than 98 percent of all classes are taught by faculty members, not teaching assistants."

I nodded. "I see. That's a good thing, for sure."

I figured him for fifty-five or sixty max. Most of his hair was gone and the few remaining streaks were heavily oiled and slicked across his wide scalp. The patches around his ears were thin and mostly gray. He wore square wire-rimmed glasses that were quite thick.

"Go ahead, have a seat," he said as he skirted around and back behind his desk. "Oh, sorry. Look at me, for pity's sake. May I have Ms. Roude get you some coffee?" He held up his own cup as he offered.

"No, thanks, professor. I'm good."

He was a short man with an accountant's pinched demeanor, a fish belly complexion, tiny black eyes, and thick sloping forehead of a killer whale. Clean-shaven, and wearing a pin-striped double-breasted suit with six buttons, his tie was navy and terribly boring. I could already tell that he was a man who thought his shit didn't flush.

"Well then, what can we do for you this fine morning, Mister Hawkins?"

"Well, I've been working on a missing person's case and your name has come up in a round-about way, so I have a few questions, if you don't mind. Won't take long."

I started jotting a few notes in a notebook I pulled from my coat pocket.

"Questions?" He leaned back in his swivel chair and laced his fingers together behind his head. "That's interesting. How in the world am I connected in any way to this missing individual?"

"Do you know a woman named Joan Vidross?"

"Joan Vidross? Oh, why sure. I know Joan. Is she missing, for heaven's sake?"

"No--not her. I'll give you a little background here, professor. We have a man in custody that was found with a prescription bottle of a controlled substance in his vehicle. The bottle of pills weren't his, but rather belonged to Ms. Vidross who says that the two of you dated. Is that right?"

Lisecki raised a single thick eyebrow. "Yes, as a matter of fact we have gotten together on several occasions. But that's rather personal, you know. I am not following you, how do I......?"

"Well, we are concerned as to how this man came by them, so I asked Ms. Vidross whom she had been in contact with--family, friends--so on and of course your name came up during that process."

"I'm sorry, Mr. Hawkins . . . I'm still not seeing the connection here." He had an oily voice, and at times his eyes glowed with the fervor of a street preacher.

"What does our dating have to do with this man you have incarcerated?"

"Probably nothing. This is standard procedure." I paused intentionally and scribbled in my book while he waited for my next question. "Are you married?"

"Married? Ha! Heavens no. How could I be married and dating Joan? No, of course not. No--I'm a bachelor. Oh, I enjoy the presence of a woman in the house for brief periods of time." He grinned. "They fall into two categories, you know--the organizers and the slobs. There's probably a third category ---the naggers, who try to get a fellow to do things, but I never ran into one of those. Oddly, I have no preference regarding organizers and slobs, as long as they don't try to pick up my clothes for me. Ha! Ha!"

"Oh?"

"Yes, basically, all women are nurturers and healers, and all men are mental patients to varying degrees. It works fine if people stick to their fated roles, I believe." He was pinching the bridge of his nose. "Marriage," he snorted. "Ha!"

His head hung low and his eyes squinted. Leaning forward, he rested his arms on the desk, poised as if to tell me a secret, then, grinning like the Cheshire cat, he noted, "I have a dear friend who made that mistake. He regrets it to this day, and he's been married to the same woman for twenty-six years, mind you. He's four years older and a dozen years slower than his wife, who has consistently reduced him to a chattering chipmunk state about once a month."

I quickly realized that bullshit hung on him like chain mail. "Sorry, I just had to eliminate the possibility of an affair."

"An affair? No, of course not, and I believe I resent the

implication, Sir. Joan isn't married either, for goodness sakes."

"Yes, I know. Is it possible that Ms. Vidross left her bottle of pills at your home in error? Perhaps they dropped out of her purse. That would be possible, right?"

"Wrong. That would be impossible, because I would have returned them to her immediately, now wouldn't I?" He leaned back in his chair. I had been listening to liars for years, and I could hear the lies in his voice.

"My goodness, Sir, what sort of questions are these?" He sounded like an old teacher of mine, and I was patiently ignoring every word of his scolding.

He tented his long fingers before him. I never was sure why people did that when they were thinking. I thought they often did it to telegraph contemplation. I watched the tension play over his face. My scalp crawled, hot sweat slicked the nape of my neck, and I heard my heart knocking as I decided to go for it.

"How about a straight answer, Professor Lisecki? Do you know Bart Hodgkins-- yes or no?" I stared at him, waiting. I searched his face for a reaction--there was none.

It's the cool ones who burn hot at the center. Authoritarian, control freaks, conservative, and obsessed with rules and regulations. It's a mechanism they use because they're frightened of their own passions, and they know what lurks beneath the suit or uniform. In reality, they have no natural checks and balances on their behavior, and when they spin out of control, they're capable of anything. Lisecki was precariously close to becoming the first name on my brand-new shit list.

Lisecki squinted, then shook his head so violently that his cheeks flapped. "Who?"

"Bartholomew Hodgkins. Do you know this man?" I pulled Bart Hodgkins picture out of my inside pocket, walked over and laid it on the desk in front of him.

I watched his eyes as he took off his glasses and leaned forward to examine the mug shot. "No. I can't say as I do. Hmmmm. I must say he is a mean looking individual. Now, how could I possibly know someone like that?" He leaned back in the chair and said, "He certainly displays a good deal of hate in his eyes, doesn't he?"

"Mr. Hodgkins is the man we have in custody. He had the pills in the glove box of his car. You're sure you don't know this man?"

"No, Sir. Heavens no. How could this man have anything to do with me . . . or Ms. Vidross for that matter? I simply can't imagine."

"Probably none, I'm sure. I just had to ask."

"No probably to it. I believe it was Hemingway who said, 'Most of us are adverbs. Few of us are nouns,' Mr. Hawkins. I'm afraid I can't help you. Please don't think it hasn't been nice."

He stood, glanced at his watch and asked, "Will that be all? I sincerely hope so, because I have exactly five minutes before I have to be available to a group of young people seeking to further their education."

Ms. Roude smiled and waved me out of the office with one hand, holding a sugared jelly doughnut in the other. "Have a good day, Mr. Hawkins."

"You too," I said.

When I worked homicide, we did a lot of psychological profiling on murder cases, especially serial killers, and it was helpful. There is an old saying among detectives: Never overlook the obvious. No matter what kind of society we create, the murderers, the bullies, the wife-beaters, the sexual predators and all the rest will always be with us and among us.

Lies are destructive and spread like malignancy to the innocent and guilty alike. The truth is only recognized as the truth after all the lies are told and discounted.

I learned two very important things from Professor Lewis Lisecki that morning. He was a liar and had a hard on for women, only it was the wrong kind of hard-on. Now, I wanted to find out how deep that hatred really was.

CHAPTER NINETEEN

When Clyde got blitzed on Captain Morgan, his short-term memory tended to vapor-lock, but not when it came to easy money. He struggled to get out of bed, showered and shaved and poured eye drops into his bloodshot retinas. He sipped strong coffee as he selected jeans and a semi clean sweatshirt, which was exactly what he wanted. Across the back, bold letters stated: Love sucks . . . true love swallows.

Friday morning dawned late under a tedious cloud cover that was the color and texture of cement curbing and accompanied Clyde's foul mood.

He felt like shit, but decided to stop for coffee at a local greasy spoon called The Golden Griddle on Ashland Avenue. It was close to a human throw-away-zone, but the food was great. Somehow, he still managed an appetite and decided to indulge himself with a full order of biscuits and gravy and three over easy. He left no tip, which was his custom, and left with a toothpick lolling in the corner of his mouth.

He'd gotten six-hundred dollars from Lewis Lisecki in order to pay the bail on six thousand dollars for Bart Hodgkins, and needed to get over to Bad Boys'Bail Bonds as soon as they opened at 7am. He drove his 1972 Dodge Ram, with the rear fender missing, and found southbound State Street traffic was still bearable. Rolling down the window, he tried to spit the toothpick from the corner of his mouth, but it pasted itself to his arm.

By 9 a.m. he had the necessary paperwork in hand, and all the required phone calls had been made by Ted Domanowski, the owner of " Bad Boys." Then, Bada-bing-bada-boom--he was clear to pick up Bart outside the county lockup within the hour.

Bart's lawyer, a Public Defender named Jerry Edelstein, had a dark beard and horn-rimmed glasses. He wore a rumpled blazer, wrinkled khakis, dirty sneakers, and possessed the weighty aura of one trying to save the world. Bart didn't trust him, or like him. Years behind bars did that to a man. But, he decided he would go along to get along--anything to get out of jail. He didn't look for trouble, but had a hair trigger when confronted with anyone looking to piss on him.

Edelstein stood outside Bart's cell with a gum-chewing deputy at 9:45 a.m.

The deputy's name was Greeley and he had spent most of his years with the department either as a crossing guard at area elementary schools or escorting prisoners from the drunk tank to court.

"Mr. Hodgkins--you have made bail," said the lawyer.

Bart lay on his bottom bunk with his hands folded behind his head. His white t- shirt was stained the color of varnish at both armpits. He leaned on one elbow and looking at the lawyer, said, "Oh Yeah? Who did you blow to get that done?"

Randall, the inmate occupying the top bunk laughed.

"Okay, Hodgkins, we all know you're funnier than a case of the clap. You've proved that much," said the deputy. "Let's go knucklehead. You can sleep when you're dead." His gum snapped in his jaw.

Downstairs, Edelstein stood by his side, as Bart collected his personal items from the property section. "Now, you have to be in court on the eleventh of next month at 9 a.m.--that's in just three weeks. Whatever you do--don't fail to be there. I will meet you that morning at eight outside the courtroom. Here, sign these papers and print your name under the signatures, too."

While Bart shuffled through the papers--signing one after another, Edelstein continued: "And, having met with your probation officer twice in the past three days, I sincerely hope you understand and will adhere to his instructions. It's very important that you do that, sir."

Bart had been assigned a new probation officer. His name was Floyd Wilhelm, a huge black man, at least six five with a wide frame that carried a lot of weight. Floyd was a sharp young man from a prominent family back in North Dakota. He had biceps the size of footballs and a scalp shaved so close it gleamed.

"Yeah, I get it," Bart mumbled.

"You are to report once a week, and each time, you will be required to drop a specimen. When you report, you will be told what day the following week will be report day. You will never know ahead of time."

Bart watched Edelstein as he stared out the only available window, hiking up his khakis that drooped in the can.

"Hey, counselor--know what you'd have if a hundred lawyers was sacked up and thrown in Lake Michigan?"

Edelstein turned around, rolling his eyes. He rubbed his jaw and slicked his hair back with both hands.

"A good start," said Bart. "Ha! Ha!"

Edelstein frowned and cleared his throat. "This policy, as you know, will remain in effect until Mr. Wilhelm feels you can be trusted, which, I might add, with your track record, will be a long, long time in coming."

Clyde was outside, waiting in his pickup, parked by the curb. He honked and waved at Bart as he came out through the thick side door.

Bart sidled over to the truck. "Who the hell are you?"

"Name's Clyde. Get in, jailbird."

"Why should I do that, asshole?"

"Look--I'm here to pick your ass up. A friend of yours paid the freight to spring you. I'm just helping out-- get in."

"Alright--nobody's complaining." He scooted around and pulled the door on the passenger side but it was locked. "What the fuck . . ."

"Oh, sorry," said Clyde. He reached over and shoved the handle down, unlocking the door, then, took his sun-glasses off and cleaned them on his sweatshirt. After checking his mirrors, he pulled out. Silence dominated inside the cab for a moment or so, until Clyde spoke.

"So--what did you do to end up in the crowbar hotel there-- don't mind my askin'?"

"Drunk," said Bart.

"What? They got you for being drunk? That ain't right."

"It is if you're behind the wheel going eighty miles an hour in a fifty-five."

Clyde laughed. "Yeah--the law frowns on that shit."

"Sonofabitch, what a night. How the hell didn't I seen it coming?" said Bart.

"Were you smokin' pot, too?"

"Nah, just the booze, is all I had that night." He scratched at his crotch as he stared out his side window. "I thought I'd die in that fuckin' place; it's been a long time since I was locked up. Who was it paid me out, anyway?"

"I can't say--not allowed."

"Why not?"

Clyde shrugged. "Just can't. Don't sweat it, okay?"

Bart waited a beat then said, "I called my Ma--see if she'd bail me out. You think she gave a shit? Hell no. My own mother left me in that fuckin' place to rot."

Bart's mother was sixty-two, the mother of three, grandmother of at least four, a lonely old woman in failing health who couldn't remember her last bit of good luck. Though she'd considered herself single for almost thirty years, she was not, at least to her knowledge, officially divorced from the miserable creature who'd practically raped her when she was seventeen, married her when she was eighteen, fathered her three boys, Bart being the youngest, then mercifully disappeared from the face of the earth.

"Ha! You want support," Clyde said, "buy a bra." He took a long breath and slipped a cigarette from his pocket and lit up. "What do you care? You're out now aintcha? Didn't cost you a dime neither." He grinned as he blew a huge puff of smoke in Bart's face. "And I made me some decent cash for just picking your ass up."

Bart stared at him. "How about taking the mashed potatoes out of your mouth, buddy. What's the big deal?" Tapping a cigarette out of a crumpled pack, he lit up, then cracked the window.

"Ain't no big deal to it, my man. I'm just saying, be glad you're out and don't sweat the small shit. Where you want me to drop you off by the way--I got other shit to do."

"Ah, I can't afford to get my car out of impound yet, so might as well take me to my place over on Waveland. I'd take Outer Drive, it was me. I've got some shit to check out there before I do anything else. Two days from now I have to report in with my new fuckin' probation officer. You believe that shit?"

"You've got to stay clean for a while, right--or else I'd offer you a hit on a doobie I got stashed in my boot."

"Shit! You just see if this probation shit stops me from partying, my friend. I'll hit it."

"Ha, you've got balls the size of melons--I'll give you that, but I heard you had some Xanax in the car when they busted you--that right?"

Bart studied the side of Clyde's face for a moment. "Yeah, that's right. Why?" He spit something out the window.

"Nothing, really, man. My girlfriend was all bent out of shape, is all, because they were her pills and she couldn't figure how you got a hold of them."

"I'm not sayin'," said Bart. "Hell, I don't even know you, man. Turn right at this light. They couldn't a been your girlfriend's, either."

"Hey, it's okay, dude . . .no big deal--everybody carries a big sack of bullshit. Let's forget about it, okay?"

For a while the moaning of the truck's engine is all that could be heard as the two went silent.

"Hey, did you hear about the sex shows they got over on South State now?" Clyde asked. "I seen a live sex show on the stage there in front of everybody-- this cute redhead and another one--a blonde, and some huge black guy with a big wanger. Hell, they just locked the door and hung a sign out, Closed until the show was over. It was so cool, dude." He paused, then so wanting to impress Bart, went into his good ol' boy rap:

"Yeah, I left there I was so fuckin' horny, I got me a little slope head 'bout as tall as a pint of piss, and I just picked her up by the ears and stuck her on my dick, then slapped her upside the head and spun her 'round my cock like the block on a shithouse door. It was like fucking a bundle of kindling, but it was better than nothing, ya' know?"

"Yeah? Turn at the next street, get over to Waveland," said Bart. He picked at a scab on his chin.

Clyde continued. "I figure there's five groups for a woman's looks--depends on how much light you want on in the bedroom. There's the three-way-bulb women--100-watt, 70-watt and 30-watt. After that you've got your night-light-only women, and finally all-lights-out."

"How did you hear about them pills, anyhow?" said Bart.

"My girlfriend told me, no big deal--you best forget about it."

Bart glared at him. His heart pounded. He was concentrating on his cigarette, bringing the ash to a point. "Yeah--sure. Turn on this next street--third building on the left."

During the day, Bart's building looked like a piece of shit, a purple-painted concrete-block two-story job with a cracked-blacktop parking lot that usually had a couple of used rubbers cooking on the tarmac. At night, it looked only slightly better.

It was a small apartment. One small bedroom, one small bath, it was an efficiency with a kitchenette on one side, a living room on the other. The Formica was scarred with burn marks from cigarettes and crack cookers. Used syringes, half-eaten bagels, filthy dish towels, and indefinable garbage clogged the sink.

There was a card table and two folding chairs, an ashtray

overflowing with cigarettes. No couch. No television. Bed unmade. Sheets looked like they had been on there since Christmas. Socks and underwear on the floor. The top bureau drawer was open. Just filth and clutter. The place smelled like pizza, tobacco, marijuana, bananas, and wallpaper mold. A single window looked over a porch roof to the street.

A sheet had been tacked haphazardly over the window. Probably to afford Bart privacy while he crushed cans of Old Style beer against his forehead and plotted mayhem.

Clyde took a chair, lit up, blew a lungful of smoke, and said, "I don't suppose you got a beer in that fridge?"

"Hell no! I ain't been here in over a month, and I ain't got no money, I told you." He watched Clyde kick back and stick out his blue-jean legs, the heels of his boots resting in the shag carpeting.

Clyde sighed and finished his cigarette, then tossed it at the sink. "Okay, well, I guess I'll shove off." He unfolded himself from the chair and headed to the door.

"No need to be pissed and leave so soon," said Bart. "I thought we were gonna hit that joint."

"Ah, right now's not a good time. I got places to go, shit to do, but, hey--we'll have to get together sometime-- drink some mash and talk some trash."

"Yeah, sure. I knew you were full of shit, but thanks for picking me up, man."

When Clyde got outside, he lit a cigarette, then sat in the cab of his truck and dialed a number on his cell phone.

"Hey, it's me" He paused. "Yeah--just letting you know I picked up your package."

He listened to Lisecki on the other end and said, "Nope-- dropped him off at his place. I'll be at your house after dark tonight to collect my money. Make sure you're there."

He paused again and answered, "Nah, that shitheel ain't goin' far. He's broke. See ya' later."

CHAPTER TWENTY

Lewis was feeling grumpy enough to bite the head off a kitten. Spending that hour with detective Hawkins made his molars ache; at times, during the interview, he had felt like wiping the smile off the man's smug face with his fists.

That fuckin' Bart caused all this. Ignorant bastard. Motherfucker. I should have my Harvard ass kicked for involving that moron.

Night always laid the foundation for overreaction and death. Lewis was motivated by forces deeper than greed. He wanted to relax in his den and dream of a lovely dancer, with long blonde hair, small round breasts and a smile that could stop an mortician's heart. Instead, he couldn't remember the last time he was so upset.

Sitting still for a time, he worked on regulating his respiration, the exercise nearly as familiar to him as breathing. His head was pounding. Pain was like a knife in his neck, and he felt sick to his stomach. Anger and resentment crushed his brain.

He found himself eyeing the telephone. His buffed nails tapped restlessly on the desk. His hand shot across to the Rolodex; his fingers tripped lightly through familiar index cards. It was an astounding trove of sources. Names and numbers, numbers and names. And so many owed Lisecki a favor. It was like a drug, this power he had. But he realized that none of his contacts could help him with this situation.

Sitting back in his chair, he swiveled around and stared, as if lost in a dream. He dreaded the call he would make now, but it had to be done. With hesitation, he grabbed the phone, dialed, then anxiously waited.

"Yeah?" said the voice on the other end.

"It's me--checking in," said Lewis. His lower lip trembled. "Seems like I've got a conundrum."

"Really? I think it's a clusterfuck. I figured you'd be calling, and a damn good thing you did. Could things get any more fucked up than they are? I understand Cleve Hawkins paid you a visit today-- that right?"

The man had a baritone voice-- slow-paced, with growling overtones that accompanied each and every word.

Lewis tilted his head and hooked the phone in the crook of his neck while he fiddled with a fresh cigar. He cupped his hand over his mouth and lowered his voice, as if to share a sordid secret with just the two of them.

"Yes, that's true, and I must admit I was strapped with fear. Maybe fear is too strong a word. After all that has happened recently, maybe fear should be reserved for life-threatening situations. But then again, maybe fear is appropriate."

"Yeah, well, in fiction, private detectives are pretty cool dudes. In reality they are, at best, retired--emphasis on the "tired"-- cops and, at worst, guys who couldn't become cops and thus are that dangerous creation known as the "cop wannabe." Hawkins is an ex-cop. Now he's a private eye. Since he left the force he swims in a bottle, and I doubt he could catch the clap in a whorehouse . . . however, he's no dummy, so watch your ass."

"Well, my impression after a while was that he's full of shit, and yet there was something about him that was alarming. Who is he really? Anyone to concern myself with?"

"Depends." The man paused. "What did you tell him?"

"I just answered his questions very carefully. Listen, I sincerely apologize for the latest developments, my friend. I think Bart Hodgkins pissed his brains out his peter on beer and hookers long ago. This Hawkins was wondering how I was connected to that bottle of Xanax they found in the clown's automobile."

"And you told him what?"

"Nothing, really. I said I used to date the girl the pills belonged to, but I had no idea how the bottle ended up in a stranger's car. What could I say? For that matter, what could he say, you know?"

"Drugs, alcohol and bad news don't mix real well," the man growled. "I'm feeling real uneasy about this guy Hodgkins--in fact much more than uneasy. The man is a fuckwit and a reprobate. He's a useless piece of shit who couldn't manage his way out of a wet grocery sack. Then you have this other hick go down there, bail him out, and run his ass home. Are you insane?"

"I know, I know, but I had no choice. I couldn't very well pick up Bartholomew myself. I couldn't leave him down there--he might start blabbing under the stress of interrogation."

"And you . . . you're a perfect asshole for associating yourself with them, Judge. You ought to have better control over your dick, then none of this shit would be happening. Listen, you are getting dangerously close to fucking up our little arrangement, you realize that, right? Remember, you are the one who will go down--not me. I'm Mister Clean if the shit hits the fan, no matter what happens, you're on your own. Do you understand that?"

"Yes, Sir. Again, I apologize. Things just got out of hand."

"Well, I can't tolerate this shit, and I won't. Now that redneck, Hodgkins is number one on the Chicago police's hit parade. He's in their crosshairs. Are you aware that this bullshit could bring them right to your expensive front door? They will put your ass in prison. Understand? Prison. Look up Statesville in the dictionary and you'll find a picture of your ass, Judge."

Lewis's jaw knotted as if he wanted to say more but was chewing the words to keep them inside. He wet his lips, the obvious awkwardness giving him the air of a little boy who had been doing something naughty and embarrassing.

"Yes, I know." There was a long pause before he attempted to speak. "I have been thinking and....."

"Shut up! What else did Hawkins ask you?"

Sweat leaked from Lewis's hair and ran down his neck. It felt like crawling ants. "Ah--he asked me if I knew Bart Hodgkins."

"What?" The silence on the other end of the phone was deafening.

"Yes. I'm afraid so. He asked me if I knew Bart and I told him no."

"And? Well, go on--what else, you educated pervert?"

"Nothing, really. He just wanted to know if I was married?"

"Married? Hmmmm. Why do you suppose he wanted that information?"

"Don't ask me. I have no idea," Lewis whined. "That was it though. He said he might be seeing me again, was all."

"Yeah . . . that's all." There was another long pause before the man spoke again: "Don't give yourself too much credit, Lisecki, there's Hawkins' way and then there's Hawkins' way. He is one tenacious motherfucker. He's also a piece of barroom furniture. But, do you see a trend here?"

"Yes sir, I know, but listen . . ."

"Shut the fuck up! You've read enough books to sound like somebody you're not, but you've got pussy on the brain. Hawkins knows how to detect, and you can bet your rich, fat ass that he's gonna take down this fucking Hodgkins. Cops can see idiots like this guy as plain as a zit on your nose."

"I know, and I warned Bart again and again about . . ."

"I said shut up, goddammit! I got the word this afternoon, as a matter of fact, that Hawkins and another cop were searching one of the victim's cars for possible DNA."

Lewis didn't reply. He listened to the labored breathing on the other end of the phone and waited.

"Remember what I told you when we made our arrangement?"

"Umm--you mentioned a lot of things, I'm not sure I . . ."

"I said, for instance, most members of the mob are stupid, and at best capable of holding only menial jobs. They typically use dog pack intimidation to get what they want, whether it involves preferential seating in a restaurant or taking or getting rid of the unwanted. Their sexual habits are childish and deviousl, their behavior is a joke. So, if they can't do better, what in the hell makes you think you can stay ahead of the law? What makes you so damned special? You're not a fucking judge anymore either-- remember that."

"I am so sorry, Sir--you must believe me."

"No! I must not believe anything you tell me." There was another pause. "You're going to make the problem disappear on this one, Judge--all by yourself, too."

"Yes, Sir."

"Are you hearing me. This is on you. You take care of Hodgkins. Now, I received further information late this afternoon, that Hawkins and another cop found three different brands of cigarette butts in the ashtray of one girl's car. A Firebird. Do you imagine the DNA on any of them might just match your friend's? You see, the boys are swarming all over this. Cleve Hawkins is a ringleader, too, even though he's not even a fuckin' cop anymore. And, people like Hodgkins draw trouble like flies to puke."

"Oh, yes. Please don't think I am taking this lightly, Sir." Lewis's demeanor became slightly gruff. "I assure you I have plans for Bartholomew Hodgkins. He simply is not aware of it yet. I have someone in mind to handle . . ."

"What? You are not listening, Judge. That's not what I'm saying. Is there static on the line or something? You will handle this one yourself. You are not getting anybody else mixed up in this puddle of shit. You understand me?"

"Yes, Sir. It just doesn't seem fair somehow, you know?"

"Tough shit! Whoever said life was fair? You don't have to be a long ball hitter every time, Judge. A well-placed bunt has its merits, you know, but you'll be wanting home run on this one."

"Believe me, I understand, Sir."

"Do you?"

"Yes. Without question--yes. However, I have never killed a man before. It is almost as if . . ."

"Well, here is an idea for you--sort of a fail safe, if you will. You have a lot of trees on that big spread of yours, don't you?"

"Yes, of course, but I don't see . . ."

"No--you wouldn't see. Close your mouth, and open your ears. You're gonna clamp down on Hodgkins like a ferret on a cobra. I suggest you immediately invest in a wood chipper. You will need to get rid of some of those dead branches laying around, won't you?"

There was a long pause before Lewis said, "Oh?"

The skin on his back prickled. "I can get one of those, of course--I've seen them advertised by Sears."

"No shit, yeah, you got it. Get yourself a heavy duty model, as well as plenty of large, extra strength garbage bags. Am I making myself clear here?"

"Very clear, Sir." Lewis sat back in his chair, swiveled around, and stared. He felt like he was going to puke as he broke his brand new cigar in two.

"Good. You will do this immediately, right?"

"Yes, of course." Lewis's voice trailed off.

"What? I couldn't hear that."

"I said, yes, Sir. Immediately. Tomorrow I will purchase one."

"Excellent. And be sure you do that cleanup as soon as you get it. By the way, on another front . . . the last I checked, your monthly premium still hadn't arrived in the Cayman account. Is there a problem?"

"Oh, no, sir. Sorry--I've just been busy. Absolutely no problem though. It will be available within the next forty-eight hours, I assure you."

"Good. Have a pleasant evening, Judge. I'll check back with you in a few days. You damn sure better have some good news for me. Sleep well." The line went dead.

When he hung up, Lewis's hands were tingling with fatigue and his mouth was dry, His hair was damp with sweat, as though his old courtship with Malaria was being revisited. Fear riddled his entire body.

He paced around in circles for an inordinate amount of time, and began planning. After a while, he drifted upstairs to his bedroom. A walk-in closet contained a secret wall safe. He shoved some suits aside and cleared the way. At first his sweaty fingers wouldn't work in coordination with his memory of the coded numbers, but then after he rubbed his fingertips on his shirt, he tapped in the coded combination and opened the safe.

He reached in and pulled out a Smith & Wesson, .38 caliber Military and Police model pistol. It was located in the back of the safe, underneath a King James Bible.

Picking up the gun, he turned his wrist back and forth to admire it. It was a beauty--never been fired except that one time, on the range, so very long ago. He felt its weight in his hand. The unfamiliar coldness of it. Then it was as if the heft of the gun usurped his anger in some magical way. Lewis felt strong-- powerful, almost invincible. All of this was underscored by a low hum of tension, and the dark, sinister sensation of falling into a deep black valley passed over him.

He seemed to spend a moment contemplating the inside of his eyeballs as he thought about killing another human being. He shivered. Like the hunter, he thought-- one must feel the adrenaline surge of pleasure at having robbed the province of God.

Yes, this gun would do the job, he thought. As he pointed it at the mirror across the room, he wondered when Bart would call. Surely, he won't wait long. *He'll need money, won't he? I must get him out here right away. I have to finish this.*

CHAPTER TWENTY-ONE

I felt I should be setting an ambush for Professor Lewis Lisecki--flashing my badge, barking out the Miranda, scaring the piss out of the bastard. Granted, I wasn't sure how, but suspected that Lisecki and Hodgkins knew each other. I had a gut feeling that Bart would fall apart and start blubbering if we could put him in Chelsea's car somehow. I looked forward to the moment.

The sun was a thin scarlet smudge on the horizon when I got back to town.

Earlier that day, after I'd left Lisecki's office, Officer Snyder, and the CSI crew met out at the Rohrman's place and performed a thorough search of victim, Chelsea Rohrman's Firebird. She had been seen driving it around at the time of her disappearance and we thought perhaps her killer had been in the vehicle with her.

We found three different brands of cigarettes in the overflowing ashtray and six empty Big Gulp containers from Seven-Eleven. Crumpled Misty Menthol cigarette packs were scattered on the floor, front and back, along with Burger King and Dunkin' Donut bags.

Evidence is the physical history of an event, but the absence of a physical history is its own kind of evidence. Bottom line, we bagged up what we had and hoped the lab would find fingerprints and DNA from the killer, whom we suspected was Bart Hodgkins.

The fingerprints would be analyzed almost immediately, but it would take a while to get the DNA results back from the Diagnostic Center located in Oak Park.

It had been a long time since a case stomped on my brain the way the Chelsea Rohrman killing had. For the first time in months, I felt invigorated. I was in the hunt again. I let everything about the case pass through my mind that day, and made a mental list of people I had to see and things I had to do. I would let a couple of other smaller cases wait. I wanted to nail Bart Hodgkins to the wall, but so far we had little to go on.

I got a call from Phil Andrews while we were finishing up with the car. Bart Hodgkins had been bailed out. I worried about that possibility, and now he was in the wind as far as I was concerned. I couldn't touch him anyway--not yet. I suggested Andrews put a tail on the guy, but he wasn't sure he could.

There was no doubt, Bart was a player and so full of shit. I realized he had been born with a vivid imagination, a quick tongue, and an innate inability to tell the truth. The man could lie. And as for Professor Liseccki--he was an educated fool, but he wore his breeding like a rented suit. I believe he was capable of anything, so I'd try and set things in motion. Make the shit fly and see where it stuck.

When I got home around seven, I lay down on the bed, crossed my ankles, put my hands behind my head, and thought about taking a nap. Later, when I woke up, I fumbled around and found my watch on the nightstand. It was damn near eight-thirty. I couldn't go back to sleep and I was hungry.

I lay there for a few more minutes and stared at the ceiling. I thought about a shot glass with two fingers of Johnny Walker. Drinking was a time thing, thank God. When it was five minutes to five, and I was off the wagon, when the clock inched towards five, my thoughts came in frosted mugs. Either that, or tumblers of ice and bottles that were smoke-colored, dark green or reddish-black and glowing with an amber warmth. I had missed the time frame and it was just as well.

It wasn't too late, and I thought about calling Maureen. Maybe she could use some company; I knew I sure as hell could. I figured I'd stop by after a while.

I headed out at nine, and drove through a light, cold drizzle. The rain was steady and the windshield wipers beat their rhythmic half-circle swipes; it was mesmerizing listening to them whacking back and forth. Pulling into a seven-eleven, I Grabbed my Cubs cap, went inside, and bought a large black coffee. None of their junk food looked good. I knew the coffee wasn't fresh either, but I didn't care. It was so strong; I could almost feel my pulse rise with each swallow.

A mile or so later, I was still mulling over the case when I decided to pull into a Subway. Two young sandwich makers, both sandy-haired, were visible through the front window. Nobody else was in the shop. Inside smelled of pickles and relish; the clean watery odor of lettuce mingled with the yeast smell of bread. A few minutes had passed and the rain slackened, but eating an Italian sub with one hand is sloppy business. I managed to drop some tomato juice and oil on the front of my shirt. *Great--smooth move, Ex-lax.*

I wondered if it was too late to drop in on Mo, even with my soiled shirt. Then, a chain reaction got me to thinking about what we used to have together and how wonderful our last get-together had been. It really was a special deal. Recalling the first time I met her, I caught myself smiling. I hadn't made detective yet, was still in uniform, with my partner, Kris Branoff.

She was so pretty, in a reserved sort of way, and when our eyes met, they went "clink," like eyes sometimes do. At Five-seven, around a hundred and thirty pounds, only twenty-eight, but looking ten years younger than her age, Mo had classic good looks, with piercing eyes, the color of blue dye number 2, like they use in ice pops,

The sex had been unbelievable. It still was, but maybe I should show her there is really more to it than hopping in bed--maybe take our relationship more seriously. I liked her a lot--in fact I was pretty sure I loved her and felt she really did love me. She was a tough, wised-up, honest woman, with a big loving heart. What more could a jerk like me ask for?

Her folks were fine people. They lived in Sylvania, Ohio. Her stepfather was a retired postal clerk from Toledo, and they spent most of their time square dancing and traveling in a Winnebago. Her mother was a talker, though. If I asked her what time it was, she'd end up telling me how the clock was made.

I thought again about calling, but then decided it would be best if I just showed up. If she was home, she was home--if not, oh well. I figured it would be harder for her to say no if I was on her doorstep.

I had a hell of a time finding a place to park, but eventually made it to her door. She must have seen me through the peephole, because she opened the door in her robe and smiled while she waited for me to speak.

"Hope you don't mind me stopping by, I've been tied up all day. I probably should have called first, huh?"

"No, you're fine. I just got out of the shower. Come." She let me in, and I figured I was damned lucky. We held each other and kissed beforeI took off my wet cap and jacket. I went over and sat down while she sidled out to the kitchen and brought back two drinks--a Scotch and Soda for me and her glass of white wine.

"Will you be okay with this?" she asked, handing me the drink.

"Yeah, I think that problem is behind me now."

She kissed me lightly on the lips as she sat next to me on the couch, curling her legs beneath her. Her hair was wet and the drops of water glistened like diamonds in the indirect light from a corner floor lamp.

She smiled as she slid a cigarette between her lips. That gesture alone turned me on, although I didn't like her smoking.

"Let's see--where have I heard that 'shoulda' called' story before Detective Humbug?" She paused and stared at me for a moment before her smile turned to a frown. "I'm . . . I'm tired of

167

being treated like an adverb in your life, Cleve."

"Aww, come on, Mo, I said I'm sorry for not calling. You know me, and it must still be obvious, I care about you a lot." This time I was the one whose words hung up in my throat like a tangle of fishhooks.

"Oh, really? That's funny; it's not obvious to me."

The unlit cigarette bobbed up and down in her mouth as she talked. She shook her head as she fired up the thing while still scowling. She inhaled deeply and exhaled through her nose, without removing the cigarette. I never liked her smoking, but I wasn't about to bitch. I wanted to change the subject though, pronto.

"Ahhh. I don't know, Mo-- lately, my brain's been doing too many push-ups. It's incredible, if you think about it, how much trouble is caused by people putting Tab A into Slot B. You know the way it is-- anything could be out there, in the thick woods, waiting for you. And yet, where is anybody really safe these days?" I paused and sipped my drink. "Anyway, we searched the Rohrman girl's car today. I'm hoping our suspect's DNA will be on some stuff we bagged up."

"Huh? I didn't even know you guys had anybody figured for the killings."

"Well, we're pretty sure on this guy. He was fingered out of the mug shots, but the guy who identified him is in a coma and can't do a lineup. In the meantime, our boy got himself bailed out." I paused again. "Then there's another guy that might be involved somehow--a college professor, believe it or not."

"A professor? Seems like he might be an intelligent, wealthy sort. Is he?"

"Believe me, this guy is the capitalist's wet dream--but, also the kind of man made me want to wash my hand after shaking his. It's pretty involved. I went out to see the good professor-- put a hot-plate under his balls. We're being very cautious, but I just feel there's something there. We'll see. I have a clandestine reputation to uphold, after all."

We were silent for a moment. "This case is like trying to get cobwebs out of your hair, isn't it?" she said, as she blew a geyser of smoke.

"Yeah--it really is." I felt awkward and paused before I spoke again. "I just have to keep poking around until I find out something useful. I just hope I'm smart enough to recognize a clue when I step on one." I sat back, and tried to act relaxed. "So, how have you been?"

"Fine . . . Really, okay," she said, nervously twirling a strand of her hair.

"How's work treating you? I honestly haven't had a chance to stop in and see anybody. Everything's been by phone."

She shrugged. "I understand."

"How's Kris treating you--he's a good boss, eh?"

"He's fine. A little different though since this serial killing epidemic has hit--busy is all. The press drives him nuts with their nagging questions."

"Yeah, he's got his hands full at home too. How is Jeannie doing by the way?"

"His wife? Well, you know that situation. Her MS is tearing them both up, but Kris is doing real good, considering. Good thing there's no kids for her to take care of anyway. Poor thing, I feel so sorry for her--she's too young for that. She's not doing that well and it's costing them a fortune."

"How about Andrews? You gettin' along with him okay? He looked sort of stiff to me when I met him--know what I mean? A straight-by-the-book cop. Is he as tough as he looks?"

"Not really." She grinned. "Andrews is a good man, I think. Kris is the one who gets moody lately, but of course the shit all ends up on his desk--you know that, right?"

"Right, of course."

"We've got Connie with us now. Remember her? She used to work the desk for Vic Myers in Vice."

"Oh, yeah. She's working with you guys now, eh?"

"Just barely. Connie Withers was born with a hairbrush up her ass. She thinks she should be in charge."

"Well, that's a poke in the eye. Is there a line to kiss her ring?"

We both laughed and Mo gazed at me for a long moment. She looked at my eyes and raised her mouth, and I slipped my arms around her shoulders and kissed her. It was a long, deep kiss the kind you never want to end.

She slowly got up and dropped her robe, then walked naked over to the bar and retrieved an ashtray as I stood up. She had such a beautiful body; it seemed sculpted, glowing with the light from the lamp. I felt myself getting hard.

She strolled back and drank half her drink, still standing naked in front of me. Taking a deep lungful of smoke, she let it escape and ground the cigarette out in the ashtray. She set it aside as she stepped close against me so that her stomach touched lightly against my loins, and moved her palms over my back.

She opened and closed her mouth while she held me and kissed me, and then she put her tongue in my mouth and I felt her body flatten against me. Her mouth never left mine, nor did the fierceness abate as I carried her to the bed. I pulled the drapes closed and undressed without speaking, as if words would spoil it.

Kneeling, I ran my hands over her ass and her thighs, then leaned up and gently bit her shoulder as she wrapped one calf inside my leg and rubbed her hair on the side of my face. I kissed her breasts and took her nipples in my mouth and traced my fingers down the flatness of her stomach. I felt her reach down and take me in the palm of her hand. She stretched her legs out along my body and ran her hands along the small of my back, down my thighs. My body was rigid and hot.

When I entered her, she moaned and hooked her legs in mine as she laced the fingers of one hand in my hair and kissed me as her other hand pulled hard on the small of my back. I felt her hot breath on the side of my face, then her tongue on my neck, the wetness of her mouth near my ear. We moved slowly, with the rhythm and tempo of an exotic tango.

She stopped her gyrating hips and held me tight, while she planted small kisses on my face. I wanted to move, but she wouldn't allow it.

"Let's not hurry," she said quietly, almost in a whisper. "You're mine now, nothing to worry about." I heard myself groan.

She said, "here," and tapped on my arm signaling me to climb off. Brushing her hair out of her eyes, she straddled my loins and kissed me on the mouth, before she rose up on her knees and put me inside again.

Her eyes closed and opened, she tightened her thighs against me, and propped herself up on her hands and looked lovingly into my eyes. She groaned and her breathing became loud and raspy. In complete control, she came before I did. Her face grew intense and small, her mouth opening like a flower and she moaned again and again. "Oh, my God! Oh! Ooooh!"

"Mo," I said hoarsely, as I felt my own release building faster and faster. spray inside of her wetness.

"It's okay, Cleve. Go ahead," she whispered. Pressing both palms on my chest, she urged me on, pulling me deeper inside with each stroke.

I felt the explosion coming--the rise and swell in my loins--the explosion-- and then, the gradual ebbing, like waves back to the sea.

"I've got you," she whispered, while I felt her pulsing around my hardness.

We kissed as the passion ebbed from our bodies. I felt tears well up as I looked in her eyes and said, "I love you, Mo."

"Oh, I love you, too, Cleve. I love you so much." She snaked her arms around my neck and we kissed again.

She lay in my arms under the sheet, her fingers tangled in the hair on the back of my head. I lay my head down on her pillow where I smelled the sweet scent of her perfume, sex and sweat.

In the early hours of the morning, I drifted off to sleep, growing ever more confident of our relationship. I felt her body curled up against mine and listened to the shallow rhythm of her breathing. I knew then, I could never take her for love for granted again.

CHAPTER TWENTY-TWO

Bart held a cell phone and steering wheel with one hand, while using his other to eat a turkey sandwich. He twitched, jerked, and rattled his mouth across half of the city with a glob of chicken salad stuck to the corner of his mouth. He was in a foul mood, frustrated and angry. Driving with the windows down, he finished the sandwich and swiped the sleeve of his shirt over his mouth.

Traffic on the Stevenson Expressway was a wretched crawl, winking brake lights as far as the eye could see. Heavy trucks, their engines hammering, roared past him, their air brakes hissing. The cars in front of him were inching along in maddening spurts. As therapy, Bart jammed both fists on the horn. In the station wagon ahead of him, a frizzy-haired young woman flipped him the finger.

"Yeah--and fuck you too, bitch," he yelled as he maneuvered around her and nearly careened off the rear-end of the new Corvette in front of her. He smiled crookedly when he yelled; the lower half of his face sagged like the mouth of a bottom feeder. He didn't realize he had pushed the talk button.

"What? No--I was yelling at some dizzy bitch, gave me an Italian hand signal that didn't mean left turn. Now, what was you sayin'?"

"Pay close attention, Bartholomew. I said, where did you get the phone you're using? Are you driving around with one of those insipid, state-of-the-artless cell phones in your hand?"

"Hey, Lew, don't sweat the petty shit, okay? It's the same cell I had when they locked me up. I got it back is all."

"I see." Lewis seemed to be thinking for a moment. Meanwhile, Bart got off at the exit ramp and kept driving on a four-lane highway.

"What? Did you say something?" Bart yelled, as he proceeded to pass as many cars as he could. "You're just going to turn to stone on me? Go ahead. What was you sayin'?"

"Nothing. I just wondered if the thought occurred to you that the police may have inspected that phone? They may have even inserted a bug of some sort before they returned it to you."

"Aw, shit! You worry too much. They don't do that. You been watchin' too many fuckin' James Bond flicks. And, even if they did-- so what?"

"So what? Your calls can be traced, that's what, Bartholomew. Why on earth wouldn't you go purchase a new one to be safe?"

"Yeah. Like I got a ton of money. Alright, if it'll make you feel any better, I'm getting rid of the phone right after I hang up. I'll smash the motherfucker so nobody can trace shit, unless they want to glue about a hundred pieces back together. Ha! Ha! Good luck with that."

"That would be an excellent idea," Lewis sighed. "And you'll do it somewhere out in the country, right? Not on the corner of State and Madison."

"Knock it off. I'm not stupid, you know. Give me some credit for once. He punched at the steering wheel and shouted. "Hey--I want a nice cold one waitin' when I get there, too. I just ate a shitty sandwich from Seven-Eleven, and after I bought gas, I didn't have enough to buy a brew. I'm as thirsty as a nag that just finished the derby, so I'll be wanting a lot more than one beer--follow?"

"Yes, of course, my friend. I understand, and I'll have a drink waiting for you. How much longer do you think you'll be?" He paused. "It's getting late, you know."

"Well, that's the way the toilet flushes sometimes, Professor. I'm doing the best I can. I just got out of city traffic a few minutes ago. It's a bear tonight. Where in the hell do all these fuckin' people go, anyway?"

"They have homes and families to go to, my friend."

"Yeah, well I wouldn't know about that shit. It's only about seven-thirty--not that fuckin' late. Jesus H Christ. Chill out, will ya?" He pulled a cigarette from the wrinkled pack in his shirt pocket and put it in his mouth, but didn't light it.

"You can't blame me for worrying, Bartholomew. And speaking of worrying, please assure me that you haven't brought anyone with you. None of your surprise gifts, I mean."

"Hell no, professor. I'm not that lame. Nope. I'm all by my lonesome tonight. Damn, I haven't had time to do anything else. I'll be needing some green when I get there too, by the way. That's why I called in the first place." He rolled his window up, and resting his arms on the steering wheel, lit the cigarette..

"Why are you so abusive with me, Bartholomew. You are downright nasty, do you realize that? You should be grateful for me bailing you out. My God-- what did you do for kicks as a child-- swallow thumb-tacks? And, what on earth did you do with the four-hundred dollars I gave you the last time. I remember paying you handsomely for the gift you brought me. Surely, being incarcerated, you didn't have a chance to spend it."

"Ha! What the fuck do you think I'm driving? The jack off cops wouldn't give me my wheels. They're still holding that car at the police impound yard. Besides with the goddamned towing and impound charges it would cost me more than that piece of shit was worth."

"So you purchased another vehicle?"

"Let's just say I got a good deal for a coupla' hundred bucks from a friend, okay? But I have rent and shit, too, you know. I have to eat, too."

"Sad story."

"How's that? What in the hell are you talkin' about now?"

"Pay me no mind, my friend. I'm going to hang up now," said Lewis.

"What?"

"I said, I'm hanging up. We'll talk when you get here. Goodbye."

Bart drove eight miles over the posted speed limit of fifty-five until eventually, his car's headlights washed over the pines alongside the highway. He rolled the window down and tossed the phone in a ditch, just a few miles from Lewis's house. With the cigarette dangling from the corner of his mouth, he mumbled, "There asshole-- that good enough?"

Lewis slammed the receiver back on the hook. He knew it was just a matter of time before Bart would be looking for money, and sure enough, he was on his way. *Miserable cretin.*

After he hung up, Lewis got lost in his worrisome thoughts. His memories were his cocoon. His nasty eyes were red, but not from booze or partying. He hadn't slept. Pacing slowly behind his desk, he puffed blue smoke from his eighth cigar of the day. His nerves were jangled. He realized that he deserved better than tolerating trash like Bart.

He snapped on his reading glasses and went to the bar. Bottles of rum, gin, bourbon and vodka were there. He held each bottle up to the light. They were all better than half-full. He needed plenty of choices for his guest. However, he made a point of leaving just one bottle of beer in the refrigerator, not caring if it pissed Bart off or not. He'd mixed a double Martini for himself, using his private stock of Nolet Reserve which he kept snuggled away in the bottom drawer of his desk.

He studied himself in the mirror mounted behind the bar. Today he had worn a light gray three-piece suit with a pale red plaid pattern, a white shirt, and a silk-finish wide red tie. His shoes were patent leather loafers. The clothes usually gave him an air of cockiness, but not today. He had removed his tie and rolled up the sleeves of his shirt. He had nobody to impress for the rest of the night.

Despite everything, Lewis caught himself smiling. He'd summoned the courage to shoot Bart. At least he thought he had.

But, let's face it. I'm a coward. I don't like confrontation--never have. It all came down to the right opportunity tonight. He shuddered at the thought of using the wood chipper to dispose of Bart's body. He regretted his hastiness in purchasing the STANLEY 15 HP, 420cc Chipper Shredder, he bought at Home Depot in a panic.

Still, some things just had to be handled. *Oh my God. What choice did the man give me when he called, anyway? Absolutely none.*

He knew better than to cross that man; who was capable of scaring hot piss out of an ice cube.

Lewis had thought long and hard on all of it, and now he had a real plan. The .38 was in his desk drawer, loaded and ready. He slowly slid the drawer open and stared at it for what seemed like the tenth time since he'd put it there. He had made up his mind. If Bart got violent, he would defend himself. *I will summon the courage to shoot the bastard. I swear I will. Everything hinges on that idiot's actions when he arrives. And the timing . . . Yes, oh yes . . . the timing.*

Bart parked his Activa in the driveway in front of the professor's three-car garage. He no longer had the key to the garage. Lewis had taken it back. It was dark as Bart scampered across the lawn, being careful to stay in the shadows. He disappeared in the thick yews and forsythia bushes that ran like sentries along the front of the house. He stood still as a statue until the front door opened.

"Come in, come in. Hurry up." Lewis yanked on his shirt-sleeve. Insects spiraled in from the night, hungry for the light.

"Why didn't you wait, I would have opened the garage for you? I'd rather you didn't park in the driveway, you know that."

"What was I supposed to do for chrissakes, blow the horn? You got no fuckin' neighbors anyhow. What's the big deal?"

"Never mind, I was watching for you. Go pull it inside," said Lewis. "I'll open the door." His hands were growing sweaty, and his pulse banged in his eardrums. Just the sight of Bart kicked his loathing into high gear.

After he parked the car, Bart strolled in through the side door with a swagger and headed for the bar. "You'd better have a beer back here?" He watched the tension play over Lewis's face.

"Uuuuh, yes. There should be a few bottles in there."

Bart leaned down to look in the refrigerator behind the bar. "Nope. Just this one, is all I see. Shit!" He bent over to look closer. "Nah, there ain't no more down here." When he straightened up he was red-faced from the bending." He snapped the top off the bottle of Heineken and took a long swallow. Foam slid down the inside of the neck when he removed the bottle from his mouth. "Man, that's some good shit. I was dying for one of these when I was sittin' in Cook County. You shoulda' got a twelve-pack. One brew isn't gonna do it tonight, Lew."

"Sorry. Yes, I can imagine a man would be craving a lot of things while he's incarcerated." Lewis was trying his best to be congenial. He wouldn't even mention that Bart's hair was growing back in, and he'd done nothing about his red eyebrows.

"However, no sense in getting drunk, you know. Remember the last time you left here with a load on, you got arrested. You don't want to do that again, Bartholomew. We don't want or need the attention. Consider yourself lucky for escaping your last infraction."

"I'm right there with you on that, Professor. Hell, no. I'm not going back there again. You don't know the half of it. Man, there were some real assholes in that city lockup. Mean motherfuckers. Some of 'em could make good football players. Thanks for bailin' me out by the way.."

He fiddled with an unlit cigarette, twiddling it like a pencil between his nicotine-stained fingers as he dropped into an overstuffed arm chair. He lit up and blew a cloud of smoke at the ceiling.

Lewis cringed. He shook his head once, as if there were a horsefly on it. "Must I tell you again about calling me Professor and Judge?"

"All right, all right." Bart waved a hand at him, as if to dismiss unwarranted whining. "Don't get your panties in a knot. I know you only bailed me to save your own ass." He took another long swallow of the beer and emptied the bottle. "I need another drink. Hey, ain't you glad to see me?"

"Yes, Of course, Bartholomew. I missed you. We did have our little arrangement you know, and it has been a very long time since we've had company."

Bart grinned. "We can still do that, we gotta wait though, like you said before." He belched. "So, have you spotted any decent puss since I've been away? I'm hornier than a two-peckered Billy Goat right about now."

"Well, I've not really paid attention, but you are about as subtle as a rock through a window," my friend. Lewis eyed him steadily, however he wanted to be careful to avoid confrontation tonight of all nights.

"Oh, bullshit."

Lewis feigned a smile. "Well perhaps I have seen a few prospects. I observed one young thing on campus who caught my eye. She had some excellent headlights. I personally wouldn't mind examining her high beams. But that's too close to home as they say."

"Yeah, well, as soon as things cool down--I'm going to get us some for sure.

"But we must be--for chrissake, discreet. I mean dis-goddamn-creet. Understand?"

"Yeah, don't sweat it," said Bart. "It'll be awhile anyway. The cops are hot for me right now." He got up and sauntered over to the bar. "Shit! What else have you got to drink back here?"

"Ah-- as you can see, there's plenty of liquor. Captain Morgan, Jim Beam, Beefeater's and some Absolut vodka. My Grey Goose of course. Plenty of mix back there on the lower shelf too. Help yourself. Just don't get carried away. Remember you have to drive back tonight."

"Yeah, but I plan to make up for lost time. I'll have me some Captain and Coke if you got any Coke back here--not just this fuckin' Pepsi."

"It's down there, right behind the Pepsi as a matter of fact. I believe there's a couple of bottles."

Lewis watched him pour a tall glass--half full of rum--the other half Coke. "This is the only way to drink this shit-- half Morgan, half Coke. Thanks, pro...fess...or. There--is that better? I didn't call you Judge--professor. Ha! Ha!"

Lewis frowned. "You know, your chattering reminds me of an old line I frequently tell my students--'never miss a good chance to shut up'."

"Well, I'll be damned. Talk about the cold shoulder, my shoulder's frozen all the way down. You're as dull as a dog turd, ya know that?"

A little over an hour and two stiff drinks later, Bart's alligator mouth began to overload his hummingbird ass.

Lewis had taken a seat behind his desk with his gun just inches away from his hand as Bart rambled on and on about everything from the feasibility of killing the mayor of Chicago to the possibility of Spiderman being a real person. He was all over the place, lost in the debris of his past and future.

"I think you've had enough to drink, Bartholomew" said Lewis as he stood.

Bart's glass wasn't empty, but he proceeded to head for the bar. "Don't fuckin' tell me what to do, old man. I'm not one of your snot-nosed kids from school."

Lewis quickly scooted around the desk and stood in front of him. "Whoa. I'm telling you for your own good. You have to drive. Enough is enough."

Bart lowered his voice and spoke very slowly, as if giving street directions to a tourist: "Get . . .the. . . fuck. . . out. . . of. . . my. . . way, Judge."

Lewis buzzed around him like an angry wasp. His hands trembled, stomach acid scalded the back of his throat, and his bowels felt loose. "You . . .you must leave now, Bartholomew."

Bart glared at him for a moment. "Ah, fuck it. It's no fun being here with your old ass anyway. I'm outa' here." He threw his drink at the mirror behind the bar and sprayed the entire area with liquor and shards of glass. He shoved Lewis out of the way and staggered to the side door that lead lead to the garage.

Lewis quickly opened the garage door and locked the side door behind him. He cringed as he heard the roar of Bart's engine, then the squealing of tires on the road as he sped away.

"Thank God! Goodnight, my friend, Lewis murmured as he settled back into his favorite leather-back chair and smiled. And goodbye, he thought. His chest swelled with pride. Everything had gone as planned.

Unlike other forms of murder, poisoning is fast and easy and doesn't require strength or a good aim, and if it's done properly, by the time Bart realized he'd been poisoned, it would be too late, he'd be dead. What could be better?

Lewis made sure every bottle of the liquor was contaminated, because he wasn't sure what Bart might drink at any given time, but he knew he would drink anything if the beer was gone. If it was alcohol, Bart would abuse it with pleasure.

Through his research, Lewis had eliminated strychnine, arsenic, hemlock and many others. He used Methyl alcohol, which is distilled from fermented wood and is extremely toxic. It's the same ingredient they use in perfume, antifreeze, paint removers, and varnish. When ingested, it metabolizes into formaldehyde in the body. Within twenty-four hours it damages all the vital organs.

Bart's brain would swell and he'd die from respiratory failure. By putting it in his drinks, he wouldn't 't feel any symptoms for twelve to twenty-four hours, and Lewis knew it was practically impossible to detect through toxology testing. Perfect. *He will not die anywhere near my home. I cannot be held responsible.*

There was no final act; to Lewis, it felt as if someone had unplugged the projector in the middle of a movie.

CHAPTER TWENTY-THREE

Sometimes in police work you get an undeserved break. The bad guys do something really dumb. Or they turn out to be more deranged than you thought they were. By the grace of God, law enforcement now has tools to help us no matter what the felons do.

DNA is a blessing. Three days had passed since Hodgkins made bail, and I was beyond anxious, waiting for the lab results, before our boy Bart thought about skipping town.

I held a bottle of Old Style and leaned back in the recliner with my eyes closed. It had been a confusing day at the end of a confusing week. Now I just wanted to let the Charlie Parker jazz sounds move through me and clear out my insides. I felt sure that what I was looking for I already had in my possession. It was a matter of getting rid of the unimportant things that cluttered the view.

Monday morning Maureen called me at my office to tell me the good news. It was not quite eight-thirty in the morning, but she wanted to call before her office was in full swing. The DNA results for the Camel cigarette butts found in Chelsea Rohrman's Pontiac

Firebird, as well as those found in Hodgkins' impounded Chrysler, were back from the lab.

Our conversation was unofficial, but Mo knew I was chomping at the bit to get the information, and I was grateful to say the least.

"So, they matched the sample your guys got from Hodgkins while he was in lockup?"

"Absolutely--ninety-eight percent result, but you didn't hear this from me. You know that--right?"

"Of course not. I'll wait to hear from Branoff." I couldn't help but laugh. At last we had the sonofabitch. "Thanks a lot, Mo. I owe you, big time."

She lowered her voice. "I'll take it out in trade . . . How's that, Columbo? Call me. Gotta go. Bye."

That morning, I awoke feeling good and the good news made my day. I went to the gym and worked out in the weight room. I hit the light bag and the heavy bag, then ran three miles round the indoor track, before I took a shower, changed clothes and went to the office. The temperature was supposed to reach eighty degrees that day, but it was misty and chilly--a typical late spring morning. I decided to wear my blue blazer with some tan slacks, no tie. My mood couldn't have been better.

As much as I hated it, I would have to wait to hear from Branoff. I was anxious to get rolling. Everybody, including the press, was screaming for action on the serial killings. I wanted to be right there when they slapped the cuffs on Bart. Just the thought of it made my heart beat so fast, I feared my blood vessels would explode.

I had sent Deckle out for donuts and had my third cup of coffee while I waited for the phone to ring. Mulling over the case, I knew that once we had Bart, the pieces would all come together. We would make a plea deal with him and he'd tell us everything. That asshole was the type that would give up his own mother if it benefited him. Was my hunch correct? Was that professor Lisecki involved? We'd see.

Branoff and his homicide division were under the gun. Any leads they had either fizzled out or had yet to be explored.

Forensics was still plugging away, but so far had come up empty. Relying on tips is almost always a waste of time, but they have to be checked out. A lot rested on getting the DNA thing verified so they could arrest our prime suspect, Bart Hodgkins. Everyone, it seemed, was scrambling for a chair before the music stopped.

I made up my mind, I would carry a piece when we went to arrest Bart. I'd take my Glock as well as my .25 strapped to my ankle holster.

I finished the cup of coffee, took apart the Glock, oiled it, reamed out the barrel with a bore brush, reassembled it, and stuck a full clip back up into the magazine. Then I opened a box of hollow-points and inserted them one at a time into a second clip. When they flatten out the rounds can blow holes the size of baseballs in an oak door and leave a wound in a human being that no doctor can heal.

Yes. Guns kill, and I always hoped I wouldn't have to use mine. But you never know. The arrest would, for the most part, be handled by the cops, but I was sure Branoff would allow me to come along, and it's better safe than sorry when dealing with scum like Hodgkins.

Deckle stumbled through the door with the bag of donuts and a small bottle of Mountain Dew mixed with something alcoholic. "Sorry it took so long," he said as he handed the sack of donuts to me.

"It's okay, Deck. I fished out a chocolate-covered one and handed him the bag. "You weren't gone that long. Keep the change and have one of these-- go ahead."

"I bought me this here bottle of Dew for later, hope you don't mind," he said. "Thanks for the change, too."

"That's okay. Go ahead, have a donut though."

"Nah, that's okay, I gotta be someplace," he said as he headed for the door.

"Yeah, I understand. You go ahead; I have to leave pretty soon myself. I'll see ya', Deck."

He suddenly stopped before he reached the door and turned around. Snapping his fingers, he said, "Oh, I forgot to tell ya', Cleve, some guy was hanging around out here the other day."

"Huh? What do you mean?"

He shrugged. "I don't know his name. He was sitting across the street--down a ways, like nobody was supposed to see him-- know what I mean? Sneaky like."

I was puzzled. "No, Deck. I don't know what you mean. Who was it? What kind of car?"

He waved me off. "Ah, I don't know who it was. Just some guy. He was in the car all by himself though. Oh, yeah--it was a brown car-- you know, one of them phony cop cars--unmarked, you know the kind I mean?"

"A Crown Vic. Go on, Deck. What else? What did the man look like?"

"I couldn't see his face; I just know it was a guy cuz he looked big and was smoking a cigar. I could see that through his windshield, but that's all. I gotta go, Cleve." He turned again to leave.

"Wait a minute, Deck." I moved closer and got a good whiff of his alcohol breath. "How long was this guy out there?"

"I don't know for sure, but it was for a long time, I was sittin' on your steps but, then I got up and headed towards the car to see if maybe I could help him out someway, ya' know? When he saw me coming, he took off. Just like that, he took off, Cleve."

"That's it, eh? I waited for more, but finally said, "Okay, Deck. Thanks a lot. Keep your eyes open though. Let me know if you see that guy again. Use somebody's phone and call me or tell a cop. You still have my number?"

He went for his coat pocket. "Yup. I always keep it right here. I got it. I'll watch for the guy, I promise I will. Yes sir, Cleve. I gotta go, now. Bye."

"Yup, Sure thing. See ya' Deck.."

I sat there wondering about what Deckle had just told me. It could have been an undercover cop, I supposed. But that didn't make sense. Why would they stake out my place? I was inclined to believe it may have been a figment of Deckle's fuzzy imagination. I'd worry about it later.

Andrews called shortly after Deckle left. He informed me that they had the DNA results and said Branoff told him to call and see if I wanted to ride along with them to pick up Hodgkins. I told him I was on the way.

At headquarters, four of us piled into an unmarked Chevy Trailblazer and headed for Hodgkin's last known address off of Waveland Avenue, on the north side of the city.

Lenny Fallon, the uniformed cop who drove, was slender and totally bald, with soft brown eyes hidden behind thick glasses, and a mouth that seemed too wide and too sensuous for his small pinched face and little button nose. He was maybe thirty-five with a thick blond mustache and his police cap was crushed like a bomber pilot on his fifty-third mission.

Detective Jim Snyder rode in the front with Fallon, while Phil Andrews and I sat in the back. Snyder had taken Kris Branoff's place for one reason or another.

Snyder was in his late fifties, over six-feet-tall, with a ruddy complexion. He had sandy hair that was thin on top, and when he talked his nose wrinkled and his upper lips rose to reveal four large upper teeth, all the same size. I could see his shoulder holster and snubbie .38 under his sport coat.

I noticed Andrews was like a cable stretched too tight and beginning to fray. He sat sullen-faced in a corner of the back seat. I had the feeling he didn't want this detail for some reason or another.

"So we got this sonofabitch for sure, eh Phil?" I said.

"Looks that way. We can definitely put him in both cars with the DNA. We've notified his lawyer, Edelstein. He says that prick is due to check in with him tomorrow, 9 am. I told him we'll have him in custody today if we can find him."

"He can't go far," said Snyder as he laughed. "His probation officer is clinging to his ass like Bounce in a dryer." He reached over and took a cigarette from Fallon's shirt pocket. "Sorry--I'm tryin' to quit," he said, and grinned. "So far I've quit buying them. Thanks. Got a light, Lenny?"

Fallon handed him a lighter. "Jesus, Jim, you haven't got

anything but the habit, do ya'?"

"So what's the plan when we get there, Phil?" I asked.

"Ah, I figure after we gain entry, you and me will go up to his apartment on the second floor. Then, Lenny and Jim can set up at both the front and back doors of the building in case this fucker makes a run for it. You got any better ideas, Hawk?"

"Hell no. That sounds good to me. I just want to nail this scumbag."

"Yeah, that's for sure. Just remember, Cleve, I have to make the arrest. That means I'll do the Miranda bit and cuff him--everything. You can't touch him, know what I mean?"

"Yeah, I get that."

"Good." Andrews turned in his seat and stared out the window. Traffic was heavy and steady, but a half hour or so later we pulled up and parked just down the street from Hodgkin's place. The sun had come out and burned off the haze. I was already sweating; my blazer would be too warm before long.

According to his probation officer, Hodgkins lived in this apartment building on a dead-end street where every front lawn, without exception, had an automobile on cement blocks. In front of the building was a rusted Ford Victoria with a holly tree sprouting from its dashboard. Beer cans, crushed plastic cups and fast-food containers were scattered across the entire area, and at least one dirty plastic diaper lay on the ground near the cracked sidewalk leading to the front door.

The doorbell. Dangled from two wires. Andrews knocked.

An elderly woman answered the door. Her white hair was in curlers, her cheeks slathered in oily yellow cream and her broad, pointy-shouldered frame was draped in a short terry-cloth robe. Her legs were bare and mottled, her feet appeared too big in scuffed-looking men's loafers. She held up her hand to shield her eyes from the morning sun.

Andrews flashed his badge. "Good morning, Ma'am. I'm Detective Andrews. This is investigator Hawkins. We need to see your tenant, Bartholomew Hodgkins."

"Police? Oh, my. What in the world has he done now?"

"I'm not free to say, Ma'am. If you would please just give us the key and direct us to his apartment, that will be fine."

"Oh, of course. She went back into her apartment and came back with the key. "I'll take you up there. He's on the second floor-- 201."

"No, Ma'am. We'd rather you didn't. Just give me the key and stay down here, please."

We left her standing bewildered at the door and cautiously mounted the squeaky stairs leading to the second floor. My heart was thudding loud inside my chest.

There was no peephole, and I stood on one side of the door, Andrews on the other. He planted his feet firmly and stood sideways to the door, then, raising his left arm, he bent the elbow to less than thirty degrees and hit the door with the fleshy side of his fist. No answer. He knocked a second time, harder this time. Nothing.

"Bart Hodgkins--this is the police. Open up."

There was still no answer. *Did Hodgkins skip already?* The landlady was trying to sneak a peek from halfway down the stairs. I waved at her, signaling to go back downstairs.

Andrews tried again. "Hodgkins. Open up, now!" We waited, then I put my ear to the door and shook my head.

"Enough of this shit, Probable Cause," said Andrews, and he used the key.

The light was dim and the smell was stifling; something was rotting.

I held a handkerchief over my nose and mouth as we began to search the filthy lair. I followed Andrews as we proceeded with guns drawn. He pointed for me to go one way while he went the other. We separated and began to sweep the apartment. The linoleum floor creaked under our weight. A poorly cut rug of orange shag, like something the Brady Bunch would have considered too garish, covered the far quarter of the room.

The place smelled like Goodwill furniture, laced with pizza and immersed in a Burger King deep fryer. Cigarettes and body odor. No, it was actually worse than that. The place smelled foul. Even with my nose covered, I quickly realized the predominant odor was that of a dead body.

Andrews called out. "Hawk--in here!" He had a handkerchief over his nose and mouth when I entered the bedroom. The smell was stronger now and I gagged. Where's the Old Spice when you need it, I thought.

"There's our boy," Andrews grunted as he pointed. "What the fuck? Look at this shit. His fuckin' head is swollen up the size of a basketball. Looks like it tried to explode, don't it?"

It was Bart Hodgkin's alright. His body was sprawled on the floor next to the bed. His head laying in a puddle of puke and blood. His mouth was locked open in the shape of a big "O." His skin looked like alabaster, hard and red along the bones.

Strings of vomit smeared his mouth and chest, and it was obvious that his bowels and bladder had let loose. He was naked except for the faded jeans that hung just below the knees as if he had been trying to get them on and failed. His milky-looking eyes stared vacantly at the ceiling.

I kept my handkerchief in place and squatted next to the body.

"I'm not a pro at this, but I sure as hell don't see any bullet holes, Phil. What the hell?"

"Rigor has already set in though," said Andrews. "Look at that arm--it's like he was reaching for the bed or something."

"Yeah. His hand is twisted in the sheet. But I don't see any cuts or contusions either, do you?"

"Uh uh. Most likely overdosed on some shit. Who knows? Let's get the hell out of here, I've got to call the M E," said Andrews.

I glanced at the ceiling on the way out. Over Hodgkin's unmade bed was a framed Hooter's Girl, signed by a model with a lipstick kiss next to her ass. I shook my head and said, "They should have done an autopsy on him while he was still alive."

I almost felt like puking. The whole situation was like a dream. But where do I go to wake up, I thought?

To be alive was to be afraid. To not be afraid was to be dead. I couldn't feel sorry for the poor bastard. When a predator like Bart catches the bus, people have parades. I couldn't help but wonder if Professor Lewis Lisecki would be applauding.

CHAPTER TWENTY-FOUR

They say death is the mother of beauty. Some say you're dead when they send your fluids to a drain at the end of a stainless steel trough. That's dead. Bart Hodgkins would never know that's the way it's supposed to be.

The findings weren't conclusive yet, but my intuition told me Bart's death was not an accident. To the coroner, another human being is just a buckct of guts sewn up in a sack of skin. But, I don't believe in coincidences, and didn't think the deceased was dumb enough to overdose on some recreational drug. I wasn't sure how, but he was murdered. Somebody killed the man in order to shut him up. Now, the cops had to find out exactly what killed him, and moreover who did it. It was no longer my problem. It hadn't been for days, but I still couldn't let go.

I no longer felt Hodgkins was the only one involved. Why did Professor Lisecki's face keep popping up in front of my eyes like a mirage from hell? When I focused on everything I did and didn't know, my heart pushed up into my throat, feeling larger than a clenched fist.

After the discovery of Hodgkins' body, I felt down, like somebody had stuck a pin in my ass and let the air out. I didn't sleep that night, but then, insomnia and I were old companions. Yes, Bart was dead, but I decided, as they say in the old west, I had to get right back on the horse that threw me. I had some other ideas to pursue as well as the sense that the dead were about to rise and tell it all.

Whoever had orchestrated the death of Bart Hodgkins knew what he was doing. Contrary to popular fiction and movies, most criminals weren't that accomplished and couldn't so easily outmaneuver the police at every turn. The majority of murderers, rapists, burglars, robbers, drug dealers and other felons are usually uneducated or scared, drugged-out punks or drunks terrified of their own shadows when off the needle or bottle, yet demons when high.

They left many clues behind and were usually caught, turned themselves in, or were ratted out by their friends. They were prosecuted and did jail time or, in rare cases, executed. They were in no sense of the word, professionals. All investigations run the same course: You follow the trail of a person's life to see where it crosses with another.

Men like Lewis Lisecki lived and worked in a shadow world that I knew little about; they paid cash and were paid in cash, lived under other names, and moved in circles so clannish that they were known in their true lives by very few others. Hodgkins had been my main target in the disappearance of Chelsea Rohrman--that is, until I interviewed the good professor.

I knew Florence and Betty Rohrman would be on my private-detecting-ass very soon. I couldn't blame them; it was their habit to call every few days to find out where I was on the case. I knew in truth, Florence wanted her daughter back, but finding her killer would give her some comfort, and I was determined not to fail her. I didn't know what to say. It wasn't my place to tell her that you have to let go of the dead or the dead will carry you down. Talking about it was like looking down the wrong end of a telescope at someone else's life.

I couldn't admit that I didn't actually know which way to go now that our prime suspect was lying in the morgue. "Working on it" became words she and her daughter Betty, were sick of hearing. The sun was low and I could feel the day shedding heat in layers as I drove over to meet Kris Branoff and Phil Andrews at *The Parking Lot Tavern* for a cold one the next day. The evening streets had been choked with traffic going nowhere at a glacial pace.

When I was on the beat, *The Parking Lot* was a favorite watering hole for cops. Still was. Kris Branoff had given me a call, and said they would meet me there around seven. Nothing official just shoot the shit and discuss whatever. It always came around to talking shop though, and we all knew it. I hadn't seen Branoff much at all since the bodies were discovered and I was anxious to catch up with my old partner.

When I walked into the bar, the after work crowd was in full swing. The music was deafening; the crowd was packed shoulder to shoulder and wall to wall with college kids and yuppie types. The jukebox was blaring with the Eagles' Hotel California.

Brady was bartending, which was not the norm. He was a short man, with a head slightly too large for his body, the size emphasized by a wild thatch of curly black hair, shot through with silver. He was dark-eyed and olive-complected, with a predominant gold front tooth, which patrons got to see a great deal due to his winning smile.

Not seeing either one of the guys, I ordered a Guiness and stood at the end of the bar, by the front door, so they'd be able to find me. Branoff and Andrews came in about fifteen minutes later.

Andrews wore an ill-fitting blue blazer over a collarless black shirt and gray slacks. His clothes had the worn and rumpled look of a thrift store sale. Branoff, on the other hand, was decked out in his usual on-the-job attire. I saw him just as he opened the door; he wore a gray suit and a gray and red tie. The wind blew his tie over his shoulder before he got inside. I was glad I was casually dressed in my blue Don Henley shirt, jeans and Cubs cap.

Branoff knew how to dress and carry on chitchat over cocktails, but his forays into society were temporary as far as I knew. He ordered a Bacardi and Coke while Andrews ordered a draught. We stayed huddled together for lack of room. We didn't want to yell at each other over the hum of the crowd.

Branoff loosened his tie and flipped the brim of my cap with his fingertips. "You still praying for those losers, eh?" He chuckled.

"Always, Kris. You know that. Cubs corner, all the way.

"You should root for a real team like the Sox," said Andrews. "At least they stand a chance."

Branoff paused and said, "Sorry I missed out on the big discovery at Hodgkins place. I had an early morning press conference; I thought I'd never get out of there." He took a long swallow of his drink and continued, "Shit! If I only knew, eh? I didn't find out about our perp's demise until after the meeting, or I coulda' told those reporters we had our serial killer--end of him-- end of story." He shook his head in disgust.

I said, "Nah, I don't think so, Kris."

"What? What in the hell do you mean, Hawk? Hodgkins was our guy--we know that."

"Oh, he was a killer alright, but I think he was taken out to keep him from talking, is what I'm saying. He had an accomplice in his killing spree."

Branoff shook his head.

"What makes you say that?" Andrews asked.

"You know I interviewed that Professor out at the college. All I can say is that bottle of Xanax, Hodgkins and the professor are connected in some way, and I intend to find out how. I still know how to detect, and I mean to keep digging until we put the noose around that pervert's neck."

Branoff thought for a long time. He checked his glass, rattling the ice. "Lisecki, eh?" I saw a vein high on his temple start to tick. He smiled and said, "Bet you didn't know forensics found red hair fibers on the bodies of two of the vics. Turns out, they matched our boy Hodgkins' DNA. It's a done deal, Hawk. That asshole was our killer. He just got too juiced for his own good and overdosed. Goodbye serial killer."

"Hmmmm. I hadn't heard about the hair thing yet, no. Good

work, by forensics, that's for damned sure. Great in fact, but it just proves he was in on it for sure. I never doubted that much. But, for instance, did you know that Professor Lisecki used to be Judge Lisecki for Cook County? I've checked this guy out. He smells bad no matter which way you look. I think he and Hodgkins had some sort of deal going."

"Ah, it sounds like semi-horseshit but it might hold up okay, I guess," said Andrews.

Branoff saw me look at the side of his face . He bit off a hangnail, spit it off the end of his tongue and signaled for the bartender. After he got another drink, he took a swig, looked at me and swung his head to the side, signaling me to join him outside. "Come on out, Cleve. I wanna' puff on a cigar."

"I'll come along," said Andrews. "I want a smoke, myself."

"No, Phil." Kris smiled. "You stay right here, if you don't mind. I want to chat with Cleve alone for a minute."

Andrews shrugged. "Okay--sure. I'll have another beer. You guys can play catch up when you get back."

Outside, Kris took an expensive-looking cigar from the breast pocket of his jacket. After stripping the cellophane, he plugged the cigar into the corner of his mouth and stared me down as he lit up and blew out a huge bloom of smoke.

"Just what the hell gives you the right to start playing OK Corral in my jurisdiction, Hawk? You have managed to piss off a bunch of people in Cook County, you know? That ex-judge is well connected in this town. I let you in on some of our stuff because of your client and the missing girl, but you are starting to ruffle feathers and if anybody's gonna do that it will be me. I'm the cop, remember?"

Kris's words made me freeze. He puffed on his cigar and we were silent for a beat.

I slipped my hands inside my pockets and shrugged. "Yeah, Kris. I know you're in charge. I'm just trying to find leads here. So far, I haven't got much. Neither do you, really. I'm telling you Lisecki stinks. He lies and he's wearing guilt like a cheap suit."

I felt like an idiot talking to hear my head roar.

"That's just a hunch you have, Hawk. And I'm telling you our perp is dead. Bart Hodgkins was our serial killer. I think he overdosed, but if somebody did his shit in, too bad. Probably a revenge killing if anything. Hodgkins should have thought of the possibilities before he unzipped his fly. Look, Hawk, we've got to leave Lisecki alone unless we get something more concrete-- understand? And I do mean we, the Chicago Police Homicide Division--not you, Hawk."

"If I get anything on him, will you get a warrant to search his house?"

"Sonofabitch!" He hiked his eyebrows. "What did I just say? You be careful whose toes you step on, Cleve. No shit--I mean it." He paused and watched the traffic whiz past us before he said, "What are you going to do now?"

"Well, I was figuring, I'd go back out to see Joan Vidross. I think she'll open up like a ripe melon if I work it right. I think she knows something she's not telling."

He grinned. "Your gut again, right?"

"Call it that if you want--yeah."

He turned and went back inside to collect Phil Andrews, who looked at me now, as if I was a suspect.

"See you later, Hawk," said Branoff as he tapped me on the shoulder. "Don't take it personal, Buddy."

"Yeah, Kris, see ya."

"Catch you down the road, Hawkins," said Andrews. "Stay in touch."

I edged through the crowd and worked my way outside where I watched them as they melted into the crowd and disappeared down the street.

I was getting very pissed off now, almost uncontrollably so. I could feel the rage surging as I hustled down the overcrowded streets to my car. I sat behind the wheel, breathing, unable to move, feeling apart from my own body as if the ass-chewing had just happened to someone else. *What the hell just happened?*

I blew the air from my cheeks as the hopelessness of the situation set in. *How in the hell hadn't I seen this coming?*

I thought about all of it. Branoff's words wouldn't leave me.

Now what? Joan Vidross, that's what. And who bailed Hodgkins out? I needed to talk to whoever that was and fast.

CHAPTER TWENTY-FIVE

I knew Joan Vidross and her redneck friend, Clyde, had to know more than they were letting on. But, then, maybe I just didn't ask the right questions. I had to go back out there. The last time I talked to them, I simply wanted to find out about the Xanax, but now I needed more, and that need followed me like a guilty conscience.

It was late Tuesday afternoon when I drove out to the outskirts of Elk Grove Village. Her place was in the middle of an ordinary neighborhood with kids on bikes, moms talking in front yards, and dads cutting the grass. Knowing that she worked as a lunch waitress at *Olive Garden* and would probably be gone during the day, I made it a point to go out there late in order to catch her at home.

I remembered she had a Chihuahua and I heard it yapping when I knocked on the rickety screen door. She had the dog wrapped in her arms when she opened the inside door. It trembled and continued to yap until she wrapped her fingers around the dog's snout.

"Shhhh. Quiet, Princess."

She wore designer jeans and a sleeveless aqua-colored blouse; an unlit cigarette dangled from her lips. Her dark hair was pulled tightly behind her head, and her big brown eyes added to her look of surprise. Wearing very little makeup, Joan Vidross wasn't beautiful, not cute, and evidently determined not to be so.

She stared for a moment, and said, "Oh, it's you again? What do you want this time, detective?"

"Good afternoon, Ms. Vidross. I don't mean to be a bother, but I wonder if I might speak to you again for a few minutes."

"Hmmm. What was your name again?"

"Hawkins--Cleve Hawkins." I flipped open my wallet and showed her my ID. "Private Investigator."

"Oh, yeah. Well, I just got home from work, so it's not really a good time, Clive. Maybe you could come back on my day off. That's Thursday. I'm off all day, so if you'll excuse me . . ." She began to ease the door closed, and the dog yapped again.

"Ma'am, I really need to speak to you and Clyde now. It's something that can't wait. I promise I won't take much of your time."

"Clyde's not here anymore. I gave that asshole the boot over two weeks ago." She sighed. "I guess I can spare a few minutes. What's it about this time? Are you bringing my bottle of pills back?"

"Ma'am, may I step inside?"

She hesitated, then shoved the screen door open. "Yeah, sure. Come on in." She scooped up a newspaper that was fanned out over the coffee table. I spotted a large pizza sitting on the table in the kitchen.

"Sorry for the mess, like I said, I've been working a lot of hours. It's been a bitch of a day too. We were swamped,"

"Yes, Ma'am."

"Enough of that Ma'am stuff. Call me Joan, for Chrissakes. There," she pointed to the Lay-z-boy. "Cop a squat."

A stack of folded clothes sat in a laundry basket next to a pile of towels on the couch. She put her dog in an adjoining room and closed the door. After lighting her cigarette, she shoved the clothesbasket over and sat on the couch.

"So, what's up, Clive?" I caught her eyeing the pizza.

"It's Cleve, Joan, and I need some more information concerning your relationship with Professor Lewis Lisecki."

"You're kidding, right? What about him?" She seemed surprised, but then gave me a look that would boil cheese, and crossed her arms over her chest. She blew a plume of smoke up towards the ceiling. "I don't need any trouble with that asshole."

"What do you mean? What kind of trouble are we talking about?" There was a long, silent gap.

"Ah, let's just say . . . asking anyone to go one-one with Lewis would be like putting a guppy in a piranha pool."

"I'm not sure what you mean by that? Tell me about him."

She shrugged as she stood and retrieved an ashtray from the dining room table and returned to the couch.

"Well, he used to be a judge, you know?" She paused and blew more smoke. "You ever met him?"

"Yes. I interviewed him out at the college a couple of weeks ago."

"Well, then you know what he looks like, but you don't know him like I do." She paused. "I don't know if I should be talking to you about him to tell the truth, Clive."

"It's Cleve, and everything you tell me will stay with me, Joan. It's all off the record, I assure you."

"Well . . .I was never really attracted to him. As you saw, Lew is one of those fat guys who hardly has an ass on him." She paused and shook her head. "I could never figure why none of the fat went there. Anyway, he's got milk-white legs and walks like his balls are sore. He has little feet, pink ones" She smiled. "The thing is, the man is a boozer, too. I'll bet you didn't know that, eh?"

"No, I didn't."

She nodded. "Lew's priorities are women, cocaine and scotch, and I believe in that order. Plus he smokes them damned stinkin' cigars. Oh, he's got the money, that's for sure, and he showed me a good time, so I closed my eyes to his faults, know what I mean? That fat little shit can twist some keys whenever he wants. He's got a lot of pull. He helped me out of a bad deal one time. I don't want to go into it, but it's amazing the shit he can do."

"I'm not sure what you mean, but can you tell me when the last time you saw Lisecki?"

"Why?" I noticed, her fingernails were bitten down to the quick, and she seemed to be getting stressed. She stubbed out her cigarette and lit another.

"I have reason to believe he may be involved in a case I'm working on."

"You mean my stolen pills, for Chrissake?" She feigned a laugh.

"No. This is much more serious than that, Joan."

"Oh, I was going to say, Those damned pills can't be that big a deal. What in the hell did he do, anyway?"

"Sorry, I'm not free to say at this point. It's just speculation."

"Ha! Well, the last time we saw him was at his house over three weeks ago."

"You visited him? I don't mean to get too personal, but was that for a date?"

"Hell, no. Me and the professor never had anything serious going on. No sex, that's for sure." She grinned. "He probably couldn't find his dick with a pair of salad tongs."

She stared into my eyes with a crooked smile that slashed her face as if she, and only she, had discovered that everything in the world was about sex, and Lisecki had never seen anything like her before. She shifted her eyes to a point between us for a time. "He was hot for me, alright."

"So, why did you visit him? And you said, 'we'. Who's we?"

She sighed. "Oh, I guess it's okay to tell you now. Like I said, Clyde is history as far as I'm concerned. Me and Clyde went over there. I was pissed off because I thought Lew had given my bottle of Xanax to somebody. You were the one who tipped me off to that possibility, you know. Remember? Some asshole had them in his glove box when he got busted, right?"

"Yes, and I remember asking who you dated and you told me Lisecki had been the only one. Right? Besides Clyde, I mean?"

"Right. And that's why I figured he might have had them, but he denied knowing anything about them."

"So, were you satisfied with that?"

The yapping started again, but when Joan went to the door and yelled "Hush, Princess!" the dog obeyed.

Joan blew a geyser of smoke and sat back on the couch. Curling her legs underneath her, she draped one arm along the top of the couch before she answered.

"Yeah, I guess so. We had a few drinks with him. I really don't think the little weasel would lie to me. He might try to screw me-- but he wouldn't steal from me. He doesn't need to, like I said he can get whatever he wants. Rich prick."

"Did you ever notice anything out of the ordinary while you were there? Something unusual, I mean? Something he may have said about his other relationships with women, for instance?"

Joan shook her head. "No, I know Lew and Clyde made some kind of deal that night. I'm not really sure what it was all about, but Clyde told me Lisecki was paying him two hundred dollars to do him a favor."

"And you don't know what that was about?"

She was leaning forward, biting down on her lower lip with her upper teeth. Her eyes were wide and fixed on me. "No. Well, that's not exactly true. Clyde did tell me he was going into the city to pick up a guy for Lew and he would get two hundred for doing it. Clyde would do anything to make a buck as long as it didn't involve work, I mean."

"You don't know who Clyde was supposed to pick up though, right?"

"Nope. Clyde just said he was supposed to pick up this guy at the Cook County Jail."

My insides flipped. This was the break I'd been waiting for.

I held up my finger, signaling her to wait, then I said, "What about this Clyde guy. Is he a good pal of the professor's?"

"Not really. I introduced him to Lewis a couple of months back at a party Lewis had."

"And, where did you meet Clyde?"

"At my other job, the grill. I worked there before *Olive Garden*.

Anyway, he kept coming in for breakfast. Sometimes lunch too. He kept hitting on me, and we finally started going out."

"Clyde seemed to think it was pretty serious between you two, last time I was here."

"Yeah, *he* thought that alright. But, no, Clyde is not my type. It took me a while to realize it, but he's just not."

"Drinker? Lazy? What?"

"Both. How did you know?"

I shrugged. "Seemed like the type when I met him."

"He's a couple of sandwiches short of a picnic, too," she said.

"So, where is Clyde now? Where is he staying?"

"Ha! That's easy. He's out in that big trailer park in Wheeling."

I took out my notepad. "What's the name of the park, do you know?"

"Sure. He told me last weekend when he called, wanting me to go dancing with him. Asshole. He's got two left feet and he can't stay sober past nine at night."

"So, what's it called--this park?"

"Highland Estates. His mother lives in the same park. I don't know the address. Listen, are we done, I 've got to eat. My pizza's getting cold."

I put my notepad and pen away and got up. "I think that's all I'll need for now, Joan. I appreciate your time."

"No problem," she said as she stood. "I'd sure like to know what's going on though."

"Maybe later, Joan. Thanks again--enjoy your pizza."

I smiled as I fired up my car, and my heart hammered in my chest. I was on my way to a trailer park to see that shit-kicker, Clyde.

CHAPTER TWENTY-SIX

I was on the right path to take down one of Chelsea Rohrman's killers. Homicide investigation is a pursuit with countless dead ends, obstacles and huge chunks of wasted time and effort. I knew that every day of my tour as a cop, but when I caught a break I took advantage of it with the aggressiveness of a shark that smells blood.

I had plenty of time to think on the way out to Clyde Hargrove's place. I could only hope I had gotten solid information from Joan Vidross, and the redneck would, in fact, be home at the trailer park near suburban Montgomery.

The Cubs had managed to lose the ballgame to Cincinnati, so I put in a CD by Miles Davis. The two-lane highway was rough. Its asphalt was thin and the concrete seams had become disjointed by time and disrepair. The surfaces were crumbling and my Crown Vic tires banged hard, sometimes making the music inside jump.

On the way out, I passed a long sequence of miscellaneous enterprises, on the left and the right: a hardware store, a liquor store, a bank, tire bays, a John Deere dealership, a grocery, and a pharmacy.

Clyde's trailer park was on Highland Circle across the street from a tavern called *The Hole*. It was parked in the very back of the park where the lineup of double-wides ended and the smaller units were parked like abused stepchildren.

His trailer had a permanent lean, and looked as if a decent breeze could flatten it. Except for the buzz of horseflies, the place stood silent. A '72 model Dodge pickup sat on an angle in front of the trailer and a couple of used truck tires leaned up against its skirting.

A similar trailer was next door and on the other side was a vacant cement slab. There was nothing behind the trailer park but farm fields. I parked next to the pickup and looked around as I slowly got out.

Heavy metal music was coming from the rear of the trailer. I rapped on the screen door and getting no answer, knocked again.

"Hey! Come around back," I heard a man's voice yell. I stepped to the side and craned my neck around the corner in order to see who it was. Clyde flipped his sunglasses up onto his forehead and waved. I had met him once before at Joan's house; it was Clyde alright.

"Oh, it's Dick Tracy. Ha! What do you want?"

He was bare-chested, wearing shorts with dancing elephants on them, flip flops, and a baseball cap with NRA lettering above the bill. He moved out of my sight for a moment and when I came around I found him drinking a bottle of Heineken while he flipped a steak on a flaming grill. A portable radio blared classic AC-DC from its position on a set of small steps under the back door.

He put down the tongs and forced a wide grin as he fiddled with an unlit cigarette. Twiddling it like a pencil between his nicotine-stained fingers, he decided to light up.

"What's up, Ace? Don't tell me you can't find your drugs again? Ha! If that's the case you can leave now. I'm a good boy--don't do drugs." Maybe he actually thought the realization of assholedom was the beginning of wisdom.

"How's it going, Clyde?"

He didn't ask me to sit in any of the three lawn chairs that were clustered a few feet away from the Weber grill, nor did he look at me directly. Instead, he swallowed hard and burped loudly, without the slightest trace of hesitation or embarrassment. Smacking his lips, he frowned as though he swallowed vinegar, and moved away from the grill.

Taking a seat at an umbrella-shaded table, he tossed the cigarette and stuffed his mouth with what looked like chili. Continuing to scoop some of the stuff into his mouth, he took another long pull on the bottle of beer and belched. With the back of a beefy hand, he wiped a smear of chili from his chin before he acknowledged me.

"It's supper time, case you didn't know, pal."

"Yeah, I know."

"But you've decided to bother me anyway, right?" he said as he stood up.

I was wishing that he would put on a shirt. His tufted breasts were drooping and mole-covered, and I spied what appeared to be a fresh bite mark above his left nipple. His big belly hung over his belt, nearly covering his fly. His face was slightly flushed, with cheeks that were flecked with tiny blue and red veins. He wasn't wearing a bra, but should have been.

"Sorry to interrupt your space, Clyde, but I just left Joan Vidross' place, and she seemed to think you might be able to answer some questions for me--better than her, that is."

"Well screw that bitch, and damn her! It takes balls to send you over here?" He moved around with his hands in his pockets, squinting, with his wraparound sunglasses on the bill of his cap.

Shaking a finger at me, he said, "Talk about not knowing nothing, that broad don't even suspect nothing. God knows what she'd say. She certainly was happy to get me to jump her bones. Ha! Ha!" He paused and shook his head as he looked down at his feet. "What kind'a questions, anyway?"

Finagling a pack of Marlboros out of his pants pocket, he tapped one out and lit up. His mouth drew up in corkscrew fashion, and he squinted in an attempt to keep the smoke out of his eyes.

Glaring at me, he said, "I'll give you until my steak is done, then it'll be time for you to hit the road, Ace."

"Does the name Lewis Lisecki ring any bells for you, Clyde?"

"Louie who?"

"Lisecki . . . Lewis Lisecki, don't you remember that name?"

"Uh uuh. Why? Should I?"

"Sure, you know him, Clyde. He's the guy Joan used to go out with before you. Remember, the professor?"

He grinned. "Oh yeah." He snapped his fingers as if a light came on in the deep recesses of his skull. I believe he had a Mixmaster in his head instead of a brain.

He licked his teeth with his tongue and spit. "Oh,Yeah, he's the guy was porkin' Joanie before me." He tapped his temple. "I got him. I couldn't remember there for a minute. Yeah, yeah, but what makes that looney bitch, Joan-- or even you-- think I know anything about him?"

"Oh, just a hunch. Let me ask you another question, just off the record, what do you do to make a living?"

"Huh? Well, I do all kinds a things. I hang drywall, paint, fix cars. I'm a jack of all trades, like they say. Hell I get my food paid for. Food stamps, you know. I keep busy too, else I couldn't afford to keep this here place up." He swung an arm around in a circle, as if he was pointing out a hundred acre farm.

"Didn't you live with Joan for a while?"

"Yeah, sure I did. You knew that--so what?"

"Nothing--just making sure my info is correct."

"Well, you know what, Ace. I think you're too fucking nosey; what do you think of them apples?" He edged in close to me, practically toe to toe. His breath was a mixture of beer and spicy chicken wings. He snorted like a broken diesel as he flicked his cigarette and it landed with a hiss in a rusted pail of water sitting by the back steps.

"Just chill out, Clyde. You're getting too excited."

"Damned right. You got no business coming around here bothering me about my personal shit."

"Just answer this, Clyde, and I'll be on my way. What did Lisecki pay you two hundred dollars for?"

"What?"

"Two bills, what did Lisecki pay you to do for him?"

"Says who?"

"Says Joan. She was right there when you two swung the deal, remember?"

"Bullshit!"

"I don't think so, Clyde. As a matter of fact, I already know, but I wanted to hear it from you. Or, maybe you've got Italian Alzheimer's; that's when you forget everything except who pissed you off."

"More bullshit, Mister detective."

"Yeah, just like you're bullshitting me right now, Clyde."

"No, no, no, not ever," he said, making a wide-arm gesture like an umpire calling a runner safe at the plate. "I wouldn't bullshit you, man. I don't want anything to do with it anymore." He flicked a hand that said, you people are flies. "My steak is getting cold. Shame I ain't got some to share, Ace. If you don't mind I'm gonna dig in; time for you to split."

"Okay, tell me what you did for the professor and I'll go away."

He ignored that and said, "I don't mind you watchin'." He flipped the steak onto a paper plate and brushed his hands in the air, ready to go. "Yeah, man, I'm starved."

"I'll wait," I said, and took a seat in one of the chairs.

After he took a few bites, Clyde sighed. He became sort of agreeable without admitting anything: calm brown eyes set against a ruddy face. A half-hour earlier he had been able to joke about my questions. Now I had him by the short hairs and he knew it.

He spoke out of the corner of his mouth as he continued to wolf down the steak.

"Okay. He paid me the two-hunnert to pick up some guy at the jail in the city."

"Uh huh, and who was the guy you picked up? His name?"

There was a long pause between us and nothing was said, then he looked me in the eyes. "I don't want no fuckin trouble, understand, Ace? I don't need no shit from that little asshole."

"You won't be fingered for anything, go ahead."

He stopped eating. "I got your word on that right? You could still stick it in my ass. How would I know? I'm tellin' ya', I don't need no shit from Lisecki or the guy I picked up."

"Who was the guy, Clyde?"

He took another slug of beer and continued to chew his steak.

"Was his name Bart Hodgkins?"

He hesitated, then said, "Yeah. That's what his bail papers said when I picked him up. Tall dude, has short red hair, right?"

"That's him."

Clyde took another bite of steak. "This fuckin' meat is tough now," he said as he threw his fork on the table and it clattered to the ground.

He fished around in his pocket and retrieved his cigarettes again.. "I don't like neither one of them jokers--understand?" He lit up and exhaled the smoke in one long puff.

"Can't say as I blame you."

"Yeah, that professor ever comes around here, I'll be all over him like a bad smell."

"Gotcha."

"And that asshole I picked up--if that son-of-a-bitch's heart caught on fire, I wouldn't piss down his throat to put it out."

"You won't have to worry about that, Clyde . . . he's dead."

"No shit?" His mouth hung open. "When?"

"I can't give you anymore on that." I stood to leave. "Thanks for the information." I threw two twenties on the table in front of him. "Sorry about the steak, have another one on me."

I was relieved as I backed up and headed out of the park. Let the professor lie his way out of this one. Now, I needed to get into his house--with or without a warrant.

CHAPTER TWENTY-SEVEN

I was as taut as a strung bow, as I drove home from Clyde Hargrove's place. I knew I had Professor Lisecki right where I wanted him. The pieces of the puzzle were coming together like leaves settling to the bottom of a pool.

The setting sun behind me was red in the mirror as I drove back to my place. As much as I hated it, the showdown at Lisecki's home would have to wait until the next day. It would take some planning, and with no warrant I couldn't afford to screw up.

I knew Lisecki would be working at the college during the day, and although I thought about pulling a B&E on his house, I was sure he had security systems in place that would nail me before I got to his door. I decided the best way to gain entry without setting off alarms, would be to have him let me in the house. No warrant would be a huge issue, but I figured Branoff would cover my ass with that if I found anything. He'd better.

Timing would be critical, so I called the university and was told Lisecki's last class was at two-thirty in the afternoon; I figured he'd be home by four-thirty at the latest. I had the entire day to prepare before I went out there.

When I got back to the apartment, I checked the machine for messages. There were none, and although I was disappointed that Mo hadn't called in a few days, I had no right to consider that since I hadn't called her either. I was sure she would understand. I needed time to think and analyze everything Clyde Hargrove had told me and figure my plan for when I gained entry to Lisecki's place.

Grabbing an Old Style from the fridge, I turned the radio to some blues on WGMR and went out onto the balcony. I stood in the warm night air and enjoyed the cold beer. The smell of a neighbor's freshly mowed grass was still strong in the early evening, and automatically carried me back to my teenage years of doing yard work. Good times for a young man with no direction in sight.

I watched the sunset turn into long strips of maroon clouds, back dropped by a moment of robin's-egg blueness on the earth's rim. As light drained from the sky I listened to the distant hum of rush-hour traffic on Lakeshore Drive. Leaning my elbows on the railing, I ruminated about my plan for the next day.

I couldn't depend on the cooperation of the Chicago Police Department. At least not yet. My former partner, Kris Branoff, had made it crystal clear that I wasn't to mess with the professor. I was to stay away from him, and in fact, Branoff had suggested he wouldn't even consider getting a warrant to search Lisecki's house, no matter what. I knew that was bullshit, but he was the man in charge, so I'd pretend to go with the flow.

Eventually homicide would have to get involved, whether Branoff liked it or not. I was disappointed in my former partner because he allowed an asshole like Lewis Lisecki to control his investigating capabilities. Having no warrant when I went out to the professor's place could make for an interesting situation when the shit hit the fan. Nevertheless, I had my mind made up, I would take Lisecki down by myself and worry about consequences later. Branoff could kiss my ass.

I didn't know if my plan was clever or just plain stupid, but I was determined. I went inside and got another beer. I felt a bit jittery about the whole deal; it was times like this when I wished I hadn't quit smoking and scotch and although scotch seemed like a good idea, I discarded the thought, pronto.

Plain and simple: Lisecki was guilty. He lied about knowing Bart Hodgkins. Not only that, but he had paid to bail the scumbag out of jail. Why? I could only conclude that Lisecki put up the money because he was worried about the possibility of Hodgkins opening his mouth. Who knew what Bart would do under intense pressure of interrogation? Perhaps confess to something incriminating, including the admission that Lisecki was his perverted partner . I even toyed with the idea that Lisecki may have had something to do with the unusual circumstances surrounding Bart Hodgkin's death.

Since we already knew that Bart was a killer, it followed that Lisecki was probably involved too. It seemed impossible in so many ways, He thought himself untouchable, but I had the feeling I could stick thumbtacks deep into his scalp with relative ease if I handled it right. He was most likely the brains behind the abductions of the women who were ultimately raped, tortured and killed. In my mind it all fit, but I wasn't sure what I would find in Lisecki's house to prove it.. At best it was a crapshoot and I knew it, but I had always followed my gut.

Four beers and a couple of hot dog sandwiches later, I fell asleep on the couch, watching reruns of *Everybody Loves Raymond*.

Before I left the next afternoon, I slipped my 9mm Glock in a shoulder holster and pulled my right trouser leg up over my sock, exposing the hideaway .25 that was Velcro-strapped to my ankle.

Lisecki's house was located on the outskirts of Rolling Hills. It was a huge place, a tri-level, that appeared white and towering. A wide porch swept across the front and around the side of the house. was It stood by itself on roughly twenty acres, with a pine plantation at the far end, and a half-dozen pear trees clustered in an expansive back yard. I wondered if he owned all of the surrounding land. It was certainly isolated. Interesting.

The driveway was concrete, and at the entrance there was a mailbox with a hand-painted sign on an adjoining pole that said

"Home Of The Brain" Egotistical bastard.

I noticed the flower beds along the front of the house were weedless and obviously received constant care. Between them and the road the long wide lawn was thick and manicured. To one side of the house there was a neglected apple orchard, the trees barren and twisted like broken fingers in the air. Knee-high field grass surrounded the dying trees.

A forest-green Mercedes was parked in front of the three-car garage. I pulled my Crown Vic up alongside and hesitated a bit before I got out and walked to the front door.

A fan-shaped, stained-glass window highlighted the door. I rang the bell and heard loud chimes ring inside. Lisecki opened the door. He wore a pale gray Italian suit with an open-necked black dress shirt. Somehow he looked different without the tie and glasses I'd seen him wearing at the university. A tasteful gold bracelet clung to his left wrist just below a diamond Rolex.

He was soft-looking, overweight and pasty-faced. He looked shocked at first; then there was a small glint of hope in his eyes before he sagged. Opening the door just a crack, he said, "Yes--can I help you?"

I flashed my ID for him. "Yes, Professor, I'm Cleve Hawkins, remember me?"

He was obviously caught off guard. "Ah, yes, Mr. Hawkins . . . what can I do for you?"

"Well, for starters you could show some manners and allow me to come in for a moment."

"I beg your pardon, Sir. I don't see why I should do that, after all, I . . ."

"I do," I said, as I shoved the door aside and brushed past him.

"Hey! Who do you think you are, Mister Hawkins? You can't just come barging in here like some storm trooper. You either get out of here right now, or I'm calling the police." He was pissed off, and his left eye flickered with unexpected tension.

"Oh I agree, we're gonna call the cops, Professor, but not just yet." I crowded him, and he backed up. He retreated out of the foyer and hurried down the hallway that gleamed with a polished oak-floor. I followed him.

We passed a winding staircase, and I looked up to admire the cathedral ceiling as Lisecki unintentionally led me to the inner sanctum of his den. Determined to get to the phone, he marched straight to his desk and grabbed it. I smacked his hand when the receiver was barely off the cradle.

"I said later, Professor"

He studied me as if he were deciding whether or not I would back down. "How dare you strike me! That's assault, Hawkins. You just assaulted me."

"Not yet, I haven't, but if you don't sit down and shut up, I'll show you assault."

"I don't appreciate the intrusion, Sir," he huffed and struggled to get his breath as I edged past him and walked around, taking in the surroundings.

"Nice digs you've got here, Lewis. Make good money, do we?"

"That's none of your damned business and I want you to leave this instant. You have no right to come . . ."

I whirled around to face him. "I 'll ask the questions. Sit down."

He shifted his weight on his small buttocks and wet his lips, before with an exasperated gasp, he dropped into the swivel chair behind the desk. "What is it?" he said, looking stung. "What do you want here?"

"I'm here to look around, Lewis. I want to see what you're up to when you're away from that bevy of co-eds." I continued to wander around the room as I talked.

"What? What do you mean by that? I'm not hiding a thing. I don't have to. "For your information I looked into you, Everybody said you thought you were tough and funny. Oh, and a drunk. I figured that though."

"Good natured and handsome, too, Lewis."

"No. You are an abrasive, mean man, and, I've also learned you're a killer. That's why they took your badge, isn't it."

I had worked my way back to the desk. "Why are you so obnoxious? Is it because you're fat and ugly, or is it because you're fat and dumb? It's a mystery to me." I grinned. "I know you're a liar, Lewis."

"Says who?"

"Says me." I crowded in and bent down. Just inches from his face, I gritted my teeth and said,, "I say so. You told me you never heard of Bart Hodgkins, but I can prove you not only know him, but you're fuck buddies with him."

"You're wrong. I said I don't know him, and I didn't."

"That's not what Joan Vidross says.

At first Lewis remained calm, like a spider waiting at the edge of its web, but then, his cheeks turned red and his eyes narrowed. His chubby face collapsed into a pile of gravity-ravaged tissue that pulled his eyes, nose and mouth downward into a scowl. He shrugged as if he didn't care.

"Ha! You can't believe anything that woman says. An miserable and unstable woman, that one. She was doomed from the moment she tumbled from the womb. Joan's a member of the Women's Wine and Whine Club. She lies and will do anything or say anything to get what she wants." His mouth opened and closed like a goldfish pecking at the surface, and his breathing was labored.

"Really? Well, she was right here the night you made your deal with Clyde Hargrove. Remember that, Lewis? The night you paid Clyde two hundred dollars to go into town and bail Bart out of jail?" I leaned over the desk. "By the way, I noticed you used Bart's name in the past tense. How are you aware that something happened to Hodgkins?"

Lisecki slowly snuck his middle drawer open and came out with a gun. I was ready for him, and slammed my Glock down on the back of his wrist. I thought I heard bones crack and he yelled, "Owwww! Damn you!"

His gun rattled across the desk top and fell to the floor. "You scared me, Lewis. The only thing that would have scared me more would have been if you threatened to flog me with a noodle."

He doubled up over his hand and made a repetitive grunting noise, rocking back and forth in his swivel chair. He was drooling and making sounds that were very much like crying.

I scooped up his gun, yanked him out of the chair and shoved him against the wall, pinning him like an insect to a board. His breath came in broken, disjointed spasms and he turned his blubbering face away from me.

"Now, my perverted friend, you're going to take me on a tour of this house, room by fucking room." I shoved him. Let's go!"

CHAPTER TWENTY-EIGHT

Lisecki smashed into the wall and hung there like a broken doll before he slumped to the floor. He blubbered like a baby with snot running from his nose.

He stared at me as if I was an alien creature who'd come to haunt his nightmares. His uncontrollable trembling and the sweat that ran down the sides of his face showed his terror.

Seeing him right there on the verge of cracking, I knew I was right, he had a lot to hide, and felt I would find something to prove his involvement in the serial killings. He looked appalled because he knew I was about to challenge his notion that the planets revolved around him and not the sun.

I holstered my Glock, grabbed a handful of his shirt and hauled him up to a standing position. "Come on, Lew, let's take a look around, shall we?" I shoved him out in front of me.

"You . . . you can't do this. I have my rights and you need a warrant to do this." He cradled the hand I'd smashed and stared at me as he pondered the situation, thinking he was just about the smartest guy on the whole continent because he knew his rights.

"You lead the way, let's go, counselor. Walk slow and easy," I told him as I gave him another little shove.

As we went from room to room, I was on high alert and noticed that Lisecki had a strong interest in modern art; there were pieces of it in every room except the library, which was a shrine to himself with his bowling trophies and numerous framed photographs, diplomas and certifications.

"You a bowler, are ya', Lewis?"

"No--not anymore. It's been years since I . . ."

"Okay, I don't want your entire strike and spare history." We were still in the library. "Any closets in this room?"

"No, and if you leave now I will forget that you were here." I glanced his way and saw pleading eyes.

"Not gonna' happen, Lew." I studied the bragging wall where most of the framed certifications were mounted. I didn't see any family-type pictures anywhere, which was no surprise.

Tapping an Appreciation Award with my fingers, I said, "They called you a Judge on this one. Why did you leave that cushy job anyway, Lewis?"

"Not that it's any of your business, but I wanted to retire."

"To teach at the university? What the hell for? Lots of young stuff running around out there, huh?"

"No." He edged away from me. "That's not it at all." He paused. "It's . . . it's a long story."

Two of the four walls in the library were taken with bookshelves. Law books took precedence, but I spotted volumes by Dickens, Melville and other classics on two of the shelves.

"No false partitions that move or some such secret shit?" I said, as I ran my hands here and there on the walls and bookcases.

"Don't be ridiculous, Detective." He stopped whining and had a smug look on his face. "I don't know what you're looking for, but you won't find it in my house, I assure you."

"Keep moving, Lew." I shoved him in the direction I wanted as I checked things out. I didn't really know what I was looking for but I knew it would be obvious and incriminating when I found it.

"I don't want to hear it right now, but I'll bet you schmoozed some sort of sweet deal for your friend, Bart, while you were on the bench, didn't you?"

Lisecki rolled his lips back from his teeth, thinking, but then sighed and said, "You are so wrong. I never let any of the felons who appeared before me get away with anything. I have honor, sir."

"Yeah? Bullshit. Remember, Lew-- you told me you didn't even know the man."

We finished touring the living room, den and kitchen, and so far, coming up empty, I followed him to the bar, which was complete with a gold-trimmed mirror mounted behind it. The bar top was at least eight feet in length. Two beer spigots marked with Miller Lite and Sam Adams logos were prominent in the center, and I noticed room below for two kegs. A good-sized refrigerator was built in at one end, and a wide selection of top-shelf liquor occupied a ledge behind the bar. Fluorescent lighting shone behind the bottles when I flicked a switch.

"I'm pretty proud of my bar," he muttered.

"Drink much, do ya, Lew?" I continued to look around and watch him at the same time.

"Of course not. This is for the convenience of my guests."

I had to laugh. "Probably a houseful every weekend, right? Okay, rich boy, let's have a look at the bedrooms." I pointed. "Upstairs, I take it? How many are in this palace of yours, anyway?"

"There's three, and yes, they're all upstairs, but do we really have to do all of this? You see nothing is out of order. I no longer wish to deal with this absolute nonsense. Just go."

"Shut up, and let's go." I gave him another shove and he led me up the spiral staircase. I kept my distance behind him, just in case he got brave.

He led me into two small bedrooms first. The dressers and nightstands were white, and both rooms had queen-sized beds. A feminine decor of pink and white in one, and lavender and white in the other. I knew he wouldn't be hiding a body under the beds, but I had to look, keeping an eye on Lisecki at the same time. I also checked the closets but found them empty except for unused hangers and empty luggage.

A bathroom was situated between the two rooms and I urged him in there. It was complete with a heart-shaped tub and shower. Again, all feminine tastes in towels and faceclothes. Everything seemed prim and proper, especially for a bachelor. On the vanity was a hand-held mirror and women's hairbrushes--several of them. Checking the medicine cabinet, I found a bottle of Advil, band-aids and a box of Midol. Somebody had left behind a disc of birth control pills.

"You must have a lot of female guests, huh, Lew?" I grinned.

"These bedrooms are set up for whomever should need to stay over. I try to make things as comfortable as possible. Anything wrong with that?"

I flashed the birth control pills in his face. "No, but I'd imagine some woman was pretty pissed when she discovered she left these behind." I tossed them on the counter. "Come on, show me your room."

As we moved out of the last guest room, he turned to the left and looked over his shoulder. "This is such an invasion of privacy." He dared to smirk. "You are going to cost the city one damned big lawsuit when I get done. And you'll do some time in jail, too, you cop wannabe."

"I really don't give a shit, Lew. Keep moving before I whack your other hand and do your skull while I'm at it. Shut the fuck up. You're pissing me off. Move!"

His room was plush. A four-poster bed with a burgundy canopy was the highlight on the far side of the room. The Berber carpeting was beige. All of the furniture appeared to be Chippendale walnut or oak, I wasn't sure which. A fake fireplace was on one side of the room, between two separate bay windows. Velvet-looking drapes were pulled to the side.

"So this is what a pervert's playpen looks like, eh?"

"Pervert indeed, you bastard. I will have your badge, I promise you that. Get out of my house, now!"

I looked under his bed, but saw nothing except slippers and shoes. I dusted my hands. "I'll leave when I'm damned good and ready, how's that?" I said, as I spied a closet door next to his private bathroom. "Let's have a look in the closet."

"What for? Haven't you snooped enough?"

"I'll let you know when I'm done, Professor. Open the door."

He opened it and stepped aside. I shoved him inside. "Get in there and turn on the light."

It was a walk-in that had a rack full of suits, slacks, ties and so on. I shoved the clothes back and forth, looking behind them while he stood off to the side.

"Well, what have we here?" I said. There were stacks of porno magazines piled all along the back wall. "Give me a handful of that shit, Lew. Go ahead, bury your head in there and pull some out. Let's see what you're into."

"Just magazines I collect, like any other man. Don't you?"

"No. I'm too busy to jack off, Lew." I looked at the covers that were mostly Bondage and S&M. I thumbed through one. "This is some sick shit, Lew. You like to tie women up, do you?"

I felt claustrophobic at that point and craved fresh air the way a desert nomad seeks water. I tossed the magazines on the floor. "Why am I not surprised by your tastes?"

After I checked the bathroom I said, "Let's go back downstairs, bondage boy."

Back on the first floor I stood by the door leading to the garage and directed him out that way. A fifty-seven Chevrolet was partially covered with a tarp in one of the open bays. A tool bench was situated along the back wall and I noticed a new-looking wood chipper sitting in the corner. A full-sized window faced the back yard. Keeping Lisecki close by, I looked out there.

There was a big backyard that featured a brick terrace, raised flower beds, brick walls about five feet high, and a few pieces of wrought-iron furniture on a good-sized patio. I opened the back door and pushed Lisecki out ahead of me.

As I walked around, with him still in front of me, I looked to my left and saw a cement stairwell. I walked a little further and saw a steel door at the bottom of the stairs. A basement? Sure, this was a tri-level.

I shoved him ahead of me and we went down the stairs. The staircase steepened and appeared to drop into darkness. A steel door was at the bottom. It was locked with a Master Lock that required a key.

I snapped my fingers. "The key."

"I'll have to see if I can find it," said Lisecki. His face grew taut and his eyes blinked as they fixed on me.

"Bullshit. Give me the fuckin' key."

I gritted my teeth as he fumbled around in his pocket and handed me the key. "Oh, I forgot I had it with me," he said. His hand trembled as he handed it to me.

The key fit and I turned it in the lock and opened the door. It squeaked on its hinges.

I shoved him harder than before. "You first, professor."

"No, I'm not going to do that. There's nothing in there."

Blood pounded in my temples as I realized I'd hit the jackpot. "I'll be the judge of that. Now, you lead the way and turn on the first light you can, understand me? I'm sure you remember where the switch is."

He shrugged and nodded. "I will, but I don't understand why. It's just a basement."

Even as he spoke, his eyes didn't come off their distant focus over my shoulder.

The room was dark and still. It throbbed with emptiness. There was enough light in the room from the outside, but it was dreary, bleak kind of light, like a light in the garage that didn't reach into the corners.

"Turn on a light, Lisecki. Now!"

"Okay, okay." He flipped a switch off to his right. He quickly turned and started to run.

"No you don't, motherfucker." I grabbed him by the shirt and yanked him to within inches of my face. "Try that again and I'll break your fuckin' legs." There was another door, a thick wooden one. "Open it!" I growled. Lisecki fumbled around in his pocket again until he came up with the key. "You need a key ring, asshole."

Holding him by his shirt-collar, we moved forward. I squinted at the harsh fluorescent lighting that shone down from an acoustic tile ceiling. As it brightened I saw that it was yellowed with cigarette smoke. The place stunk like dirty sweat socks.

I saw an odd-looking king-sized, four-poster bed centered in the room. I'd never seen one like it. I shoved Lisecki aside so I could examine the bed. "What have we got here, another guest room?"

I slowly turned around and saw an entire wall plastered with eight by ten glossy pictures of women. Obvious victims. Most were very young, twenty-something. My brain immediately told me to search for Chelsea Rohrman among the pictures, but there were too many, and I was still looking at everything enveloping me. I felt my breath catch in my throat.

Some victims were on their knees, bound and gagged. Some were spread eagle on the bed, their hands and feet tied to the posts of the same bed I stood next to. Some of the pictures were close-ups showing the absolute terror in the victims' eyes. Still others had cuts on their faces, hands, legs and backs. One woman had an apple stuffed in her mouth. It was held in with a black bandana.

I turned and saw a Panasonic video camera mounted on an aluminum tripod at one end of the room; behind it, was a small bank of lights.

When I turned to face Lisecki, his manner was one of subdued excitement. His entire body was shaking, his head bowed, staring at the floor.

"I underestimated you, Lisecki. You're a fuckin' monster."

I turned to the bed. The four corner posts were locked into position, but appeared adjustable for desired height, with a slot in the top rails. It was obvious the room was set up for extreme sexual activity.

Chains hung from the walls and restraining black cuffs were draped over the posts on each end of the bed. BDSM made easy.

Torture made easier.

My pulse banged in my eardrums. I felt a cold sweat on my brow.

Lisecki stood motionless in the darkest corner, a cockroach trying to blend into the cork. His breathing was labored as he pressed his back against the wall, clinging there as silently as a piece of ridiculous art.

He began to sob, and then suddenly lurched for me and I hit him with an openhanded slap to the face that caught him off guard and knocked him on his ass. He was in shock when he hit the floor, too stunned to speak, too frightened to protest.

I pulled my Glock and aimed it at his head. I stood that way for a moment, then retrieved my cell phone from my jacket pocket and punched in Branoff's number from speed dial.

It rang four or five times as I prayed he would answer.

CHAPTER TWENTY-NINE

Like a boxer in his corner between rounds, I wasn't thinking about the earlier rounds and the punches missed. I was only thinking about answering the next bell and landing the knockout blow as I waited for Branoff to answer the phone.

The last time I'd seen my ex-partner we were outside of McGuire's Bar, where he chewed my ass and left me standing there like an orphaned dog.

Lisecki blew out his breath in exasperation. My Glock was still pressed against his forehead.

I turned and looked behind me. Rings and hooks were bolted into the walls on either side of the torture bed. A strong metal frame for suspension held chains and a sling or swing and the seat hooks onto brackets on the bed headboard at different heights.

Yanking Lisecki up on his feet, I dragged him over to the wall of pictures. Still covering him with my gun, I looked for a picture of Chelsea Rohrman. Pacing myself, I took my time while my phone continued to buzz.

In police work, I had seen many kinds of photos, some taken in booking rooms, others at crime scenes, some in morgues. But the kind you are never prepared for are the pictures of either the victims or the ambivalent smirk of the perpetrators.

Some of the women in the pictures would most likely be difficult to identify, even by their own mothers. But, it didn't take long before I recognized Chelsea, despite the pleading eyes and bruised cheeks. I ripped it from the wall and elbowed the professor under his chin.

"Owwww!" He screamed and whined like a baby as he whipped back against the wall.

"You sick bastard," I heard myself growl.

In her school pictures, Chelsea looked like a girl that had been loved and who believed the world was a good place where the joy of young womanhood waited for her with each sunrise. I would make sure her mother didn't see the picture I held in my hand.

People wonder why cops booze it up, take pills, become sex addicts or eventually eat their guns. Even among the most tarnished of police officers, unless they are sociopaths themselves, there are moments when they witness human evil for which no one is prepared. It causes them to wonder if some individuals in our midst are possessed by Satan himself. That's what we want to believe because the alternative conclusion would rob us forever of our faith in our fellow human beings.

Branoff answered his phone and I came out of my dark reverie, realizing I was still on the phone, waiting.

"Hi, Hawk. What's up?"

"Hey, Kris, where ya' at right now?"

"I was walking out the door. Lucky you caught me, I wanted to get out of here over an hour ago, but everybody had to stay for a meeting with the Captain. Why? What's up?"

"Well, I've got your serial killer. He's located at the business end of my Glock, as we speak. I suggest you bring the lab guys and come out to Professor Lewis Lisecki's house, right away. It's in Rolling Meadows--easy to find. Look for his Mercedes and my Crown Vic in front of the garage."

There was a long silent gap.

"Kris?" I heard a whoosh of breath on his end.

"Jesus! What the fuck are you doing, Cleve? I specifically told you to keep your distance from Lisecki. Remember? If you're in his house, this is all fucked up. You've got no warrant." He said it like I was some kind of squatter or other nuisance who had previously been warned to move on and never come back.

"What the hell, Kris. Did I spit in your soup or something? I'm in his house, alright, but before you climb on the cross you might consider this: I didn't need a warrant. The good professor let me in through the front door. I'm a guest. I'm not the law, Kris, but you are. I suggest you wake up a judge and get that warrant for probable cause. There's enough shit here to make sure Lisecki gets the needle."

I shifted my weight from foot to foot like a boxer in his corner waiting to answer the bell.

There was another long pause and I heard Branoff sigh before he said, "Alright, but this better be damned good, Hawkins. You're in a shit load of trouble, my friend. But, I'm on the way . . . see you in about twenty or sooner."

"Right." I closed my phone and checked my watch, then shoved Lisecki toward a set of wooden stairs on the opposite end of the room.

"Let's go up those stairs, asshole." I don't know how I had missed it, but what I had mistaken for a bookcase, was actually a revolving door. One good shove and we were in his den. I turned and played it back and forth with my free hand.

"Pretty clever setup, Lisecki. You must have thought you were real smart when I missed this earlier, huh?"

Shoving him ahead of me, I picked up his .38 that still lay on the floor by the desk. Checking it out, I found all the chambers other than the one under the hammer were loaded and it appeared unfired. I dropped it in my coat pocket and shoved him down into his swivel chair, then, I sat on the edge of the desk, my gun still aimed at him.

"Joan Vidross had your number, didn't she, you asshole?"

He shrugged and replied, "She's not so smart. That one has

more money on her tits than I have on this house." He leaned forward. "I remember when the bitch got a pumpkin up her dress, and I knew the name of the Romeo who put it there."

He became smug all of a sudden, as if he didn't have a care in the world and continued, "I made him pay for the abortion and then some. That cunt didn't have a clue about how to handle it."

I quickly grabbed his face with one hand and squeezed as hard as I could. His nose was buried between his cheeks. "Just a footnote for you, professor. If you ever refer to a woman like that in my presence again, using that particular word, I'm going to forget you've got rights and use this gun to smash out all of your teeth."

Lisecki shuddered and slumped back in the chair.

"As it is you're damned lucky, Professor."

He glared at me and said, "What do you mean?"

"Well, I was considering doing you the way the mob boys do when they discover scum in their midst."

"You wouldn't dare kill me."

"Well, far be it for me to be graphic, but you know how they usually do it?" I moved my Glock from place to place. "One behind the head, one in the ear, and three under the chin. But I wouldn't have to do all that. The boys don't either. You see, they just have the asshole drop his drawers, give him a dull knife, and make him cut off his own dick at gunpoint."

I checked my watch every so often and finally, nearly a half-hour later, I heard a car pull up outside.

Edging over to the front windows, I saw Branoff looking out his open window as he parked his blue Blazer. I expected the lab van would be right behind him, and probably a few blue and whites.

He strolled in without ringing the bell. He'd gotten a haircut since I'd last seen him and wore his gray hair in a crew cut. He wasn't wearing a tie and his white shirt lapels lay flat so that his chest hair stuck out like a tangle of wire. Branoff always carried an aura about him, a sense of confidence and knowledge, like a guy who knows he's two moves ahead of everybody else.

My pulse spiked, the adrenaline was soaring, but those internals were all under control as I waited and Branoff stopped just inside the door to the den.

"Cleve." He stood as still as a statue and stared at us.

"Glad you could come out tonight, Kris. Look what I've got here." I shook Lisecki by the back of his neck.

Lisecki suddenly squirmed around. "Oh, thank God you're here," he wailed. "This Neanderthal has attacked me and searched my home. Kill him! I'll give you more . . .anything you want, just kill him now!"

I couldn't believe what Lisecki said, and I watched Branoff as he strolled into the room and came within a few feet. He looked at Lisecki uncertainly, a pocket of air in one cheek and sighed as he shook his head dismissively. Everything suddenly happened in double time. Lisecki stood up, shoving my gun sideways.

At the same time, Branoff yanked his Glock out of his shoulder holster, shoved me aside, and shot Lisecki, once in the forehead and once in the chest.

Unlike in the movies, a bullet doesn't blow a man backwards several feet. A man drops where you shot him; makes him crap and piss his pants, plunges him to the floor without a word. Lisecki's body jerked as he fell into his swivel chair. It tried to spin around in a circle until it caught on the desk.

Before I could get it together, Branoff stepped back and aimed his gun at me.

"What in the hell are you . . .?"

"Lay your gun on the desk, Hawk. Do it real slow n' easy."

CHAPTER THIRTY

I was pissed off to say the least when Branoff ordered me to lay my Glock on Lisecki's desk.

He glared at me; his eyes looked like dark tunnels, the color of bruises on bananas. I had seen the same eyes on other cops cruising the edge of a burnout. My ex partner was in the zone; amped up, wrung out, and surging forward like the Terminator with mission lock. When you get in the zone, your thinking grows fuzzy. It's a good way to get killed.

It didn't look like that mattered to him. I knew he could handle himself, but so could I. He had always stayed in shape and had the physique of a linebacker: about five-eleven, maybe two-hundred pounds, chest like a drum, arms like cable. I had to catch him off guard.

He stood less than ten feet away, and I didn't move. Holding myself absolutely still, my heart hammered, but I barely let myself breathe. The thought that a rogue cop had been monitoring my moves froze the adrenaline into tiny icicles in my veins.

I looked down. Blood was splattered everywhere. Lisecki's head was thrown back, mouth agape, and his eyes stared vacantly at the ceiling. His arms dangled like shoelaces over the arms of the chair.

My mind was in a whirl as I stared at Branoff. Why in the hell did he kill Lisecki?

"Now take that jacket off," he ordered. His attempt at confidence came across as cockiness. I realized Lisecki's .38 was still inside one of the pockets. However, I had no choice but to hand it over. As I did, Branoff backed up another four or five paces, putting plenty of space between us. He kept his Glock pointed at me while he searched the jacket. My notebook tumbled out onto the floor in front of him, and, at the same time, he discovered the other gun. He ignored my book and tossed my jacket off to the side.

"What have we got here?" he said. "This Lisecki's piece?"

I nodded as he slowly checked the gun. "Loaded, too." He sighed and shook his head from side to side as he holstered his Glock and kept the .38 pointed at me. "We have a problem," he said as he moved in and grabbed my Glock off the desk. He shoved it in his belt.

"Ha! No shit, Kris. Ya' think? Why are you pointing that thing at me? I don't get it. What in the hell is going on?" I nodded toward Lisecki's body. "Why did you kill him?"

"He dealt it."

"So, he did. Him and his red-headed buddy did the killings, but now you've fucked it up and we'll never get the whole story. Where's the warrant and where's the lab guys? You gotta see the basement."

"No. I think we've got the story alright, and the two perps are history now. You and I both know they were guilty. I just spared the taxpayers a lot of money."

"Well, fine. Now, quit pointing that thing at me and give me back my piece." I took a step towards him.

He held the .38 with both hands and aimed. "Hold it right there, smart guy." I froze. "What the hell? You're losing it, Buddy. Come on, give me the gun."

"Shut the fuck up!" he yelled, as he waved the .38 and began to pace back and forth. He stopped and studied me before he went on.

"It's a long story, Hawk--something you would never understand." There was a long pause before he continued: "You just couldn't stay away from Lisecki, could you? I warned you in every way I could to leave his ass alone. But no--you couldn't do that. Not Detective Hawkins. You had to go snooping until you stepped right in this pile of shit."

"I don't believe this. What the hell's wrong with you?" I said as I started moving towards him again.

"I said stay back and I mean it, Hawk." He paced some more as he said, "You always thought you were the smart one. Sherlock Hawkins, a killer cop--more clever than the rest of us, right, Hawk? You're a sneaky fuck. So smart, but you couldn't keep your badge, could you? Yeah, that's smart."

"I don't get it, what's going on, Kris? You've got everything ass backwards here. We're supposed to be on the same team, we . . . "

"Knock it off," he said. "If I want to listen to bullshit, I'll go to a city council meeting." His eyes fluttered like two trapped moths and his mouth hung loose. Beads of sweat began to cover his forehead and his face was drawn and pale.

"What in the hell are you going to do?" I said. "You want me to go along with this murdering of Lisecki?"

I thought it was back-up when the front door blew open with the sound of a Cadillac hitting a picket fence. Instead, we heard high heels clicking in the foyer, just before Maureen barged into the den.

She saw me and moved quickly toward me as though we were lovers meeting for a tryst. I turned towards her, but she saw Branoff holding the gun and Lisecki in the chair. She covered her face with both hands for a moment.

I turned back around to face Branoff. "Mo!" I backed up slowly and stood in front of her, my arms extended in a half-assed protective mode.

"Jesus Christ, Maureen! What the hell are you doing here?" Branoff screamed. "Get the hell out of here. This is police business. You have nothing to do with this; stay out of it." He waved the pistol. "Go! Now!"

"He's right, Mo. Get out of here," I said over my shoulder.

Mo had lowered her hands, but didn't budge. She said, "I followed you out here, Kris. I hoped what I suspected wouldn't be true, but obviously it is. You're a dirty cop. You were on a pad with Lewis Lisecki, weren't you? He was paying you a ton of money to stay away from him in the investigation."

I couldn't believe what she said. Glaring at Branoff, I said, "Is that true?"

"I know you told him to get a warrant and bring back up, Cleve. But he ignored all of that, didn't you, Kris? I saw him tear out of the office and I followed him."

Branoff held up his hand to silence her. His brow furrowed as he concentrated. "Shut up, Maureen!" he yelled and looked at me. "Your lover here is quite a gal, wears pinstripe suits, silk ties and sometimes has an enormous chip on her shoulder." His eyes shifted to her. "But, many of us suspect she also wears a jockstrap."

Mo moved closer and squeezed my arm. "We've got everything we need to hang him, Cleve."

I was stunned. "So, that's the deal, Kris? You turned over on us? That's what Lisecki meant when he said he'd pay you more and told you to kill me? You had to shut him up, didn't you?"

I've never understood our collective unwillingness to question the authority of a predator who manages to acquire a badge or insignia or a clerical collar or who carries a whistle on a lanyard around his neck. Without our permission, these pitiful excuses for human beings would wither and die like amphibians gasping for oxygen and water on the surface of Mars.

Branoff's hands were shaking, and now, tears were visible in his eyes. I'd never seen the man this way in all my years knowing and working with him.

"It's a long story, Hawk. Something you would never understand."

"Try me."

He dramatically chopped the air with his hand. "They don't pay us enough to deal with this shit. You know that, I bust my ass to get these animals off the street and get peanuts for all the hassles and mental bullshit. If I fuck up in my position, I could be handed a cardboard box and told to clear my desk within twenty minutes. The bottom line with these people is respect. Appearances. Balls. Yet some fat-assed judge smacks them on the hand, then goes home at night to read The Wall Street Journal.

I clutched Mo's hand and made a calming gesture with my free hand. "Money was never what it was about, Kris, you know that. It's a job. Hell yes--it's a tough one, but still a job. I didn't quit because it was tough, you know that."

"I said you wouldn't understand, and you don't. You don't have a dying wife to go home to everyday, do you? Hell no. My Lori's MS is incurable. You haven't got the slightest idea of how it feels to see the woman you love shrivel up and die before your fucking eyes."

Tears streamed down his cheeks as he paused and went on. He wasn't aiming the gun at us any longer. It was pointed towards the floor. I could have jumped him, but I couldn't. Not just then.

"Who do you think pays to keep her alive, smart guy? The insurance company? No--not nearly enough. She's dying. I got fed up with it and did what I had to do."

He raked tears off his cheeks with the back of his hand and shook his head back and forth. "It's all fucked up, can't you see that?"

"You used to be a good cop, Kris," said Mo.

He looked at both of us and his face became a portrait of wonder.

"Used to be," he said. "This is what it adds up to. I want you to wipe down this .38 and put it in Lisecki's hand. I don't want to go down as a coward."

Before I could move, Branoff raised the .38, pointed it at his heart, and fired.

The noise, the incredible ringing so close in the room-- sounded like a bomb had exploded. Mo grabbed hold of me and screamed. Branoff dropped.

CHAPTER THIRTY-ONE

Things were dead quiet. When Branoff dropped I didn't move. I felt cold. My breaths were short, and I felt myself slow like I had been drugged; as if my heart and breath and the blood in my veins were winding down like a phonograph record when you pull the plug.

Tears welled up in my eyes, coming as if they were being squeezed from my heart as I looked at my ex-partner's bloody body on the floor. I could have cared less about Lisecki.

Mo was in shock. Her arms were wrapped around me, with her head on my chest while she sobbed. Looking up at me, her face darkened and a single vertical line cut her forehead. She glanced away, then looked back, and seemed to be studying me. I could almost see the furious motion of wheels, cogs and levers behind her eyes as she struggled to comprehend what had just happened.

Neither of us spoke for a while, each lost in thought.

I held her until she slowly pulled away. Glancing at the bodies, she wrung her hands and tried to collect her thoughts. Stress twisted her tear-stained face; streaks of mascara ran down her cheeks like spider webs.

I had to get it together. Both Lisecki and Bart Hodgkins were dead, but they had escaped the justice system. The certainty of nailing the scummy bastard, Lisecki, had fallen apart like a dream interrupted by an alarm clock. I felt as if I would shatter from the horrendous rage that suddenly made me brittle.

I wanted to scream my guts out. Without a warrant, where in the hell would this go?

I knew that most cops, usually at midpoint in their careers, come to a terrible conclusion regarding their career. They fear they are in danger of becoming like the twisted individuals they had always pitied as abnormal. Then they find themselves checking their own lives and perspectives. At that moment you either reaffirm your belief in justice and protection of the innocent or you don't.

I stepped back from Mo and raised my hands in an 'I give up' gesture. I grabbed a stapler from Lisecki's desk and heaved it as hard as I could across the room. It struck the mirror behind the bar and the glass shattered with the sound of a load of dishes dropped in a diner.

Mo could tell I was straddling the fence, hanging on by my fingernails, and getting whipsawed from both sides-- right and wrong. The woman could see around corners.

There was a silence, not long, a few moments, and she said, "What now, Cleve?" She paused before she continued: "Oh my God! What about Kris's wife, Jeannie? She won't be able get his pension now."

"Yeah, she will." I clasped both hands on her shoulders and looked into her eyes. "Listen, Kris was a good cop for almost seventeen years. He just wasn't always sure of himself and sometimes instability seemed to have been wired into his metabolism. So-- he stumbled . . . big deal. We're all human, aren't we? We can't let him go down as a coward, Mo. Damn sure not for perverted scumbags like Lisecki and his buddy. You agree?"

She nodded. "Yes."

I continued to study the situation until I came up with a plan. I didn't like what I was prepared to do, but I had no choice as I saw it.

It was the only way the pieces would fit.

Maureen looked at me as if she'd just stepped in something. "What are we going to do, Cleve. I'm so scared."

"Shhh." I put my arms back around her and patted her back. "It's going to be alright, I promise. Just hang in there. I need you to be strong right now, Mo." I pulled my Glock out of Branoff's belt and took Mo's hand. "Come with me."

With her in hand, I walked over to the entrance to the den, turned, and fired two shots at the wall beyond Lisecki's desk. I really didn't care where they hit. Mo screamed and covered her ears.

"Shhh. It's okay," I said as I held her again. "You'll see why I did that in a minute. Stand over there." I pointed to the bar. "And don't move."

I went back over and knelt down by Branoff's body. I took my handkerchief and pried Lisecki's .38 out of his hand and laid it across my shoe before I pulled Branoff's Glock out of the holster under his jacket. I put it in his hand, making sure my prints were wiped away first. Then, I put his finger on the trigger, aimed about three feet over Lisecki's body, and fired two rounds. I glanced over at Mo and saw she still had her ears covered.

I thoroughly wiped Branoff's prints, as well as mine, off of the .38 and went over to Lisecki's body. I remembered I'd seen him holding a pen at the college the day I visited him and knew he was right-handed. With Mo safe, I put the .38 in Lisecki's right hand and wrapped his fingers around it as best as I could.

Fortunately, neither of the men were in rigor yet.

Putting his trigger-finger on the trigger, I aimed to the left and right several feet above Branoff's body and fired off four rounds. The .38 slipped from his hand, but it didn't really matter.

I stood back and thought things through to be sure I'd covered all the bases. When I was satisfied, I turned towards Mo. "I'm done," I said, and went over to her. Looking in her eyes, I held her shaking body in my arms. "You going to be okay?"

"I don't know. I'm scared, Cleve, and I'm not sure what you're doing."

"Okay so here's the story. First of all, you need to get out of here. Go home. You were never here and you don't know anything except what I am going to tell you now. We have to be clear on this."

She nodded. "But Kris will be . . ."

"No. Listen carefully, Mo, this is key, because State and local cops will be involved here. Media too. They'll be swarming over this thing like ants on a marshmallow. Okay, so here's the story: Kris left the office late this afternoon. He told you he was going to the professor's house to question him. He claimed he would call for back-up if he needed it, understand?

"Yes."

"So, later on, I called the office looking for Branoff and you told me where he went. That's where it ends for you, okay?"

"Yes."

"Good. Then, I came out here,heard shots, and walked in on a gunfight. When I saw what was going on, I shot at Lisecki, but obviously missed. Kris nailed him about the same time that Lisecki hit him in the heart. No changes. When the cops and lab guys get a load of what's in the basement, they'll realize what was going on and Kris will look like a hero cop who nailed the serial killer. I don't like it anymore than you do, but we know this is the only way, don't we?"

She nodded. "Yes, of course. Do you think it will work?"

"It better. I think so, because it's the only way the pieces will fit. Now, I've got to call this in, it's time for you to go." She kissed me long and hard before heading for the front door.

I used Lisecki's desk phone to call the homicide division of the Chicago Police Department. I told the dispatcher, "This is Cleve Hawkins. You'd better scramble some people, pronto-- Detective Branoff has been killed in a shootout.

Everything went down just the way I'd planned. I went by a few days later to see Chelsea Rohrmans mother. Her sister Betty was on hand too when I told them that Chelsea's killer had been found and he was killed during apprehension.

They cried, but they were tears of joy as they hugged and

thanked me. They invited me to stay for dinner, but I took a rain check.

Three weeks later, Mo and I were having dinner at Geja's, one of our favorite places over on Ashland Avenue.

Mo smiled and raised her glass toward me. She was absolutely beautiful, wearing a necklace of gigantic beads that matched the colors in her dress. Her teeth were very white and her smile was wide.

"You pulled it off, gumshoe" she said. "You are some sort of hero, I think. At least to me and the Rohrmans' you are for sure. I can't help feeling a bit guilty though. I know you must."

I nodded. "It's all for the best, Mo."

"So, you think you might consider coming back to the department?"

"No, Mo, I can't come back. I sort of like this private eye stuff, being my own boss, ya' know? Have nose will travel."

She smiled. We both sipped our drinks and looked at each other over the rims of the glasses and our eyes held. I could feel the wonder and the force of their promise.

"Forever," she said. "And then we'll see." She extended her hand and I held it.

Purchase other Black Rose Writing titles at <u>www.blackrosewriting.com/books</u>
and use promo code PRINT to receive a 20% discount.

CPSIA information can be obtained at www.ICGtesting.com
Printed in the USA
LVOW04s2129180315

431155LV00015B/273/P

9 781612 964867